W9-AUI-890

ALSO BY

JENNIFER A. NIELSEN

MARK OF THE THIEF TRILOGY

Mark of the Thief

Rise of the Wolf

Wrath of the Storm

THE ASCENDANCE TRILOGY

The False Prince

The Runaway King

The Shadow Throne

A Night Divided

The Scourge

Behind Enemy Lines, Book Six in the Infinity Ring series

JENNIFER A. NIELSEN

WRATH OF THE STORM

MARK OF THE THIEF

Book Three

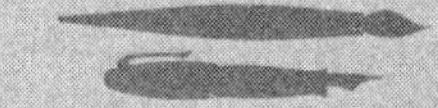

SCHOLASTIC PRESS · NEW YORK

Library of Congress Cataloging-in-Publication Data

Names: Nielsen, Jennifer A., author. | Nielsen, Jennifer A. Mark of the thief ; bk 3.
Title: Wrath of the storm / Jennifer A. Nielsen.
Description: First edition. | New York : Scholastic Press, 2017. | Series: Mark of the thief ; book 3 | Summary: Nicolas Calva has Caesar's magic bulla, the Malice of Mars, and he has hidden the dangerous Jupiter Stone, but he still has to find a way to defeat The Mistress, a dragon who contains the soul of the vestalis Atroxia, and who hates Rome, and save his mother and friends, and maybe even the Empire itself—and he is troubled by his sneaking sympathy for Atroxia, who was unjustly condemned.
Identifiers: LCCN 2016024019 | ISBN 9780545562072
Subjects: LCSH: Magic—Juvenile fiction. | Amulets—Juvenile fiction. | Slaves—Rome—Juvenile fiction. | Dragons—Juvenile fiction. | Adventure stories. | Rome—Antiquities—Juvenile fiction. | Rome—History—Empire, 30 B.C.–476 A.D.—Juvenile fiction. | CYAC: Magic—Fiction. | Amulets—Fiction. | Slavery—Fiction. | Dragons—Fiction. | Adventure and adventurers—Fiction. | Rome—History—Empire, 30 B.C.–476 A.D.—Fiction. | GSAFD: Adventure fiction. | LCGFT: Action and adventure fiction.
Classification: LCC PZ7.N5672 Wr 2017 | DDC 813.6 [Fic]—dc23 LC record available at https://lccn.loc.gov/2016024019

10 9 8 7 6 5 4 3 2 1 17 18 19 20 21

Printed in the U.S.A. 23
First edition, February 2017
Book design by Christopher Stengel

A note to readers: Latin words will be italicized upon their first appearance in the text.

To Mrs. Riley, 8th Grade,
who returned to me what the
locksmith took away

·ONE·

If I was lucky, I still had another hour to live. Of course, if luck had ever played a role in my life, I wouldn't have been here in the first place.

Only the gods knew how long I'd been trapped beneath a pile of rubble from what had once been a temple — and a tomb. Atroxia's tomb.

Was it hours? Days? I really didn't know.

I had destroyed this temple, hoping to destroy Atroxia as well. But she was so much more powerful than I had expected. My plan had failed. I had failed against her and, in doing so, had lost everything.

My magic was gone. Every time I'd awoken, I'd hoped to find a spark within me. Yet I was still waiting, still hoping. It was gone.

I'd also lost my mother and my sister. I had no idea if they were safe, or where they were now.

My friend Aurelia was probably safe, but she was lost, at least to me. In order to save her own life, Aurelia had agreed to marry another of our friends, Crispus. That agreement had etched a wound within me that no kind of magic could heal.

I'd even lost Radulf, who had traded himself to Atroxia to save me. No matter how often I had tried to understand why he'd done that, I couldn't. Something in the complicated relationship with my grandfather had changed. I just wasn't sure what it was.

I'd lost all of this because of Atroxia, which was her name while in her human form. The Praetors knew her differently, as a cursed dragon named the Mistress who was bound to serve the goddess Diana. At times, they spoke as one voice, but not always, I'd learned. The dragon controlled the girl.

It was obvious why Diana had chosen to curse Atroxia this way. Atroxia had once been a *vestalis,* a holy woman. But she was nothing of the sort now. Instead of honoring her high position, she had betrayed it centuries ago, an act that resulted in the murder of Emperor Julius Caesar by one of Diana's descendents. The punishment for her crime was to be buried alive. While she still breathed, Diana changed her into a dragon, powerful enough to withstand centuries of punishment. It saved her life and, at the same time, destroyed her life.

Thanks to my foolishness, she was loose now and would carry out Diana's plans to bring down the empire. The Praetors of Rome would help in that fight. It was a war that had started with Caesar's assassination.

And I suspected that one way or the other, it would end with me.

Time was not on my side.

For once, it wasn't because of the gods, or my failed attempts to reclaim any feeling of magic.

No, my problem now was far more simple.

I was running out of air.

I needed to escape.

But first, I would sleep again.

I couldn't help it.

TWO

Nicolas Calva, where are you?"

The sharp voice snapped me from my sleep and was accompanied by a pained scream that seemed to echo in the rubble around me. I felt the scream inside my bones, as if whatever had caused it was also happening to me.

It was completely dark down here, but I didn't need light to confirm that I was still alone. The voice had been in my head and had belonged to Radulf. He was calling out for me. And then had been punished for it.

Viciously punished. I knew that because I had felt it too. My heart was still pounding. The tips of my fingers felt like they were on fire, but I couldn't move enough to do anything about them.

The Mistress had taken Radulf away, believing he had the Malice of Mars. Just to look at it, the Malice appeared innocent enough, only a silver armband for the forearm, similar to what a gladiator might wear. But anyone with magic would sense its great power, enough to topple an empire. More than anything in the world, the Mistress wanted that Malice.

Except Radulf didn't have it. I did, somewhere nearby in this darkness.

My eyes wanted to close again, wanted to return me to the deep sleep that had claimed me so many times already since I had become trapped down here. This was Diana's curse on the temple, no doubt, to cause anyone trapped here to sleep, preserving their life and, at the same time, refusing to allow them to live.

I had to get out of here.

My right arm was trapped beneath a large rock and had long ago lost any feeling. I tried making a fist and thought I had been successful, but I wasn't sure. It was completely numb. My left arm was nearer to my body. My wrist wouldn't bend, and then I remembered the Mistress had broken it. So as far as I could tell, I still had both limbs, but they were useless. My legs were below me, twisted and contorted around crumbled temple stones that at one time had each been as large as a grown man. Equally useless.

The Malice was in here too. I vaguely remembered collapsing the temple with the Malice in my hands. Bringing several tons of marble and brick down over my head had been a dangerous move, but it seemed better than allowing the Mistress to get it. Now I wasn't so sure. The best choice would've been not to seek the Malice in the first place, though that might never have been an option for me. Eventually, I'd have been forced into coming here. Diana's curse must still rest upon this temple, or I'd probably be dead already.

Collapsing the temple had been only half of my stupid

plan. The other half was to use the Malice to escape again. Unfortunately, it had fallen out of my reach. I hoped it wasn't far away.

I closed my eyes, searching for any feeling of magic within me. I had lost my magic once before, when Radulf took it from me in the amphitheater, and on multiple occasions I had spent so much of my magic that I was unable to use it. But it had always come back. It would come back to me one more time. I hoped.

The Divine Star marked my shoulder. It was still there and could heal me. Where was the *bulla*?

I vaguely felt its weight on my chest, but the metal had gone cold. I inched my left wrist upward, then clenched my teeth as the broken bones protested the movement. During the battle with the Mistress, how many times had I healed that wrist, only to break it again moments later? Why couldn't I heal it one more time?

I could. I just needed to touch the bulla, and since my right hand was probably flattened like a squashed bug, my broken left hand would have to do the work.

I took a few deep breaths to summon enough courage to raise the arm, then lifted it suddenly, pushing through crumbled stones and pockets of loose dirt. I didn't get far before I had to stop to catch my breath and mumble a few curse words. But no matter how it was screaming at me, my wrist was above my waist now. One more move and it would reach the bulla.

My whole arm throbbed, and waves of nausea washed over me. I didn't want to move again. If I only relaxed, I knew I could fall asleep as I had every time before. This place wanted me to sleep, to disappear forever here.

But when Radulf had sacrificed himself to the Mistress, I had vowed to go and find him, to save him from whatever the Mistress might do. However long I'd already allowed him to remain within her clutches, it was too long. I had to get out of here.

So before I could think better of it, I jerked my arm upward again. The wrist snapped against a sharp rock that had been in its way, but my arm pushed past it. I cried out, only to fill my lungs with dust that the wrist had swept up with it. Choking, I pressed my arm against my chest, then felt something change.

My left hand had landed on the bulla. It couldn't grip anything, but the same sharp rock that had given me so much pain now propped my arm perfectly in place against the gold amulet.

A familiar heat lit within my chest and quickly spread through me. I had been shivering before. Interesting that I hadn't known how cold I was until now.

The instant the bulla's power reached the Divine Star, its healing powers began to flow through my chest down to my legs and arms. The warm magic seeped into the bones of my wrist, strengthening them and bonding them back together. Making me whole again. A quick, painless wiggle of my wrist confirmed that.

I was still trapped, and I doubted the bulla could get thousands of pounds of rock and brick off me. But I knew something that could do it.

Magic can always sense other magic in the area, and I used that power to search for the Malice nearby.

The bulla had originally been given to Julius Caesar, filled with Venus's powers. Upon Caesar's death, Venus's power left the bulla, and Diana replaced the magic with her own, hoping it would be used in her war against the gods. The fact that I had the bulla and was using it to stop that war probably infuriated her.

As a rule, having a god furious with you is not a good thing. How well I understood that.

Nor did it help that I had the Malice . . . more or less. The Malice came from the god Mars with the power to end that war. To end any war, really. Use of the Malice guaranteed its bearer victory in battle.

If Diana resented my having the bulla, I could only imagine how she felt about the Malice. But she had no claim upon that amulet. I did. The key to finding it had been given to me. She'd have to destroy me to get it back.

What a pleasant way to begin a day — with the reminder that one of the gods had specifically targeted me for destruction. I grimaced, deciding that at least Diana would not kill me here.

I felt the Malice's magic slightly below my right hand. I pressed that hand downward and heard a shift in the rocks around me. They were more delicately balanced than I had imagined. Perhaps my right hand was keeping them in place.

So, more carefully, I lowered my hand farther and felt a small quake of rocks tilting overhead. It was difficult to imagine myself in a worse position than my current one. If she could see me now, Aurelia would rightly accuse me of great stupidity.

"Picture where you want to go," I whispered. That was what Radulf would say. Indeed, that was how I had gotten myself here in the first place, for better or worse. Where did I want to go?

Home.

I didn't have a home of my own, but I could go to Radulf's home. I pictured my room there, with the frescoes of Minerva in battle with a draco, the statues that lined his hallways, and even the *triclinium*, where he and I had eaten as we faced off in numerous battles of will.

But most clearly of all, I saw Radulf's atrium. Painted in the rich colors of Rome and surrounded with tall marble columns made to look like serpents climbing the walls. Considering the cruel serpent that had trapped me down here, it wasn't the most welcoming thought, but anything was better than this.

My left hand had finally healed enough to clasp the bulla. I held to it tightly as I pictured the atrium, every detail of the room so sharp in my mind that I could hear the steady drops of water falling into the pool. It must be raining outside. How I missed water. Now that I was awake, I was terribly thirsty. When was the last time I'd had a drink? It felt like months.

I reached for the Malice again, and this time the rocks above me shifted. My predicament was becoming clear. Any more movement, and those rocks would fall, crushing me.

It had nearly cost my life to get the Malice the first time. For all I knew, it would still cost Radulf his life, and maybe others whom I loved. I would not let that be in vain. I refused to leave the Malice behind.

I closed my eyes again and let Radulf's atrium come into focus. That's where I would go, disappearing completely from this rubble before it collapsed.

Had I ever been this tired? I didn't think so, not even when I was a slave in the mines of Rome. But I could not allow myself to sleep now. If I did, I might never wake up.

I pushed all my weight downward while the fingers of my right hand searched for the metal edge of the Malice. Rocks continued crumbling above me. I felt their weight and used the bulla's strength to push against them. I couldn't give much magic to the effort — what little I had was needed to get me to the atrium.

Then my fingers touched the Malice, and with one more stretch downward, my hand closed around it.

"Go," I whispered, clenching my eyes shut.

Rocks tumbled above me. Smaller pebbles moved out of the way for the larger boulders, but I wasn't there to see what happened next.

I heard running water and briefly opened my eyes, long enough to see the painting of the serpent inside Radulf's atrium. Someone called my name.

And I fell asleep again.

THREE

I awoke in a dark, silent room and would've thought I was back in the rubble again except for the soft bedding that covered me. I stirred a bit and felt a cup press against my lips.

"Drink this."

I accepted the cool water that slid down my parched throat, restoring life as it flowed. Nothing had ever tasted so good.

"Careful. Not too much too fast." And the cup was removed.

I didn't recognize the voice. Not at first, but with some effort, I opened my eyes. "Mother?"

Silence followed my question, but then the dim light of an oil lamp was lifted higher, illuminating my mother's face.

She was as beautiful as the goddesses themselves. Long golden curls framed her face. Her cheeks were naturally rosy, and her eyes were warm, like Livia's. She had seen much sadness in her life, yet her face betrayed none of that, at least not at the moment.

When I was younger, my mother used to say I looked more like my father, with his dark hair and brown eyes. I wondered if that was still true and whether there were other ways in which I was like him. More particularly, I wondered if my mother wanted me to be like my father, and his father before him.

The Malice was in my right hand, and I kept hold of it as I sat up on one elbow to see her better. Tears filled my eyes. No cage bars separated us, or chains, or slave masters. It was just us, as it used to be years ago. I wanted to say something; I just wasn't sure what.

"You had us worried," Mother finally said.

"Us?" It sounded like I was speaking with a mouthful of sand, and maybe I was. I needed more water.

She cocked her head toward the door. "Livia and your friends Aurelia and Crispus."

"They're here? They're safe?"

My mother's smile had always been comforting. "Of course. And breathing much easier now that you're back."

"How long —" I hardly dared to ask. "How long was I gone?"

Her smile faded, obviously concerned that I did not already know the answer. "Ten days. We had almost given up on you surviving. How did you?"

Bigger questions were on my mind. "What about Radulf? Is he here too?"

I knew he wasn't. I still heard his screams inside my head, his desperate question that had pushed through my unconscious mind: "Nicolas Calva, where are you?"

Mother shook her head. "The dragon carried him away. We don't know where he is, but he's surely dead by now."

"No, he's not." I sat up and began searching through the dark room for my sandals.

"Get back in bed; you're still weak." Her tone scolded me, which wasn't fair. I'd been on my own far too long for that.

I reached for the first sandal and began lacing it. "I've got to find Radulf. I've got to get him back."

"Nic?" The door to my room opened, and Livia poked her head through it. Light streamed in from the outer rooms. I vaguely wondered what time it was.

When she saw I was awake, Livia came all the way in. I squinted from the light, but as my eyes adjusted, it was good to see my sister. Livia was a smaller replica of our mother, though I was sure she had grown even taller since I had last seen her. Her gentle nature came through with every movement she made, and when she smiled, her entire face seemed to glow.

However, Livia wasn't smiling now. She nodded toward the sandal on my foot. "Where are you going?"

"You must know," I muttered.

Livia knelt beside me. "*Pater* is gone," she said, using the more familiar term for our grandfather. "And you're in no condition to search for him anyway."

Suddenly, I was ravenously hungry. The curse that had preserved my life in the rubble of the temple was fading, leaving me with the reality of not having eaten for ten days. "Get me some food, Livia, please. Anything we have. I'll eat my sandals if you don't hurry."

With a glance at our mother, Livia stood and rushed from the room while I reached for the other sandal. Mother probably wanted me to eat them so I couldn't leave.

"He is not a good man," she said. "I'm sorry to say this about your own grandfather, but the things he has done are terrible. Even if he were still alive, he is not worth saving."

"He's changed," I said. "He traded his life for mine with the Mistress — don't I owe him something in return?"

"We wouldn't be in this situation if not for him!" she said. "No, Nic, he is not worth any further risk to us."

I didn't want to fight with my mother, not ever, but especially not so soon after having her back in my life again. I wanted to know her as I used to, from a place of innocence and pure trust. I wanted her to know me as I used to be too. But none of that was possible. I hated that every word I spoke to her now seemed to fill her heart with sadness. But regardless of what she thought of Radulf, I had to go after him.

"Is Aurelia here?" I asked.

Mother licked her lips. "She and Crispus checked on you this morning, then went to the forums for some business."

I didn't ask what sort of business the two of them might have in the forums, together. I didn't want to know.

I stood and immediately regretted moving so quickly. My head swarmed with dizziness, and I fell back onto the bed.

Mother was immediately at my side, offering me more water from the cup. I emptied the cup and asked for more. While she refilled it from a pitcher on a nearby table, Livia returned with a tray of grapes and a loaf of bread.

"It's yesterday's bread, but I don't think you'll care about that," she said, placing the tray on my lap.

"I've got to make up for ten days of not eating," I said with my mouth already full. "I'd eat ten-year-old bread, if necessary."

Her smile came from relief more than happiness, and when she sat in the chair where our mother had just been, they both watched me eat as quickly as I could. Once the worst pangs of hunger subsided, I slowed down and stared back at them.

"I am going to rescue Radulf," I said. "And I know you don't like that, Mother. I know you don't like *him*, but I understand him differently than you do. I have to help him."

Tears filled her eyes. "Please don't. If you fail, the Mistress will have you."

"I won't fail." My hand drifted from the bulla to the Malice, assuring myself it was still there.

But that wasn't enough for my mother, who said, "Even if you succeed, then what? Radulf will force you to make a Jupiter Stone for him. That will kill you."

I wanted to argue, but I couldn't. For all its power, the Malice could not save me from the consequences of making a Jupiter Stone. Much as I feared that, it was worse to stand aside and abandon the man who had traded everything to save my life.

So I only nodded toward Livia. "Tell Mother that you agree with my decision. Do you want me to try to save Pater?" It was the first time I'd ever used that term for Radulf, and though I wasn't entirely comfortable with it, I also liked the idea of having someone in my life who might deserve it.

Livia stared at me, then at our mother, torn between us. Finally, she looked back at me and nodded. "I would come with you and help," she said, "if I thought I wouldn't get in the way."

"I'll fight better knowing you're safe back here." I turned to our mother. "And if I have your blessing to go."

"On the night he tried to create a Jupiter Stone, your father and I had a similar disagreement." Mother's eyes suddenly seemed distant, as if she were remembering him, the good memories and the bad. "He knew the risk to himself, knew it wasn't enough simply to have the Divine Star's magic. Yet he challenged the lightning because he felt it was his only chance to save us. You know what happened to him."

"I'm not challenging the lightning," I whispered. *Not yet.* Not ever, if I had the choice.

"You've seen what the Mistress really is. Do you think it's any safer to fight her?"

I finished the last of the food on the tray, then stood and tested my balance. I wasn't as strong as I wanted, but I felt the bulla's growing strength within me and I had the Malice. It was enough.

I wrapped the Malice around my wrist and immediately felt the increase of magic. It filled me with more power than I could hold, like an entire sea trying to fit into a cup. I gasped from the new weight of magic within me and was surprised to find myself strong enough to bear it up.

Livia stood and finished lacing the Malice for me. "Are you all right?"

I grinned. "Absolutely!" Then I leaned down and kissed my mother on the cheek. "I will return, I promise. But a dragon is calling for me."

Before I could leave, she took my hand in hers and gave it a squeeze. "It was never my desire to leave you and Livia in that mining camp. And I always hoped to hide from you the true reason for our family's draw to magic. I didn't want this life for you, Nicolas. Please come back."

"I have no intention of dying today." I smiled down at her. "Keep my supper warm. I'll be hungry when we return."

"We'll set out a plate for you and for Pater!" Livia called after me.

If he is still alive, I thought. *Please, let him still be alive.*

FOUR

I went from my room toward the back of Radulf's home, where he had a small stable that I hoped would contain a unicorn named Callistus. Callistus had brought my mother here while I fought the Mistress at her temple. He should be here now.

Fortunately, he was, watching the door as I came through it, as if he'd anticipated my arrival. Callistus was an uncommonly beautiful animal, strong and lean, with deep blue eyes, a golden horn, and a coat of the purest white. Nothing created by the gods could ever be so perfect as him.

When I walked up to Callistus, he nuzzled his head into me as I leaned against his neck, wrapping one hand over his shoulder and the other to brush across his chest. The magic from the Malice lit within me when I did. Perhaps the power of this amulet was similar to the magic already within a unicorn.

"I need your help again," I said in the most respectful of tones. "The chariot races were difficult, I know, but I must ask more of you this time."

Callistus snorted in reply. I ran my hand down his back, then grabbed the saddle from a nearby fence. Once Callistus was saddled, I climbed up, patted his shoulder, and then directed him to leave the stables.

"Leaving without us?"

I glanced up and saw Aurelia on a speckled gray horse, waiting in the grasses just outside Radulf's stables. She had a bow and arrow slung over her shoulder and looked rather triumphant to have caught me here.

Had it been only ten days since I'd seen her? She was lovelier than I remembered. Of course, when I'd last seen her, it had been in the midst of a battle for us both. Now her clothes were cleaner, and her chestnut hair was pulled back in one long braid down her back. Had her eyes always been this blue, so bright I could see them from here? How had I never noticed they were so close to the color of Callistus's eyes?

Beside her, Crispus sat tall on an equally fine black horse. Crispus wore a brown tunic and dark gray cloak, symbolizing his mourning for his father's recent death. A sword hung at his side, one I wondered if he was strong enough to use; but then, he'd gotten up on the horse with it, so maybe he could swing it too.

I wasn't sure how to reply to Aurelia's question, or maybe it wasn't the kind of question that needed to be answered. Either way, they were blocking my exit, so I needed to say something. I didn't want another argument, not about where I'd been or where I was going, and I certainly wouldn't congratulate them on their upcoming marriage. The thought of that turned my stomach.

"You have the Malice," Crispus finally said, nodding at my right forearm. "Does it work?"

Not yet ready to answer, I only squinted back at him. "What are you two doing here?"

"You're going to rescue Radulf," Aurelia said. "I knew you would, as soon as you got back. Crispus and I just came from the forum, where we bought everything we might need to help you."

That was absurd, and my expression no doubt showed it. "Which shop at the forum prepares you to fight a cursed dragon?" I nodded at Crispus's sword. "You might as well swing a blade of grass."

"We want to help," Crispus said.

He was sincere. I knew that and appreciated it, yet I shook my head with equal sincerity. "I don't want any help."

Aurelia's face reddened. "I wasn't asking if we could come along. I'm telling you that's our plan!"

My knuckles tightened around the reins. "Whenever I'm in a fight, I end up trying to keep you safe for half the time."

"And the other half, you're thanking me for keeping *you* safe! We're coming with you, Nic."

Crispus only shrugged. "You're wasting time arguing with her. You know that she always wins. Besides, if the Malice doesn't —"

"The Malice does work," I said. "It will give me victory against the Mistress."

"Assuming she doesn't steal it from you first," Aurelia said. "*Auribus teneo lupum*. Do you know what that means?"

"That I have the wolf by its ears." I leaned forward in the saddle. "You're saying I'm so close to the danger that it will bite me, and you're right." I glanced at Crispus. "But the difference is, I'll survive the bite. You two won't."

"Even if you defeat the Mistress, that doesn't mean you'll be able to fight her and rescue Radulf. You take on the dragon. We'll find Radulf."

"He saved our lives too," Crispus said.

That wasn't exactly true. I was the one who had reminded the Mistress that Crispus was a judge now in Rome. The Mistress would never harm her Praetors. At least Crispus was one of the good ones, if there *were* any other good ones. And Aurelia saved herself the only way she could, by promising to become Crispus's wife, putting herself under the same protection.

But it was true that defeating the dragon wasn't the same as rescuing Radulf. For that, perhaps I did need their help. So I nodded my permission, and when they parted for me, I rode Callistus forward and we headed out.

"Where will we find him?" Crispus asked.

I shrugged. "Callistus probably knows. I thought I'd let him lead me there."

"Then we'll follow you," Aurelia said as she and Crispus took up positions on either side of me. It seemed like an appropriate symbol. I had come between them yet again. I glanced first at him, and then at her, where my eyes lingered longer. It was almost a relief when Callistus led me away.

The unicorn was taking us southward, keeping to the outskirts of the main population but heading toward the city gates of Rome. I'd been on this path before, most recently when he took me to Lake Nemi. There I'd met the vestalis in the grove of oak trees outside of Diana's temple. I'd fought Jupiter's eagle for the rock that was meant to become a Jupiter Stone. The vestalis had also told me a few things that still haunted my mind. She told me that to get what I wanted, I had to walk through fire. And that the Mistress, Atroxia, would teach me what I did not yet understand about love.

I stole a sideways glance at Aurelia. What I understood about love could fit on the head of a pin, but I seriously doubted I could learn it from a dragon who would soon try to kill me. Aurelia caught me staring and smiled back, but I quickly looked away. I felt stupid, especially as she continued staring. I had to say something, to cover my real thoughts.

Finally, I said, "I think I know where we're going. Atroxia serves Diana. She would take Radulf to Diana's temple."

"At Lake Nemi?" Crispus's eyes widened. "My father forbade me to ever go to that temple. It's a place of violence, not peace."

"I didn't ask you to come," I reminded him. "And there's no shame in leaving."

"We're not leaving," he said. "I'm just . . . nervous."

So was I. We'd have been fools to feel anything different.

Since Crispus and Aurelia were on horses far less powerful than Callistus, it took us most of the day to get to Lake Nemi. Still, I was grateful for at least one reason to have them along — they had packed plenty of food for the journey, over half of which I had already eaten. They didn't ask why I was so hungry or where I'd been for the past ten days. They only let me eat and drink as much as I needed.

It was dark when I first caught sight of the lake, far below us down steep, wooded hills. My eye caught some fluttering movement in the moonlight, and my heart leapt. I knew what that was.

"We should camp here for the night," Crispus said. "Then approach the temple in the light of day."

"But Radulf is a captive tonight," I said, urging Callistus to move down the hill. "We don't rest until we have him back."

"Do you ever rest, Nic?" Aurelia asked as her horse fell into a single-file line behind mine. "You're always moving, unless you're knocked unconscious."

Crispus drew in a breath. "Is that where you were for ten days, unconscious? Beneath that temple? No wonder you're so hungry!"

I smiled, ready for whatever was about to come. "If I did sleep that long, then I'm well rested now. Let's go. We're saving a life tonight!"

FIVE

When we were nearly to the shores of Lake Nemi, Crispus stopped his horse as suddenly as if it had hit an invisible wall. "We should go back. Can't you feel it, how haunted this lake is?"

Aurelia and I stopped too, and both of us stared at him. Crispus's face had drained of color, and he was holding on to his horse's reins so tightly that I thought he might snap them in half.

"Haunted?" Aurelia chuckled. "It's just a lake."

"Emperor Caligula used to spend a lot of time here. He had a floating palace on these waters, and a floating temple, dedicated to Diana."

My grin matched Aurelia's. "Let's hope he was a better swimmer than I am."

"He was mad!" Crispus seemed irritated that Aurelia and I weren't taking him more seriously. "It's rumored that while watching the games one day, he got bored because they ran out of criminals to fight the animals. So he ordered an entire section of the audience into the arena instead."

Aurelia shrugged. "That's cruel, but not mad."

"He made his horse a priest and his own personal advisor," Crispus added.

I snorted a laugh through my nose. "His horse advised him to do what, eat more hay?"

"All right," Aurelia said, taking mercy on him. "I'll agree with you. Caligula was a madman."

"And he dedicated these waters to Diana," Crispus said. "We are not safe here."

"You will be." I dismounted and brushed a firm hand down the unicorn's back, then walked closer to the waters. There was a reason we had come to this exact spot. "Come out, Caela!" I called.

There was a fluttering sound and the heavy stamp of a foot, and finally, a griffin emerged from a clump of bushes. I saw Caela's eagle half first. Her head was as large as Callistus's, but rather than a horn, she had a sharp golden beak from which she issued a screech loud enough to be heard from miles away. Her wings were white and made of the softest feathers. The rear half of Caela was a lion, with muscles strong enough to propel her high into the air before she ever needed to fly.

Caela glanced at Callistus and gave an angry caw. Was that jealousy? I loved Callistus; that was true. He was beautiful and powerful, and had saved my life more than once. But Caela was the creature that owned my heart, and I had missed her more than she could ever know.

Cautiously, I inched toward the griffin. Although we were

friends, I was never entirely certain that she wouldn't one day try to eat me. But Caela only lowered her head, giving permission for me to pet the feathers of her neck, then the lion fur of her back. Her wings had been spread out at first, but now they were tucked in close to her body, ready for me to ride on her back.

It would've been a wonderful evening to ride, but that was not my plan.

"I need to bring the Mistress down here to the lake," I said. "I want to draw her away from Radulf. Will you take my friends up to the temple to rescue him?"

Caela eyed them, and I might've heard Crispus's stomach drop to the ground. "You're sending us up there . . . alone?" he asked.

"Atroxia will come down to me; I guarantee that." I was deliberately keeping my voice calm, so as not to panic either Caela or Crispus. "And once you rescue Radulf, you won't be alone. His magic will get you safely back to Rome."

"What about you?" Aurelia's brows were pressed close together, and a slight smile crept to my face. It shouldn't have — what we were about to do was very dangerous. But I liked knowing she was concerned for me.

"I survived the collapse of a temple," I said. "I can survive the Mistress."

"You survived the collapse of a temple. Of course you did." Aurelia frowned. "Who talks like that? Who thinks like that?"

My grin widened, which no doubt annoyed her further. After she finished rolling her eyes at me, I motioned her over to Caela. Aurelia quickly glanced back at Crispus, who was tending to his horse, then pressed her hand over mine.

"Before Crispus and I leave, we need to talk." Her whisper was soft, but the intensity in her eyes made it feel like she had shouted.

My heart skipped a beat. "About what?"

Now her hand slid across Caela's back, scratching the fur the way I had been doing it before, letting the soft tufts brush between her fingers. But her eyes were on me. "About us. About what happened before that temple collapsed. You and I —"

"There is no you and I. That was what happened before the temple collapsed." My words sounded bitter, which wasn't my intention. Or maybe it was.

She reacted by pulling her hand away, and I knew I'd hurt her feelings. But there was no chance to apologize. Crispus, seemingly unaware of our conversation, was cautiously approaching Caela from the other side, letting her sniff him. I started forward, ready to protect Crispus if necessary. He shuddered, no doubt wondering how it must feel to be crushed inside a griffin's giant beak. But Caela only crouched lower, allowing them to climb onto her back.

I put my hands on Aurelia's waist, helping her get on first. She stared at me while I did, and I tried to communicate my apologies that way, though I wasn't sure it worked. In a more perfect world, I would've climbed on behind her to see where in the empire we might go. But instead, I backed up to make room for Crispus. He sat closely behind her and put a protective hand around her for the ride. I looked away from them, unable to bear seeing them so near to each other.

"We'll save him," Aurelia said to me. "Just don't . . . well, don't collapse any more temples over yourself."

"Be safe, Nic," Crispus added.

I nodded at them, then at Caela, prompting her to leave. Aurelia let out a joyous whoop as they soared high into the sky. I wished I could be up there, to share that moment with her.

But I had another job to do.

It began with me leading Callistus away to a grove of trees where I hoped he'd be safe. Callistus was uniquely strong and had magic of his own, certainly. But I didn't know how he'd fare against the Mistress, who possibly was mad in a way that rivaled Caligula, and I wouldn't take any chances.

Then I stood on the shores of the lake — Diana's lake, a detail that did not escape my attention — and faced the temple where the Mistress would be holding Radulf captive. Aurelia and Crispus were probably on the hillside, hiding and waiting for their opportunity to enter the temple. I had to call the Mistress away.

So I closed my eyes, searching for the place within me that had heard her cries before. Atroxia's sadness had pierced me in much the same way as when I'd heard Radulf's pleas for help.

They were both in tremendous pain. But it wasn't only Atroxia's voice in my head anymore. As the Mistress grew in power and dominance, I felt her anger too, a rage that she had been funneling toward Radulf for the past ten days. Strangely, and maybe for this one time only in his life, Radulf was innocent. He was paying for crimes . . . that were mine. I had stolen the Malice, not he.

I used the Malice now to call to the Mistress. I spoke the words aloud, but almost under my breath. It was enough. She would hear me.

"I'm here, Atroxia," I said, using her human name, not the title given to her by Diana. "If you want the Malice, come and get it."

I heard nothing in return, only a shift in the breeze that told me she had heard. And that she was coming.

My heart pounded, and I brushed my sweaty palms against my tunic. The Malice was still tied tightly around my forearm, nearly overwhelming me with its power. If it had not been for the bulla giving me its extra strength, I never could've contained all the magic inside me.

I wanted to send some sort of message to Radulf as well, to tell him to hold on for just a few minutes longer. But I didn't dare. Above all, the Mistress could not know this was a rescue attempt and certainly could not know Crispus and Aurelia were so near to Diana's temple. She had to believe this was only about fighting me.

But did she believe that? Where was she?

I closed my eyes again to call her, hoping to come up with a taunt that brought her here even faster. What would it take? Perhaps if I told her she was the ugliest dragon I'd ever seen. Or that her fire breath smelled of sardines.

The taunt wasn't necessary. Nor had it been a good idea for me to even think about her fire breath.

I felt its heat before I opened my eyes. And when I did, I saw a huge swath of the hillside suddenly light up with smoke and flame, igniting the Mistress's path toward the lake. I stumbled back, shielding my face from the heat, and saw the dragon swoop through the flames it had created. The smell was not of sardines. It was death, and I was the target.

"Thief!" the dragon roared. "You stole my Malice!"

"It belongs to Mars, not to you!" I shouted back, as if it was somehow better to have stolen from a god.

The dragon was at least five times my height and had a bloodred hide that might've been beautiful if it were not so terrifying. Its claws were long and sharp enough to pierce metal. White horns protruded from its serpent head, and its yellow eyes burned brighter just before it breathed out fire. Whole armies could fall within minutes to a creature such as this.

The dragon flew in a full circle around me, creating so much wind with its great wings that it sucked the air from my lungs. I stretched out a hand to stop it, then clutched my chest instead. My heart was still beating — always a good sign — but breathing was not a function of magic. It was a sign of life.

"How dare you wear that amulet?" the dragon said. "Who are you? No one!"

I tried to answer, though the words I had in mind were hardly clever enough to convince the Mistress I was anyone worth fearing. But without being able to draw in a breath, I couldn't even mouth the first word. Instead, I stumbled to my knees.

And the Mistress laughed. Her deep-throated snort was merciless, a way of assuring herself that I was exactly what she thought. A nobody.

"This will be too easy," she said. "I will pull the Malice off your limp arm before you even scratch me."

I doubted it would be much of a scratch — dragon hide was stronger than metal. But I refused to fall this easily, not when I had access to so much magic. And not after she said my arm was limp. It wasn't.

So on my knees, I reached out the arm bearing the Malice. Summoning its strength, I made a fist and pounded it onto the ground. It shook the earth, creating a sound almost like thunder. The air above it settled like falling stones. Losing its lift, the dragon came down too, landing hard on one wing. The ground shook again when the dragon fell, enough that I would've lost my balance if I'd not already been on my knees.

I took a few deep breaths before standing again. The dragon's large eyes were closed, but I was not naïve enough to think it was doing anything other than collecting its strength. I had to move quickly.

I shot great balls of magic toward its belly, hoping to find one spot soft enough to do some damage. The dragon reacted as if it felt the hits, though with the Malice, I had expected them to do worse than what I saw.

I came closer, throwing the magic in harder bursts. The sound of their collision against the dragon's chest echoed through the hills like rolling thunder, but I still doubted they were doing much harm. I was showing an ability to bruise a creature that could crush me. Hardly a comforting thought.

With my next step, the dragon suddenly rolled, grabbing me within its claws and slamming me on the ground. While I was still in her clutches, she got onto all fours, letting the whole of her weight press down upon me. I shouldn't have complained about how hard breathing was before; this was much worse.

"Why did you call for Atroxia, that useless, weak vestalis?" the dragon asked. "Diana has made me more than a human. I am a creature of magic, more powerful than ever before."

Why was she more powerful than before? My eyes narrowed. I knew the way Radulf had increased his power, and it was cruel. Were those her ways too?

She answered my unspoken question. "It was a simple thing to strip your grandfather of everything he had." Wisps of black smoke filtered between her teeth, and a guttural laugh filled my ears. "Well, it was simple for me. Harder for him."

She had taken Radulf's magic for herself? All of it?

When Radulf had taken my magic in the arena, it had nearly killed me. It would have killed me if he had truly taken everything. Was my grandfather still alive?

And if she had his magic, then she had powers greater than what I had faced when we fought outside the temple ten days ago. That explained why she could repel the balls of magic I'd sent at her chest.

Keeping her weight pressed down upon my body, the Mistress squeezed tightly. I heard the bones of my ribs crack and sent everything I could from the Divine Star to heal them before she pinched me in half. I was certain she could, if she wanted.

As the Divine Star flowed within me, it carried the Malice's magic with it. I was stronger than this.

I widened my arms, forcing the dragon's claws apart, then shot a spear of magic up through her leg. She yelped and released me entirely. I scrambled to my feet, ready to run forward and . . . well, I don't know . . . maybe, punch the dragon the way I had fought other workers when defending myself back at the mines. Did people ever punch dragons? I doubted it.

But she drew back and sent a breath of fire at me, hot enough to cook my flesh where I stood. I raised my hands, creating a shield between us. I felt the heat, but not the burn, and I continued pressing my way forward. The trees around me had already lit on fire. I had to be careful. When I was closer to the dragon, I repelled the fire entirely, sending it toward its maker.

The Mistress reeled backward, partially blackened from her own flames.

I started running toward the lake so that if she tried that trick again, she'd find nothing around me to burn.

Well, nothing *except* me. She breathed out fire again, and this time it lit across my back. I immediately fell into the water, dousing the flames and hopefully saving enough of my tunic to prevent any embarrassment later.

By the time the fire was out, the dragon had pounced again, standing over me in the water and trapping me between its legs and tail. I leapt to my feet.

"That's your only trick — fire?" I yelled. "I expected more from the woman who murdered Julius Caesar!"

"I did not kill him!" she roared. "Marcus Brutus was his assassin, not me. I did not deserve that punishment from the empire!"

"You are a traitor," I continued. "You betrayed the vestalis oath, and you betrayed your own people. If Diana made you into a dragon, that is no blessing. She truly did curse you, just as you deserve!"

The Mistress raised a front claw and struck my whole body, knocking me sideways into the water. The scratches went deep into my flesh, piercing my neck, ribs, and thigh. Blood pooled into the water around me. I lay there, as still as the Mistress had lain before. Above me, she snorted, trying to figure out how much damage her swipe had caused.

The answer was: plenty. But I wouldn't let the Divine Star heal me this time. Not yet. Instead, I gathered every bit of magic I could into the core of my body.

When she lowered her head to check on me, I reached up and grabbed her neck, then yanked downward, pulling both of us into the waters of Lake Nemi.

This was a deep lake. Deep enough for Emperor Caligula to float a temple and palace, and, I assumed, for the ships to carry him there from shore. Also deep enough for a boy and a dragon to battle underwater.

The Malice breathed for me and gave me strength to pull the Mistress far beneath the surface. She snorted, either searching for air, or a way to revive her fire breath, but neither of those would happen. Her neck flailed about, trying to propel me off her. When that didn't work, she tried grabbing me again with her claws, but she was floundering around so much just trying to avoid sinking any farther that I had the advantage.

Well, I sort of had the advantage. I knew I'd eventually need air too. But I also had a plan. Because I knew where to find air this far underwater, and I was pulling the dragon in that direction.

The Mistress began rolling her body in the water, hoping that would force me to let go. I kicked at her throat, which made her stop for a moment, but also increased her rage. Even with the Malice, I was having trouble keeping hold of her neck, and especially having trouble forcing the dragon in the direction I was trying to swim. We weren't too far away. We couldn't be.

Then I saw the opening I wanted. It would be a tight squeeze to get the dragon inside that tunnel. On the other hand, it would be a tight squeeze for the dragon to escape the tunnel too.

"No, please!"

It wasn't the Mistress whose cry entered my head. That was Atroxia, the cursed vestalis within the dragon. The human. She understood where we were going, and the tension in her voice betrayed the terror she felt.

The Mistress rolled again, and this time I was shaken loose from her neck. She swerved around as if to make for the surface, but I was not about to fight her on land again. So I grabbed the dragon's tail and used the Malice's strength to continue toward the tunnel. We were headed to the place where it had all begun for me.

To Caesar's cave, where I had found the bulla. Where Caela had given me the Divine Star. Where I had first gotten magic.

And the closer I came to the cave, the more my magic strengthened. Enough that against the dragon's will and with all her resistance, I was still pulling her forward.

I put my feet down on the wet tunnel floor, then gave a hard yank to tow the dragon behind me. It was nearly out of air and had lost most of its fight. Thanks to the Malice, I had not.

"Do not bury me again," Atroxia cried into my head. "I beg you not to take me here."

I remembered my fear when I first realized I was trapped inside Caesar's cave, lost in a darkness so black that I couldn't see my hand in front of my own eyes. Even for all my past crimes, I had never deserved to be here, but Atroxia did. I wasn't sure how she had helped in Caesar's assassination, but it must have been bad enough that Rome passed a sentence of death upon her. It made no difference whether her sentence was carried out in a tomb on Senator Valerius's property or here in Caesar's cave. Either way, she would get the punishment she deserved.

The tunnel took us uphill, most of which I spent in dragging the Mistress as she fought to resist me. Even with the Malice, it was exhausting work. Once we came to the stale air from Caesar's cave, I felt stronger, but worried she would too. Would she try to fight me in this dark, enclosed place? Maybe not. I felt the tremor of her heavy body collapsing onto the ground and heard her harsh panting. Hopefully, she had given up. The sooner she accepted her fate, the better.

I dropped the dragon's tail inside the cave, then found someplace a little farther on where I could heal myself from the wounds along the side of my body. From the clinking of metal below me, I was sure that I was resting on a large pile of gold coins. The first time I had seen them, I'd believed that a few gold coins could have bought my freedom, which I still wanted more than anything.

Now I doubted there was enough gold in this cave to buy me even an hour of freedom. The only way I would ever truly be

SIX

I didn't move, didn't want Atroxia to have any chance of finding me. In some ways, I feared the human vestalis more than the dragon.

I understood the Mistress. I had felt her rage, her absolute loyalty to Diana, and her sole desire to take the Malice away from me. It was easy to fight what I understood.

But Atroxia was different. The only other vestalis I'd met was the older woman who saved me and Aurelia in Caesar's temple, who showed me how to find the Jupiter Stone and who told me that there were things I had to learn from the Mistress. From Atroxia. Considering how our battle had gone so far, I had serious doubts about that.

"Nicolas?" Atroxia asked again. "Please answer me. I'm afraid."

Coins clinked beneath her feet as she walked. I couldn't tell how far away she was, but probably not as far as I would've liked. Yet the slightest move would give away my position, so I remained just as frozen as before.

Finally, she stopped walking, or at least, everything went

silent in the room. "Will you at least tell me where we are? I don't like the air." After another moment of silence, she added, "Caesar's ghost roams this place. I can feel him here."

Cautiously, I sat up, though my hand was on the bulla and I was ready to defend myself if necessary.

"His death was so long ago, and yet he still cannot rest," I said. "Why not? What was your crime?"

I waited for the sound of her footsteps coming toward me, but there was nothing. After a moment, she said, "My crime was to fall in love with Marcus Brutus. It is forbidden for vestals to fall in love."

Marcus Brutus had descended from Diana. The man he killed, Caesar, had come from the goddess Venus. I'd been told of Diana's jealousy because Caesar was the favored of the demigods. After all, if Brutus was the lesser heir, did that make Diana a lesser goddess? Perhaps Marcus Brutus was also jealous of Caesar. Jealous enough to want him dead.

I shook my head. "Falling in love might've violated your vestal oath. But that wasn't a crime against Caesar."

Atroxia drew in a sharp breath, as if holding back tears. "The vestals also protect many of the treasures of Rome. One of them was a hunting knife that had once belonged to the gods. It belonged to —"

"Diana," I finished. "The vestals had her knife, and Brutus wanted it."

"I don't think he ever loved me in return," Atroxia said.

"He only made me believe that so he could persuade me to get the knife for him."

"Sixty senators attacked Caesar on the day he was killed," I said. "Any one of them could have dealt him the fatal blow."

A sob erupted from her before she caught it in her throat. "He was stabbed by those senators twenty-three times. As a demigod, he could have survived them all. The wound that finally killed him came from Diana's blade, held by Brutus. Stolen from the vestals . . . by me."

Silence fell between us yet again. This time, I couldn't quite believe everything I was hearing. What she had done was wrong, no doubt. Very wrong. But Radulf had told me that Brutus and the other senators involved in Caesar's assassination were allowed to safely leave the city. Atroxia was not granted that privilege.

"For that they buried you alive?"

She was crying again. "Please do not leave me here in this cave. Not where I must face Caesar's ghost. Not where I am condemned yet again."

"Diana cursed you, Atroxia. You are more than a vestal. You are the Mistress."

Coins clinked beneath her feet. She was moving again. But so was I, as quietly as possible.

"She had to curse me, to save my life. And in return, I must do as she wishes. Diana is right to be angry, Nicolas. You should understand that better than anyone."

"Me? Why?"

"What has Rome ever done for you? They enslaved you — oh, yes, I know more than you think. They have betrayed you and even sought to kill you to get your power for themselves. They have never valued you, just as the gods have never valued Diana, even after all she has done. No, it was always Venus they loved. They gave Caesar honors and left Brutus to make his own way in the world."

I became aware we were no longer talking about me — if we ever were. No, this was about the feud between Brutus and Caesar. Between Diana and Venus.

"I want nothing from Rome but my freedom," I said. "I will protect the empire only until I can leave this place behind."

"And all the Mistress wants is to bring the empire down," Atroxia said. "To leave them in ruins the way they left me in ruins. She will rebuild a new empire, dedicated solely to Diana." There was a new sound in the room. It was metal, but this time a slicing sound, not a clinking one. I didn't recognize it.

"Your anger is poisoning you," I said. "That's your true curse. Until you let go of that anger, you will always be the Mistress. And I will have to leave you trapped in here."

"No!"

An arm wrapped around my throat and pulled me to the ground. Atroxia had grabbed me from behind, and now something sharp went to my neck. Some sort of blade. That was the slicing sound I had heard — Atroxia picking it up from somewhere in the room.

"The Malice must be used to serve Diana. So you will either swear to serve her, or I will take the Malice from you as a gift to the goddess. With it, she will defeat the gods and take her proper place amongst them."

I could have used the Malice to easily stop her, but I didn't yet know its magic. Would I use too much and collapse this cave room? Even if I survived it, whatever magic I unleashed might also provide a means for her escape, and I could not risk that. So instead, I contained my magic and struggled against the sharp edge. It wasn't enough. I knew exactly where it cut.

She was fumbling for the bulla, trying to break the strap around my neck, and nicking my skin with each failed attempt. "You will not leave me here," she said. "Take me away, or all your magic will be mine!"

"I will not take you anywhere!" I said. "You are evil, Atroxia, and you deserve this curse. Stay here, and sort out your complaints with Caesar's ghost. He will be your only company!"

Then I closed my eyes and pictured the shore of Lake Nemi. Dawn was rising outside; I could see the earliest hints of light. And almost as suddenly as I had imagined it, I was there.

Granted, I'd landed on my back at the edge of the shore, where each wave came up beneath me, beckoning me back into the water.

But I wouldn't go down again. Diana would drown me if I did. I felt for the Malice first, and then the bulla, and then wiped at the cuts on my neck. It stung, but the Divine Star was already at work healing them, and all other parts of my body that still felt some pain.

I stood and faced the water, then held out my right hand toward the lake. The Malice would seal up the tunnel, trapping Atroxia inside Caesar's cave. Trapping the dragon there.

But as soon as the tunnel closed, I heard Atroxia's voice in my head again, sobbing. "That wasn't me, Nicolas. The Mistress seeks to control me again. Even the best person could not fight a curse such as this. Please help me."

Her pleas would do her no good. She could cry all she wanted, but it wouldn't change her crimes against Caesar or what she had just attempted against me. Maybe the vestalis wasn't so different from the dragon after all. They were only two halves of the same angry creature.

"You are exactly where you belong," I whispered, hoping she would hear me. "And for as long as I have magic, you will stay there."

Whatever I was supposed to have learned from Atroxia was a failure. The old vestalis I had met was wrong. Atroxia had nothing to teach me about love.

SEVEN

I stood on the shores of Lake Nemi for several minutes, listening for anything else Atroxia might have to say. But she had gone silent. I was aware of her crying, but she wasn't intending for me to hear and it felt intrusive to continue listening.

When I turned to go, I scanned the hillside until I found Diana's temple, partially hidden by thick brush and the mountain itself. If Aurelia and Crispus had been successful in rescuing Radulf, then Caela would be back with them by now. Something had gone wrong. I needed to get up there.

"Callistus!" I called.

The unicorn ran out to greet me, and even before he halted, I leapt onto his back and we hurried toward the hillside.

But we weren't yet to the slope when Caela squawked overhead, a desperate caw that made me nervous. Where were Aurelia and Crispus? Where was Radulf?

Caela swooped low, directly above us, then pulled me off the unicorn's back and held me in her large talon as she flew up the hillside. Callistus turned down the hill again. When I last saw him, he was running with the horses Aurelia and

Crispus had brought here. I hoped they would return to Radulf's home together.

As we flew upward along the hillside slope, we passed directly over the massive oak tree where I had hidden the Jupiter Stone. Almost immediately past that I saw the temple, yet there were no signs of life anywhere.

No signs of life. The worry in me deepened.

Caela arced over the temple, and then we headed to lower ground again. Before we got too far away, I pointed out a pile of hay that must have been set out for any horses that'd be left here while their masters were inside. "Drop me there!" I yelled to Caela.

She did drop me, but naturally missed the haystack. Instead, I landed on the worn trail near the grove, my head knocking against a rock that jutted out from the earth. Caela had yet to drop me anywhere soft. Perhaps there was a reason she had put me so near to the grove.

Once my head cleared, and despite my hurry, I scaled down to the trees to ensure the stone was still in its place on the lower limb of the great oak. I didn't know how many rocks in this world could be used to make a Jupiter Stone. Probably not a lot. Perhaps the rock I'd found was the only one, which increased my need to protect it. But when I checked, it was gone and didn't appear to be anywhere on the ground nearby, so I knew it hadn't just blown off in the wind.

Someone had taken it, which confused me. The vestalis and I were the only ones who knew what that rock was meant to become. So either it was taken by accident . . . or someone else knew our secret.

"I know your secret," Atroxia said into my head.

And she had been here at this temple. Could the Mistress have shifted into her human form, as Atroxia, and retrieved the stone? Would Atroxia have done that? If Atroxia knew my secret, did the Mistress know it too?

I couldn't answer any of those questions, nor did I have the time to consider them now. I had to get back up to the temple immediately. I ran up the hillside, listening for any sounds in or out of my head. Surely, Radulf would know I was close . . . unless the Mistress was telling the truth and had taken all his magic. He probably wouldn't have survived that.

Diana's temple was partially built into the hillside, yet had a grand portico to allow a fine view of the lake. However, I suspected that the scenery was rarely appreciated by temple worshippers. Not if the activities that went on in this temple were as dark as Crispus had suggested.

Unsure of what I'd face when I went inside, I hesitated a moment on the steps. The thick wooden door was heavy and forbidding, an obvious warning that anyone who took the trouble to open it had better be ready for whatever might happen inside. But before I walked any farther, Crispus pushed open that same door and came running out. He stopped as soon as he saw me, looking as surprised to see me as I was him. "I was just coming to find you," he said.

"What about Radulf?"

"He's here." Crispus furrowed his brow. "Come inside. Hurry."

I followed him in. Sconces with lit torches were on the walls, and a blackened altar was at the far end of the dark room with a place for a fire beneath it. I didn't want to know anything more of the ceremonies that took place here. I only wanted to find Radulf and leave as quickly as possible.

But that was not going to happen. Every entrance into the room suddenly filled with Praetors, dozens of them surrounding us. Crispus moved closer to me and withdrew his sword while my hands flooded with magic.

"Nicolas Calva, there you are at last!" That was Decimas Brutus, walking to the front of the group. He was the grandson of Caesar's murderer by several generations and looked as cold as if he had personally held that knife. Brutus was a tall man of incredible strength, and also someone capable of great cruelty. His hair was curly and black, but his eyes were blacker still, the rims of them seeming to be lined with soot gathered from the burned lands of Tartarus. "You're finally above ground, I see."

My wishes for him were suddenly more focused below ground, preferably with several feet of dirt over him.

"You wouldn't dare use magic here." He was watching my hands carefully for any movement. "What if this ancient temple collapsed, just as the last one did? You've proved your ability to survive something like that, but would Crispus? Or the sewer girl, inside the tunnels beneath this mountain? Or your grandfather? Surely you've guessed from Crispus's expression that his life hangs only by a thread."

"I can do plenty of damage without collapsing this temple!" I said.

"And I wish I could see your little magic games, truly I do." Brutus held up his hands in a gesture of peace. "But we didn't come here to fight." Though the light was dim, I noticed something held in his left hand. At first I expected it to be the missing stone, but instead it was some sort of armband. "Where is the Mistress, Nicolas? I can feel her, so I know you've left her alive."

"She is where she belongs," I said. "Paying for her crimes against Caesar, as Marcus Brutus should have paid for his." My eyes narrowed. "And as you must one day pay for yours."

Brutus only shot back an accusing smile. "We must all pay for our crimes, no?" Before I could answer, he shrugged that away. "But for as long as the Mistress continues to serve Diana, we shall continue to serve her." He turned his attention to Crispus. "Son of Senator Valerius, do you serve the Mistress too? After all, you are a Praetor now, a judge, just as I am."

"I am a Praetor." One cautious step at a time, Crispus moved closer to my side. "But I'm nothing like you, and I will not serve the Mistress."

"Why not? Didn't she preserve your life and the life of your betrothed? Did you think there was no price for that protection?"

He held out the armband, and now I saw it better. Thin, silver, and in the shape of a curved arrow, it was the symbol of the Praetor's worship of Diana and provided them power to take my magic. It was intended for Crispus to wear.

He shook his head. "While Diana stands in rebellion against the other gods, I cannot swear any loyalty to her. And I will not help you bring harm to my friends."

Brutus smiled. "But that is the point, son of Valerius. Your cooperation might be the only way to save your friends. The slave boy can handle himself, this is true, but what about the girl inside the tunnels? Only you know where your betrothed is." He tilted his head. "She is still promised to you, yes?"

As carefully as he had moved before, Crispus nodded.

"And so she is safe . . . *if* you are one of us. But if you are not, then her life might be in terrible danger at this very moment. Perhaps some hidden threat awaits her in the darkness of that tunnel. Do you understand me?"

Radulf's life was equally at risk, I guessed. The choice to save them was being offered to Crispus.

He leaned toward me. "What would you have me do?"

As long as no Praetor got a hand on me, I'd defeat every man here. But the Malice's protection might not extend to Crispus, and it certainly didn't help Aurelia and Radulf.

Brutus walked closer to Crispus with the armband still held out. "Accept this now, become one of us, and we will leave in peace. You will allow the slave boy to find his grandfather, and perhaps save their lives. Or reject my generous offer, and force us to fight."

Crispus stepped back until he was almost behind me, though I had far more reason than him to avoid the Praetors. "Nic?"

"Go with them," I muttered.

"They will never have my loyalty, no matter what." His voice was firm, but he did sheath his sword.

"Go with them," I repeated. "Every moment we waste here risks all our lives."

"I'm sorry." Crispus scuffed his boot against the ground, barely looking at me as he walked up to Brutus.

"Kneel," Brutus commanded him.

Crispus hesitated a moment, and his hands were balled into fists when he finally obeyed. Brutus lifted Crispus's right arm and slid Diana's band above the elbow, then pressed on the edges to tighten it.

"Now you are truly a Praetor," Brutus said. "A servant of the goddess Diana, and a patron of the Mistress. You and your family are under her protection, and ours."

Crispus and his family. That meant his mother . . . and his future wife. As long as she remained promised to Crispus, Aurelia would be safe.

Crispus stood and immediately looked back at me. "Radulf is deeper in the temple. Call for Aurelia, and she'll guide you to her. You need to hurry."

I stared at him, trying to assess whether he was still a friend. I knew he valued our friendship, as did I. But the greatest danger to my life was in the form of a silver band that was now wrapped around his arm. He had become one of them. In some ways, so had Aurelia, I supposed.

"Go," Crispus said.

I turned from him and raised one hand of warning, filled with magic that wanted to force the Praetors aside, but they were already parting for me along a deep passage that was blackened by fire. This must be where the Mistress had taken refuge. It was also where I'd find Radulf. I hoped he was still alive.

Still in the main room behind me, Brutus called for his Praetors to follow him, announcing that they would go in search of the Mistress. I hoped they would try their best to find her, and all drown in the process. Except Crispus. Except Crispus, *probably*. I didn't know exactly how I felt about him at the moment. But whether Crispus helped them search for her or not, I doubted they'd have much luck.

At least they were leaving, as Brutus had promised.

Without another look back, I raced down the passageway. It was narrow and dark and felt like a trap. It probably wasn't — Praetors were running past me, away from Aurelia and Radulf as I hurried toward them. But that didn't change the growing feeling within me of being drawn into a space I wouldn't easily escape.

"Aurelia!" I called.

I hadn't gone very far before I heard her desperate reply. "Nic? Where are you? Hurry! Nic, what's been happening?"

I followed her voice, checking along the way that the tunnel truly had emptied of all Praetors. There was no way to be completely sure — Praetors had a way of disappearing like bats in a cave — but I saw nothing to arouse my suspicions.

Finally, a dim light appeared ahead, in a small room off to one side of the tunnel. I walked in and first saw the shackles attached to the stone walls, too high above the floor for Radulf to have stood there. He would have hung from these chains.

Then my attention went to Aurelia, sitting on the ground beside Radulf, whose body was stretched out on its side as if he were asleep. I knew it wasn't anything as peaceful as that, though. His eyes were closed, and I couldn't tell whether he was breathing. Possibly not, for I could hardly find a place on his body that didn't bear some sort of visible injury. If that was what I could see, I well imagined the wounds he bore on the inside too.

"Is he . . . alive?" I whispered.

Aurelia shrugged. "His pulse is so faint, I might be imagining it. Can you heal him?"

I licked my lips, then walked over to Radulf and knelt beside him. I felt for the Divine Star at his back, but nothing sparked beneath my touch, as it should have. Then I bent lower to listen for any breath. Maybe there was something, or maybe it was just the air moving in the room.

"Help me roll him onto his back," I said, and Aurelia quickly did. Then I placed my hand, palm down, directly over Radulf's heart, and began pouring into his chest every bit of magic I could. I had to be careful not to give too much; that would be like curing a man's thirst by dumping him in the ocean. But I needed enough to help him hold on to what life might still remain within him, even if it was the faintest beat.

"You save his life and destroy mine?" Atroxia cried into my head. Her desperation hit me like a rogue wave. "I am no worse than he is. Save me too, please."

I released Radulf long enough to put a hand on the side of my head and catch my breath. I hadn't expected to hear the young vestalis so far from where she was entombed. And I didn't like what she had to say. I wasn't the judge of her crimes, I wasn't the one who'd sentenced her to such a terrible fate. And regardless of who she believed herself to be, I knew her as the Mistress. That was justification enough for what I'd done.

"Don't stop yet. He needs you." Aurelia pressed her hands over mine and returned them to Radulf. She kept them in place, and even moved toward me as if her closeness would help.

It didn't. Aside from the fact that she was a growing distraction to my every thought, she was also promised to Crispus, as she had to be. That promise had just saved her life, and she didn't seem to even know it.

"Move back," I whispered. I didn't want her to. But the longer her hand remained over mine, the more I wanted to hold it, and then to hold her. Didn't she understand the effect her presence had on me? "Please, Aurelia."

She nodded and hid the sadness on her face as she released my hands and scooted away. They felt cold in her absence, but warmed as they filled with magic again, all of which I gave to

Radulf. He was still unmoving on the ground, far more dead than alive.

"Where is Crispus?" Aurelia asked. "Didn't he come back with you?"

"We'll meet him in Rome." Though I couldn't say whether it would be as a friend or as an enemy. After she was his wife, Aurelia would become the same, my friend or my enemy. It really didn't matter which. She still had the ability to crush my heart in a way that Brutus, or even the Mistress, never could.

As I continued working on Radulf, I felt strength draining from me, just as it always had before, but the Malice was replenishing it just as quickly. Once I trusted the Malice to keep the magic inside me balanced, I knew I could concentrate instead on trying to reach Radulf's mind.

"I'm here," I told him.

Nothing came in response. It made me think of when I had tried to heal Crispus's father, giving him every bit of magic within me. There had been no response then either. I'd been too weak to heal Valerius.

Was it the same now?

"Save my life too," the Mistress said. No, it was still Atroxia speaking, the human. I knew that, because in a quieter, softer voice, she added, "Break this curse upon me, please."

"We have to leave this temple." If I was going to save Radulf, we had to get farther from the lake. "There are too many distractions here."

"What distractions?" Aurelia asked. "It's only the three of us here." Then she drew back from me again. "Oh, I'm the distraction."

She was — that was true — though it wasn't at all what I had meant. But she leaned forward, still keeping herself at a distance from me. "If we disappear from this place, can your grandfather survive the journey?"

I sent more magic into him. "If you die, then I'll win," I told Radulf, sounding as arrogant and bullheaded as I could, the tone that would irritate him the most. "Everyone will say that I was stronger than my grandfather."

He grunted, or I thought he did. Whatever it was, there had been some sign of life from him.

"Nic, you fool," he finally mumbled.

"You are a fool." The Mistress's anger seared its way into my head. "When I escape this cave, you will pay for what you've done."

Radulf's visible wounds were beginning to heal, but I knew that things were far more serious on the inside. Without the Malice, I'd never have been able to help Radulf get this far. Even with it, I was starting to feel drained. If we were going to leave, we needed to do it while I had enough strength for all three of us.

I stretched a hand out to Aurelia. "We're leaving."

She hesitated. "Why are you acting so strange?"

"Take my hand, Aurelia."

She did, and I pulled her closer to me, putting one arm

around her waist to ensure she would stay with me as we left. I drew in her scent and tried to keep my focus on Radulf and where we needed to go.

"Get us out," Radulf mumbled.

"I will get out," the Mistress growled at me. "And when I do, I will find you."

"Hush!" I said.

Aurelia started to protest that she hadn't said anything, but I only shook my head at her. Then I closed my eyes and pictured Radulf's atrium. Despite the darkness in here, it was morning in Rome. A beautiful, warm autumn morning.

Disappearing from one place to another felt like squeezing oneself into a vise to be small enough to vanish. As hard as that was with one person, or even two, now I was trying to squeeze three of us into the same space. All while continuing to heal Radulf and keeping the Mistress out of my head.

The last sound in my head before we disappeared was the Mistress again. "You will kneel to me."

If she said anything more, it became lost in the journey from the cave. Finally, there was something about disappearing that I didn't hate. I just hoped we'd end up somewhere far enough away that her voice couldn't reach me.

EIGHT

When Aurelia and I arrived in the atrium, we fell apart from each other, both of us reeling from the pressure of being squeezed so close. I immediately rolled back to my knees to check on Radulf. His entire body was shaking, as if his soul was still catching up from the body's disappearance.

I pressed both hands onto his chest, sending him all the magic I could until the shaking stopped. He was breathing more easily than before, but there wasn't much life left in him.

"Mother, I heard noises —" Livia rushed into the atrium and stopped when she saw the three of us on the ground.

"Your grandfather needs to be in his bed." Aurelia was crouched beside me, balancing Radulf's limp head in her hands. "Help us carry him there."

I could have done it alone, but what strength I still had was needed elsewhere. We stood to lift Radulf, then heard someone else behind us.

"You did it." The flat tone of my mother's voice revealed her conflicted feelings. Obviously, she would be happy that I had returned, as well as Aurelia. But she was hardly bursting with joy to see Radulf with us.

"We need your help," I said.

After a heavy sigh, my mother got beside Livia to carry Radulf's feet, while Aurelia balanced his head and shoulders. I went in the middle, keeping both hands under Radulf as we walked, to take the bulk of his weight.

Radulf's bed was as fine as any place an emperor might have to sleep, and even lying on the soft mattress seemed to make him rest more comfortably. I sat beside him, continuing to work on healing his many injuries, while Aurelia dimmed the candlelight in the room and covered his windows. Livia soon left, telling us she would speak to the servants in Radulf's home about protecting the place from any Praetors.

And my mother stood beside me, her arms folded in disapproval. "You're wet," she said. "And your tunic is burned."

I smiled up at her. "It would've been more burned if I hadn't been all wet."

"And this is a good thing?"

"If I come back, then I think it's a very good thing."

She didn't even pretend to enjoy the joke. "You think because you made it back that now our problems are over? That you escaped the wrath of the Praetors, or that dragon? Have you escaped the wrath of Rome itself?"

My smile fell. "I know this isn't over, Mother. But I'm getting stronger, and smarter about how I fight them. I can win this."

She knelt on the floor beside me. "You can't win. That's what I'm trying to tell you. The price for using magic is high. Every wave of your hand, every time you disappear, and whatever else you can do that I haven't yet seen, there is a price for all of it! Your father understood that — it's why he didn't use his magic in Gaul, even when he could have. Once he did, you know how it ended. That was the price he had to pay."

"I won't make the same mistakes."

Mother took one of my hands and held it in her own. "You are too reckless with magic, like your grandfather. Since you first received the Divine Star, how many times has magic almost cost you your life?"

I lowered my eyes, hoping she hadn't already seen the answer in them. I couldn't count the number of times, even if I wanted to.

She ran her fingers over the Malice on my forearm, tracing the outline of the wolf carved into the silver. "Please, Nic, destroy this Malice, and the bulla around your neck. Or they will destroy you."

Radulf suddenly arched his back and began coughing violently. I pulled my hand away from my mother's and pressed him back down to his bed.

"I need you both to leave," I said. "Please, just let me concentrate on him."

"Your father died because of a single mistake, and with magic far less powerful." Mother rose to her feet. "Even if you think you can succeed, for my sake and Livia's — make the right choice. Destroy that Malice."

I heard her, but turned away to focus on Radulf. Or maybe I turned so that I didn't have to acknowledge that my mother might be right.

"Let's go." Aurelia held out a hand to my mother, who left without another word. After a moment, Aurelia followed, shutting the door behind them.

Free of any distractions, I used the Divine Star to find the injuries inside Radulf's body and heal them one by one. The Mistress had been thorough, and cruel. If he was still alive after all this time, it was only because she had wanted that. Without magic, he never would've made it.

And now his magic was completely gone. I knew that, because I could feel its absence. I could restore the little life he had left, but nothing in my power would return what had been stolen from him.

I reached one hand over his shoulder and pressed against his Divine Star. Mine always sparked in the presence of magic, and I hoped his would do the same, as proof of even a small remnant of his powers. But nothing was there, and it might never return. At least he was alive. Without magic, I doubted he'd care that he had survived. He'd say I had failed him. And in some ways, he'd be right.

By evening, I was leaning against a wall to rest when Radulf finally stirred. He angled his head to see me and mumbled, "Ten days. What took you so long to come?"

"I was stuck."

He harrumphed, then said, "You must have the Malice, or else I wouldn't be here."

I walked closer to him and, when his eyes opened, showed him the amulet wrapped around my arm.

"It's so much more beautiful than the false one ever was." A faint smile crossed his lips. "You should've seen the Mistress's fury when she realized what I had was fake. She —" Now the smile disappeared. "Well, she was displeased."

"What did she do to you . . . ?" I had almost ended that sentence with "Grandfather."

"You healed me," he said. "You must have some idea."

I did, and it was awful. She would have shown him cruelty that knew no limits, a depth of torture that had been intended for me before he tricked her. "The Mistress is trapped beneath Lake Nemi," I said. "In Caesar's cave, where the bulla was found."

"Sooner or later, she'll find a way out." Radulf swallowed hard, and I offered him a drink. After he accepted it, he lay back down and mumbled, "She wants the Malice, but she needs you to make it work. She'll do whatever it takes to force you to make a Jupiter Stone."

I glanced back at the doorway, half expecting to see my mother in its frame, reminding me of the price of using magic. She wasn't there, but her warning still echoed in my ears.

The stone that I'd hidden in the oak tree was missing, and I was becoming increasingly sure that the Mistress must have it, locked in a claw as she searched for an escape from Caesar's cave. All the more reason to never set her free.

"I won't help her," I said.

He continued as if he hadn't heard me. "The Mistress knows you can call in a storm. She'll convince you to make one, all the while claiming that you're protected by the bulla and the Malice. It'll be a lie, Nic. When it's over, she'll have the stone — the power of Jupiter himself. You won't survive it."

"I won't make the stone," I said. "No matter what she says or does."

"She believes there's a way to make you do it. She told me that herself." He motioned for more water, which I gave to him. After a long rest, he said, "I was wrong all this time. I was arrogant and believed magic made me invincible. My greed prevented me from seeing things clearly. Forgive me."

"Magic is not good or bad, sir. It's only what we do with it."

"And what is done to us. What will be done to you before this war is over." With a faltering hand, he reached out and touched the Malice on my forearm. "You must destroy this amulet. It won't break the Mistress's curse, but it will set you free. It's the only way to save yourself."

"If the curse isn't broken, the dragon remains. What she'll do to Rome —"

"Is not our problem." He drew in a slow, pained breath. "Nic, trust me. Destroy that Malice, or things will grow worse for all of us."

"I don't know how to do it."

"Promise me that you will find a way. And that you will never quit trying until you succeed."

I stared at him a moment. Could I give him my word when I didn't know how to make it happen, or whether it even could be done? But his eyes begged me to answer him, with even greater desperation than his words had. Finally, I said, "If it is possible, then I will find a way."

One corner of his mouth upturned, just a little. More important, he finally seemed to be at rest. "Enough now. Leave me to sleep. Those of us without magic take longer to heal."

I heard the sadness in his voice as he spoke, and left him with my heart so heavy I was surprised I could walk away.

Equally surprising was to find Aurelia outside Radulf's room. She was seated on the floor, resting against the wall, and might've even been asleep before she heard me come out. When I did, she jumped to her feet.

"How long have you been out here?" I glanced around us. We were alone.

Her eyes flicked to the bedroom, telling me she had been out here for as long as I had been in there with Radulf.

"You look exhausted," she said. "Everyone else has already eaten their dinner, but I'm sure you're hungry too."

I shrugged. "I just want to be alone. Maybe I'll take a walk through the gardens."

As I started out the door, Aurelia said, "I want to be alone too. Do you think you and I could be alone together?"

My heart skipped a beat, and I looked around us again, not sure of whether I wanted this moment to be interrupted. "That's not a good idea."

She sighed. "I'm going to come with you, Nic. It's only a question of whether I'll walk beside you or behind you. I warn you, though, if I must follow, then I'm going to throw rocks at the back of your head."

"Well, we can't have that." I smiled, then motioned for her to come with me. "Let's go be alone together."

NINE

Since his home was built on old military lands, Radulf had a lot of space to himself. Some soldiers still trained nearby, though, and they were loyal to their general. There was little risk of Praetors attempting to sneak back here. If they came — no, *when* they came — they would come like proper guests, or never get past the soldiers.

So the Praetors weren't my biggest worry as I walked back here with Aurelia. I wasn't even worried at all, not really. I only felt the dread of knowing she and I had serious matters to discuss, and that I probably wouldn't like the outcome of our conversation.

"While you were in with Radulf, Crispus sent a message to me," she began. "Is it true that he's with the Praetors? He's one of them?"

"He did what he had to do," I said. "They gave him no choice."

She spoke more loudly. "There's always a choice!"

"If there was, he would've done it."

"He should've refused them."

"He tried that."

She was becoming angrier. "He didn't try hard enough! What was so important to him that it was worth what he did?"

I stopped walking to face her. "You are that important! Aurelia, he did it to protect you from the Mistress."

"Oh."

We continued on in silence for several minutes, most of which I spent wishing I'd just told her to go ahead and throw rocks at my head. That would've been simpler.

We were deeper into Radulf's gardens when she said, "We're only friends, Nic."

Was she saying that about her and Crispus? It had been several minutes since his name had come up. Or did she mean that she and I were only friends?

I started to ask, but stopped when I heard a sound behind us. The swelling magic within me calmed when I saw a large stag in a clump of cypress trees at the edge of Radulf's property. There were deer in many places around Rome, though they weren't often seen in the city and rarely had I ever seen a stag as grand as this one. His antlers came to a dozen points and were worn like a crown upon his head.

"It's beautiful," Aurelia whispered.

I glanced over at her, and then quickly lowered my eyes when she caught me staring. When I looked for the stag again, he had vanished from my sight. At least he had been a good distraction.

When Aurelia and I continued walking, our conversation took a turn, one that made it a little easier for me to breathe. "You were wet because you pulled the Mistress into Lake Nemi, yes?"

"She's sealed up in the same cave where I first found the bulla."

"The dragon or the human?"

I shrugged. "Both, I suppose. There's no difference between them."

"There's every difference! I know how terrified I'd be if you'd left me alone in that much darkness!"

"And if I release her, then I release the dragon! What Crispus has done will protect you, but no one else in Rome."

"Of course." Aurelia pursed her lips. "I know you heard Atroxia crying when she was in the temple on Crispus's land."

"Only when I got close enough. She began crying again after I left her in Caesar's cave."

"Could you hear her from the edge of the lake?" Aurelia paused a moment, and almost seemed hesitant to ask the next question. "Right before we left Diana's temple, could you hear her then?"

"I hear her right now. She's stronger than before." I pressed a hand against my forehead. "Sometimes it's Atroxia; sometimes it's the Mistress. I think she shifts from one form to the other, trying to figure out which is more likely to get her released."

"The Mistress threatens you, yes?" Aurelia asked. "What about Atroxia?"

"She begs me to help her."

"Only you can help me," Atroxia whispered just then. "Please, Nic."

Aurelia stopped walking when I did. "Help her? How?"

It was my turn to shrug. "I think the Mistress uses Atroxia to trick me. I can't trust or believe the things she says."

"What if it's real? What if Atroxia is asking you to break the curse so that she can just go back to being a vestalis again?"

I sighed. "Even if that were true, I can't break the curse." I didn't know how to do that, just as I didn't know how to destroy the amulets or how to win the Praetor War. I didn't even know how to properly talk to Aurelia right now. Just thinking of everything I didn't know compared to the few unimportant things I did suddenly made me very tired, enough that I had to lean against a nearby brick wall.

She pulled my hand from my forehead and held it between both of hers. "Nic, are you well?"

"I was awake all night, then spent most of my strength on Radulf today. Nothing more."

"That's not it. I see the way everyone pulls at you, telling you what to do. I'm one of those people, so I know it's happening. We only do it because we care about you and about how this all ends, and we only say what we think is right. But I know it's weighing on you." Her brows furrowed, and she stepped in closer to me. "How can I help?"

I knew what didn't help, and that was having her so close. Didn't she know that her very presence changed the beat of my heart, the rhythm of my breath? If not for the wall behind me, I would've backed away.

No, I wouldn't have backed away. The wall was only an excuse. I wanted to be here with her, more than anything. But I also wanted her here without a promise to Crispus or a threat from the Mistress standing between us.

I continued staring at her and saw a stray lock of hair that had fallen free of its braid. I took it and gently folded it behind her ear, letting my hand linger there longer than it should have. I leaned even closer toward her.

"Nic?"

That was Crispus's voice. Aurelia and I backed away from each other and must've stood there looking immensely stupid when Crispus found us. His eyes roamed from her to me.

"I've just arrived," he finally said. "How is Radulf?"

"He'll live." Simple as the words were, I felt guilty for saying them because I had not been able to save Crispus's father, who hadn't been nearly as injured as Radulf.

Crispus accepted my answer without judgment. He only pointed to his Praetor armband. "We should talk about this."

"If you touch Nic, will he lose his magic?" Aurelia's question had a bitter edge to it. Any Praetor's touch would empty me of my powers.

Crispus shrugged. "I think so, especially if that was my intention for touching him. But I'm not here for that reason. I'll never do that. I'm still the person I was this morning."

"Are you?" Aurelia put her hands on her waist. "This morning, had you pledged loyalty to the man who wants to destroy Nic's life?"

The sting of her words registered on Crispus's face. He said, "While you were in the tunnels with Radulf, Praetors were there too, Aurelia, ready to kill you both. What I did saved both our lives, and maybe Nic's as well! And I spent today learning from that man about his plans for Nic. I can warn him now."

I didn't like the tone of his voice. "Warn me about what?"

"They're not finished with Radulf. They know he's lost his magic, so for the first time since he came to Rome, he's vulnerable. After they get him, they'll come for you."

Of course they would. Crispus shouldn't have needed a day with Brutus to figure that out.

"I can defend myself," I said. "The Malice will ensure that." I hadn't yet decided whether to destroy it, as Radulf and my mother both wanted. The gods had given me this magic, including the key to find the Malice.

But was that their gift to me? Or their curse? Maybe I was just as cursed as Atroxia and didn't know it.

Crispus continued, "There are no limits to what they will do to get control of you. Do you remember before the chariot races, when my father urged Radulf to get you out of the empire? It's not too late to leave, but soon it will be."

"Where would I go?" I shook my head. "I have nowhere to go. Nowhere to hide my family."

"I do." Crispus stepped toward me and Aurelia. "My family is very wealthy, you both know that. When it came time to choose a wife, many young women were presented to my father as desirable options. Do you know why he chose my mother?"

Aurelia smiled. "Love?"

Crispus snorted. "That was never a consideration. It was because my mother's family held vast amounts of property up north. When she was young, they came here from the northernmost border of the empire, in hopes of gaining power within Rome. However, they never abandoned the home they left behind, up in Britannia."

"Britannia?" Aurelia said. "It's wild lands up there, cold and rainy, they say."

"It's also very beautiful, but more important, it's outside the empire now. Some of Rome's recent military campaigns haven't gone well, and the borders have receded to Hadrian's Wall. My mother's family lands are beyond the walls." Crispus hesitated, as if I should've understood his meaning. When it was clear I didn't, he added, "Her land is no longer part of the empire."

I shifted my weight, trying to be sure of what he was hinting at. "My family could go to Britannia?"

"Yes. I'll bring my mother too, and Aurelia."

Aurelia, who would become his wife.

I shook my head. "Thanks for your offer, but I'll find something else for my family."

"I could order us a carriage for morning," Crispus said. "Within a short journey, we could be free, all of us."

"No, not all of us." I was so uncomfortable by now that I started backing away, just to move. "Not me."

"If Nic stays, then we've got to help him," Aurelia said to Crispus.

"It's not safe here anymore," Crispus said.

"Then it's not safe for Nic either!" Aurelia countered. "He needs our help."

"I don't want anyone's help!" I was surprised to find myself shouting. There was no reason for it. Crispus had just made a generous offer, one I knew my family should accept. And the arrangement between him and Aurelia was exactly what it had to be, for any number of reasons. But I was still shouting. "You will go with Crispus to Britannia! You belong with him there!"

Crispus exhaled. "We've got to discuss that too."

I held up my hands. "No, we don't. We could discuss it a thousand times and the answer would still be the same. If she marries you, the Praetors will leave her alone. And they will never leave me alone, not while I have magic they want."

Aurelia started in. "Nic —"

"I'll speak to my family tomorrow." I was already leaving the gardens, on a near run to escape into Radulf's home. "Thanks for your offer, Crispus. I'll have an answer for you soon."

I went inside through the stables, which took me past Radulf's baths, newly repaired from when Livia and I escaped his home once. Just to release some of my emotions, I shot a ball of magic into his *tepidarium*, which exploded half the water throughout the room, soaking me for the second time that day. I merely shook it off and kept walking.

"Nic, wait!" Crispus ran in behind me, though he paused when he saw the walls still dripping wet. "Everyone knows how you feel about Aurelia. Why won't you just say it?"

"What good would that do? She's promised to you."

"Only to save her life; that's all."

I turned back to him. "No, that's not all. Right after she accepted your offer, I asked her not to marry you. She would not change her mind."

His eyes widened. Apparently, he had not known that. "If not for the Praetors, I'd have released her from the promise already. You could take her."

I snorted. "As if the Praetors don't already have enough ways to manipulate me?"

"When this is over, we can sort this out, all of us together. One of us has to take Aurelia. Then I could —"

"How dare you?" Aurelia appeared through the rear doorway with her hands on both hips, and her face red as a ripe tomato. "How dare you speak of me like I'm cattle to be traded or a bargain to be negotiated?"

Crispus and I backed away from her, standing rigidly beside each other, both afraid of what she might do next.

She started with him first, marching forward to face him directly. "I don't need your protection and certainly don't want it from those foul Praetors. I hate that armband and hate that you're one of them!" Then without warning, she raised both arms and shoved Crispus backward into Radulf's bath.

I laughed only for a single second before Aurelia was in front of me. "And you! How is it that you can battle a dragon or collapse an entire building over yourself, but you lack the courage to honestly tell me your feelings?"

I glanced backward at Crispus, who was still in the water and seemed happy to remain there where it was safer. He was staring up at me, waiting for an answer.

"Well," Aurelia demanded, "do you love me or not?"

Foolish though I knew it was, I barely managed to keep a smile off my face. "If I'm being honest, then right now, I'm more afraid of you than in love with you. And I'm already wet."

Aurelia's face pinched, and she shoved me into the water too. Then she wiped her hands on her tunic and marched out of the room, muttering, "I hate you both."

When she had gone, Crispus looked at me with a mischievous grin. "That could've gone better."

We knew we were both in trouble, and each had a fair amount of work to repair our friendships with Aurelia. But not tonight. For now, we just lay in the water and laughed.

When we finally calmed down, I swam toward him and said, "You're right, my family must go to Britannia. But I will stay in Rome and end this, somehow. If you arrange a carriage to take them there, they'll leave tomorrow."

"Then I'll stay too," Crispus said. "I know Aurelia won't leave without you, and I won't leave without her. Besides, you can't do this alone, and maybe it will turn out that having a Praetor on your side is a good thing."

Maybe. But I really couldn't see how.

TEN

Over breakfast the next morning, I told Livia and my mother about Crispus's family home in Britannia.

"I won't go," Livia said. "Not until we all go together."

"I agree," Mother said. "We've been separated enough already."

Crispus was seated beside Livia and leaned forward to appeal to her first. "Nic is safer without you here. If either of you were captured by the Praetors, think of what he would give up to save you."

Mother spoke. "Then let's leave together, all of us."

I barely heard her. Atroxia had found a way into my head again, and her pleas for help were stronger than ever before. "Do not leave me here," she cried.

"It'll be safe there," Crispus said, still trying to persuade Livia. "My mother was raised in Britannia and speaks fondly of her childhood."

"Am I safe here?" Atroxia asked. "Please help me, Nicolas."

"Livia and I shouldn't travel alone," Mother said.

"Radulf is still a general," Crispus said. "He has the respect of most Romans. Even if he is not quite well enough to travel as a proper escort, he will get you there safely."

Now Atroxia's softer whispers darkened as they became the Mistress's raspy voice. "There is no safety for your family, Nicolas. Swear loyalty to me and help me use the amulets, or they will pay!"

I stood, so suddenly that my knees bumped into the table, nearly spilling my mother's drink on the table.

"What's wrong?" Livia asked. "Nic, let us help you."

"You can help me by leaving," I said. "The carriage will come to take you away soon. Gather your things."

Before they could protest any further, I hurried out the door. Aurelia had been in the atrium, refusing to come in with us. But when she saw me coming, she turned away and folded her arms. She still looked angry, but the worst she could do was push me into the atrium pond.

"I'm not speaking to you," she said.

"That's fine, but I must speak to you." I took her by the elbow and led her into a quiet wing of the atrium. "Last night, Radulf made me promise to destroy the Malice. He believes it's the only way to get the Mistress to leave me alone, to leave all of us alone."

Aurelia's fists clenched, but she was listening. "What about the bulla, and the Divine Star?"

"They're valuable, but it's the Malice she wants."

"If you destroy it, the Mistress might know you're defenseless and attack. You'll have no way of stopping her."

"Which is the best reason to keep the Malice. Without the Malice, I also never could've healed Radulf or made all three of us disappear from Diana's temple."

"Do you think Radulf is right, that if the Malice is destroyed, the Mistress will leave you alone?"

"I don't know, but he's usually right about these things."

Aurelia's nose wrinkled. "He's never right. He's the one who wanted you to find the Malice in the first place."

"That was when he had magic too. When the Mistress had him, I think she told him things that made him understand her plans for the Malice. And her plans for me." I blew out a slow breath. "Aurelia, destroying the Malice might save my life or cost me my life. Keeping the Malice could go either way as well. I don't know what is the right choice."

She shook her head. "And you want me to decide for you?"

"Of course not! I only had a question."

Her eyes narrowed. "What?"

I stepped closer to her, speaking low enough that no one other than she would hear me. "Do you want to marry Crispus? Or do you have to marry him?"

Now those blue eyes moistened, making them seem even larger than usual. "Is that really your question?"

"If you want to marry him, then you should leave with him in the carriage today. I won't follow you to Britannia, which means the Praetors won't follow either. You can have the life you want, in peace."

"And what if I'm marrying Crispus only because I have to?"

"Then you should leave with him in the carriage. And if I can, I will follow you there."

The first tear fell on her cheek. "*If* you can?"

"I will not come to Britannia if there is any chance of us being followed. Either I defeat the Mistress or destroy her reason for following me."

She shook her head. "Don't do this to me. How can I possibly know which is the right choice?"

"I'm not asking you to make that decision. Only to tell me if I should follow you to Britannia."

Her shoulders fell. "Crispus knows how I feel. How is it that you still don't?"

I smiled back and took her hand. "Come with me."

"Where are we going?"

"We're going to destroy the Malice!"

ELEVEN

I hoped Aurelia wouldn't ask how I intended to destroy the Malice, because the truth was, I didn't know. Yes, I had threatened to do it when the Praetors wanted it, but that was only a threat.

I had told them that as a creation of the gods, the Malice could be destroyed only by another of their creations — the bulla. It had seemed logical then and still seemed like my best chance. But it also felt similar to the idea of Rome putting its two finest gladiators into the arena for a battle to the death. Anything could happen. I was nervous about the kind of damage that might accompany my plan.

For that reason, Aurelia and I walked far out into Radulf's open fields, as far as possible from any homes or people.

"Where should I stand?" For about the tenth time since we started walking, Aurelia tugged at her tunic. It was one of the rare times I'd ever seen her look this nervous.

"Stand behind me, as far as you can," I said. "I won't let anything get past me." Or at least, I would try. Bringing her out here wasn't the best idea, but I wanted someone nearby in case this experiment went badly.

She helped me unlace the Malice, standing so close while she did that I could barely concentrate. If this succeeded, my connection with the Mistress would end. I would return to Radulf's home and join them all in the carriage to leave the empire. I'd be free, and my family would be safe.

I laid the Malice on a rock, then walked far from it, gathering magic from the bulla into my hands as I did. I felt the loss of the Malice's magic, but not so long ago, the bulla had given me more than enough magic on its own. If anything on this earth could destroy that Malice, it would be the bulla.

I took a quick glance back at Aurelia, who was very far behind me. Hopefully, it was enough distance. She stared at me with a grim smile. "Don't blow yourself up," she called.

That seemed like good advice, and I nodded to her, then returned my attention to the Malice. I closed my eyes and continued collecting magic, willing it into my chest and arms, down into my fingertips where I felt added weight when I moved them. The bulla was hot enough that it burned against my chest with the same fire that the Mistress had breathed onto me two nights ago. I had never before felt so much power within me. Now was the time to act.

I thrust out my hands, sending everything forward in a great ball of magic. I tried to keep it as focused as possible, aiming for the Malice and nothing more. The magic released from me as all my strength emptied in an instant, and I collapsed to the ground. Behind me, Aurelia cried out my name, but it was cut short by the sound of an explosion that seemed to shake the whole empire.

Great pieces of earth shot up into the air, so high that they became lost against the light of the morning sun. I was unable to move, so I only watched them fall in huge chunks around me, covering me in dirt. I hoped none of them got as far back as Aurelia, because if they did, I couldn't help her. The ground quaked beneath us, shuddering as if a giant had been sleeping below and decided to roll over. From as far away as I could hear, shouts of alarm sounded through the military camps, warning soldiers of an earthquake, or perhaps another Pompeii.

And then suddenly, it all went silent.

I was still flat on my back and half-covered in dirt when Aurelia ran up and helped me into a sitting position.

"Are you all right?" she asked.

At first I wasn't sure how to answer. I had given that explosion everything I had and felt the loss of strength down to my core. So although I still wasn't sure I could sit up on my own, I wasn't injured, and she seemed fine too.

"That was terrifying . . . and amazing," she said. "But mostly terrifying. I didn't know you were capable of anything that big."

"Big" failed to describe what I had done. The crater from my explosion was larger than Radulf's home. Lines of separated earth ran outward from the crater in three places, wide enough that bridges would need to be built to span them. Whole trees in every direction for as far as I could see had toppled over on their sides. If I had done this within a mile of any buildings, they also would've collapsed.

"Even having seen it, I can still hardly believe it," Aurelia said. "I'm sure it easily destroyed the Malice."

Nothing with magic was ever easy. If there was any lesson I'd learned since the first spark appeared in my shoulder, it was that. "We need to see what's left of the Malice before we can be sure," I said.

I started to my feet but faltered. Aurelia pressed me down, then said, "Let me look. You probably can't even walk."

I could walk but, admittedly, not well. This was the very reason I had asked her to come with me.

She tiptoed to the edge of the crater, paused to look back at me, then descended into its base. I didn't like not being able to see her anymore and hoped the dirt wouldn't collapse into the crater's steep walls on top of her.

After one minute, she hadn't returned. "Aurelia?" I called.

There was no answer, so I forced myself to my feet, then stumbled toward the crater. I didn't want to get too close to the edge or I'd fall in, and I knew it'd be a while until I could get out again. However, Aurelia was in the exact center of it, crouched over with her head down. Studying the remains of the Malice, I hoped.

But when she looked up at me, the light had dimmed in her eyes. She reached down and lifted the Malice where I could see it. The silver was as bright as ever, and as far as I could tell, there wasn't a single scratch or dent anywhere on the amulet. The whole of my magic had merely given it a good polish.

I sat on the edge of the crater, letting my legs dangle over the edge. "I couldn't have hit it any harder," I said. "That was all I had."

"Maybe it can't be destroyed," she said.

"Not by the bulla. But if I had stronger magic —"

"If you had stronger magic, you'd explode half the empire, judging by what you've done here." She began climbing up the crater's side. "Even if the Malice can't be destroyed, it could be sent into hiding somewhere. Like the bulla was buried in the mines, you could bury this."

"Until it's found one day, and the Praetor War begins again? No, it must be destroyed." I shook my head. "We both know the answer. I need Jupiter's magic."

Aurelia's eyes widened. "That cannot be an option!"

"What if it's the only option? Hiding the Malice just delays the war. Keeping it means I'll spend the rest of my days defending against whoever wants it next — the emperor, the Praetors, the Mistress. I must find a way to destroy it."

"We just have to keep thinking." Aurelia finally reached the top of the steep crater and sat beside me. "We'll figure this out."

She started to hand me the Malice, but we were interrupted by the sound of hooves approaching us. Crispus was on his horse, galloping at top speed and with a face in focused concentration. Slightly ahead of him, Livia rode on Callistus, and as soon as she spotted us, she called out my name.

"Nic, you must hurry!"

Aurelia got to her feet first. Even knowing something was very wrong, I was still slow to stand. But Aurelia ran through the wide crater to meet Crispus and Livia on the other side.

If they noticed the wreckage around us, that only lasted for a moment before they remembered the reason they had come.

Crispus leapt from his horse before it had fully halted, shouting, "They came sooner than I thought! Decimas Brutus is at Radulf's home, along with a large number of Praetors. They intend to arrest your grandfather!"

"What?" That got me hurrying faster through the crater. "On what charges?"

"Treason to the empire," Livia said.

My anger focused on Crispus. "You didn't tell me they'd come today!"

"I didn't know it'd be today. I swear I didn't. Do you really believe Brutus would share all his plans with me?"

"Can you stop them?"

"I've only barely begun acting as a judge, and I have no power within their ranks."

"They're inventing these charges. Why don't they charge Radulf with imitating birdcalls or overeating his dessert — those are just as much made-up crimes."

I was struggling to climb the crater as Aurelia had just done. Crispus reached out to help me, then must've realized why I backed away from him, and he lowered his hand. Still, the expression in his eyes was just as heavy as the weight I felt in my heart. "These are real charges," he said. "For real crimes."

There was truth in his words. Over his lifetime, Radulf had been many things to Rome: an outsider, a gladiator, and a Roman general. As my grandfather, he had protected me here in his home, in defiance of the empire and despite the fact that I had committed a few crimes of my own. For years, Radulf had likely also been the greatest threat to the future of the empire. Until now.

Aurelia and Livia helped me out of the crater instead. "Take Callistus and hurry back to the villa," Livia said to me. "Aurelia should go with you too, in case there's trouble. Crispus and I will follow on his horse."

I nodded and accepted Aurelia's help getting onto Callistus's back. Then she climbed on behind me. As much danger as Radulf had been in with the Mistress, something in my gut told me that being arrested by the Praetors was going to be far worse.

TWELVE

Even after we arrived at Radulf's villa, Aurelia wouldn't let me go in until she had wrapped the Malice around my wrist again.

"You need its strength," she said. "And the Malice needs your protection."

I felt magic flow into me and with it enough energy to confront the Praetors on my feet. But I wasn't strong enough yet to fight, and that worried me.

A great many horses lined the front of the villa, along with a caravan wagon, one used for the transport of prisoners. A lot of Praetors had come, all of them prepared to face me.

"I won't let them take him," I muttered to Aurelia.

"We may not have any choice," she said. "I can defend you against as many of these men as possible, but if they get a hand on you —"

"Then all is lost, I know." When Radulf had his powers, we could watch each other's back. Now, despite whatever Aurelia might do to help, I was about to face the Praetors alone.

Decimas Brutus greeted us at the door as soon as we walked in. His eyes traveled to my hands, already raised in front of me. "Let's not fight here, Nicolas, for your own sake."

"Crispus left with you yesterday, after you promised to let me save my grandfather," I said.

"And you did, I assume." Brutus's smile congratulated himself on his own cleverness. "I never agreed to stay away forever."

"If you don't want a fight, then leave this home. You have no right to be here."

He laughed. "On the contrary, I should have come sooner." He gestured around the atrium. "What terrible crimes this home has concealed. I'm not sure where to begin. Maybe I should start with you, an escaped slave, holding magic that should belong to the empire, or to the gods themselves."

Aurelia stepped forward. "He received it from the gods. The empire has no claim on Nic or his magic."

Brutus ignored her, keeping his gaze fixed on me. "Who purchased your freedom? And who purchased your mother's or sister's?"

"Leave them out of this." The bulla at my chest was warming again.

"Your sister is property of this empire, as are you," Brutus said. "And your mother belongs to me."

With that cue, seven Praetors led my mother out of the room she shared with Livia. One of them held a knife against her side. Beside me, Aurelia let out a quiet gasp and started looking around the room. Looking for a weapon of her own, no doubt.

Magic filled my hand, but I held it in with a tightly clenched fist. There was too much risk of missing my target and hitting my mother instead. "Release her," I muttered.

"Your grandfather allowed her to be sheltered here," Brutus continued. "Even after you stole her from me."

"I won her freedom, in a chariot race where you cheated."

"A chariot race where you lost," Brutus said. "I am justified in arresting your entire family. Especially you."

My eyes narrowed. "You won't succeed with them, and you won't succeed with me."

"Of course I will," Brutus said. "Do you think I didn't feel that explosion behind this home a short while ago? Whatever you were doing back there, it must've cost you a great deal of strength, even with the help of the Malice. Do you think I can't see how much effort you're making just to stand now?"

"I have enough strength to stop you," I said. That was true enough. It was the countless other Praetors here that worried me.

Brutus raised his hands. "I'm not afraid of you."

Aurelia crossed between us, ensuring Brutus could not touch me. "If I had my bow —"

"But you don't," Brutus said. "And if you did try to shoot me while I'm acting in my official capacity as a judge in Rome, that would be yet another crime in Radulf's home." He made a *tsk-tsk* sound with his tongue and pushed Aurelia out of his way, then moved closer to me. "Stand aside, boy."

I countered with a step away from him, though magic was still building within me. "You will not take anyone from this home."

He arched his neck, looking more confident than I felt. "Radulf has been charged with treason and must appear before the courts. If you continue to defy me, then I will make good on my promise to arrest everyone here."

"Touch any of us, and you'll regret it."

Now Brutus laughed. "Touching you is exactly what I intend to do."

He stretched out a hand. I immediately released enough magic to throw him against the atrium wall, where he cracked the plaster before he fell. Hearing that, a dozen Praetors swarmed in from other parts of Radulf's home, all of them with at least one weapon and with a clear coordinated plan to surround me and Aurelia. My mother was somewhere behind them. I couldn't see her anymore, which bothered me.

"Stay close," I muttered to Aurelia.

"Look behind you!" she cried.

I turned and repelled two men who had been inching forward, their hands outstretched. Then I raised a shield to protect us, though I wouldn't be able to replenish my magic while keeping that shield in place.

"What now?" Aurelia asked.

"I'm going to explode enough of this room to stop these Praetors. That'll drain me, but you'll have the chance to find my mother. Get her out of here, and Radulf, if you can find him. I'll fight with whatever I have left until you can all get away."

She scowled. "I hate all your plans, do you know that?"

By then, Brutus was back on his feet. "Surrender, Nicolas, or else!" My mother let out a cry of pain, and my heart sank. We all understood what "or else" meant.

"Release them!" Crispus shouted as he barged through the door. "Where is your authority to be here, Brutus? Where is the written order?"

"I am here on my authority as a judge in Rome!" Brutus said. "Thus, no written orders are needed. My charges are legal. You know that as well as I do."

Crispus glanced at me and nodded very slightly. His options to save Radulf would be limited.

So Crispus tried a new approach, one that required a calmer voice. "Surely, there is no need to bring a wealthy man like General Radulf to the prisons. Under the law, he is entitled to remain in the home of a friend who will guarantee his appearance at trial."

Brutus laughed. "And who is that? You?"

Crispus stood taller. "Why not? Aren't I a Praetor now?"

"You may look like a Praetor, but you do not think like one." Brutus's eyes narrowed. "I know you hired a carriage to take this family out of Rome. Indeed, I believe I heard that carriage arrive only a moment ago, no?"

I looked over at Crispus, who lowered his eyes. Yes, the carriage had come. Livia was probably already inside it.

"I will pay any remaining debt for the freedom of Nic and his family," Crispus said. "Release his mother to me."

"I will not sell her," Brutus said. "But if it avoids a fight" — he raised a finger — "I will offer Nicolas a fair choice." He nodded behind him, and men dragged Radulf from his room, looking even weaker than I felt and wearing heavy chains that must've made standing that much harder on him. "Will you save this evil man, who left you to die in the mines, nearly killed you in the arena, and once imprisoned you here in this home?" He arched a brow, amused with himself. "Or the loving mother who bore you?"

Beside Radulf, my mother tried to pull free from the Praetors who were still holding her, but it did no good. Then she looked at me and shook her head.

I wouldn't let her be taken away from me, not again. But I was also determined not to fall into Brutus's trap. "I'm offering you a better choice. In exchange for my mother and grandfather, I'll let you leave this home with both of your arms still attached."

He smiled. "Reach for my arm, then. Let's see what happens next."

"Test me," I said. "I'm ready for you."

His smile darkened. "I have surprises here that you cannot possibly anticipate, especially with your lessened strength."

"I will collapse the rest of this home if I must!" I yelled. "You saw what I did to that temple. Do you think I need nearly that much strength now?"

"Collapse a home with your family and friends inside it?" Brutus shook his head. "I rather doubt you will."

It was my turn to smile. "As I said, Brutus, test me. See what I can do."

"Enough!" Radulf mumbled. "Take your mother and sister and leave Rome." When I only stared back at him, he added, "Do as I say."

Brutus turned his attention to Radulf. "How weak you must feel, General. How useless you are without magic." Then he looked at me again. "Your choice is simple. Will you save your mother or your grandfather, a known traitor of the empire? Is this really so difficult?"

I raised one arm and shot out magic toward the men holding my mother. It collapsed part of the wall behind them, but when they released her to protect themselves from the falling plaster, she took the opportunity and started toward me. However, she didn't get far before Brutus grabbed her again and pulled her in front of him, using her as a shield against me.

"You're making things worse!" Brutus shouted. "And I promise you, they can get even worse still."

"They will only get worse for you!" The anger rising in me

was hard to control. "Release my mother. She is not part of this fight!"

"There are too many Praetors here," my mother said. "They're hiding everywhere, Nic!"

"Take someone down who has a weapon I can use," Aurelia whispered. "I'll help you."

I felt stronger now, and if Aurelia could get a weapon, then I had a fair chance in a fight. But whatever direction I might aim, I had to choose between my mother, who was being pulled toward my left side, and my grandfather at my right.

"Stop this!" Radulf's voice boomed through the atrium, though it was noticeably weaker than usual. "I like my home. I have no wish to see it destroyed. Nor a few of the people in it." He glared at Brutus. "You will also have to survive, I see. How unfortunate."

"I will not choose between you," I said to Radulf. Both of my hands were raised now.

"The choice is mine." Radulf nodded his head toward Brutus. "Release Nic's mother. I will go with you."

Brutus's eyes drifted from Radulf to me; then he released her arm. She ran toward me, but I only angled her toward the door as I said, "Go get in that carriage. Tell the driver to leave immediately, as fast as he can go. We'll catch up to you." She nodded at me, then hurried outside.

"They'll convict you," Crispus warned Radulf. "Sir, you know the penalty for treason."

I didn't know the penalty, but seeing the color drain

from Radulf's face gave me a good idea of what it would be. Even for minor crimes, the empire's punishments were short on mercy.

"Lower your hands," Radulf said to me. "Nic, I am your *pater familias*. Do as I say."

"We have to let him go," Aurelia whispered.

Inside my head, the Mistress laughed. "Pledge to serve me, or I will eventually take everyone from you, as easily as I'm taking this one."

"No!" I wasn't sure who I was shouting at, but at the moment, it applied to everyone equally.

Radulf broke through that with a louder voice than before. "Nicolas Calva, there will not be a fight over me! You will lower your hands!"

Finally, I did, hating the feeling of having lost. Once I did, Brutus motioned to his men. "Take the general away," he ordered.

"I'll go with them," Crispus said. "I'll do everything I can for him. You and Aurelia can still catch up to the carriage, if you hurry."

I shook my head in reply. Obviously, I would not leave Rome while Radulf was facing a trial. But I did move aside for the Praetors to lead Radulf from the home. Too many still remained in here, which bothered me more than I wanted to admit aloud.

"Go outside," I muttered to Aurelia. "Go with Crispus."

She mumbled about how I couldn't force her to do anything,

which was frustrating, but equally comforting. Because this wasn't over.

Brutus's smile returned again, and he seemed eager for the words he spoke. "Now, Nicolas, shall we discuss *your* treason to the empire? A second prison wagon is on its way here, for you. I warn you, the punishments are much worse for our slaves. Runaway slaves are treated the worst of all."

"Find us a way out," Aurelia whispered. "We need to get out now, or it'll be too late."

Yes, we did. The only remaining question was *how.*

THIRTEEN

The fact that Brutus had attempted to deceive me was hardly a surprise. Expecting him not to lie was roughly the same as expecting a hen to not lay eggs. Radulf had just been the first step in their plan.

I had enough magic to make myself disappear, but I wasn't positive I could bring Aurelia with me. I only needed another minute or two.

If I had that long. Brutus crossed toward me, and so I countered in the opposite direction. Aurelia stayed close to my heels. I felt the tension in her steps and knew she was kicking herself for not having her bow nearby.

"I will allow you to bargain for your freedom," Brutus said. "Tell me where the Mistress is, and perhaps you can walk away from here."

My eyes narrowed. That was yet another lie.

He was stalling too, giving enough time for Radulf to be taken away, and for the rest of his Praetors to gather here in the atrium. They entered from all sides, surrounding us, and were as wary of me as I was of them.

"The Mistress is cursed," I said. "If I killed her, it would remove the curse, but also kill Atroxia. There must be another way to stop her."

"Of course there is."

"Tell me what it is and I'll free her."

Brutus laughed. "You cannot believe I would tell you that! Atroxia chose to follow Diana and chose to be the Mistress. Becoming a dragon is Diana's gift to her. If only I were so fortunate!"

"I wonder what her gift will be to you," Aurelia said. "Give you warts perhaps?" Her eyes narrowed. "Or *more* warts?"

"Charming young lady," Brutus said, casting a dark eye toward Aurelia. "Your betrothed has accepted his place with the Praetors. When will you accept us too?"

"If Crispus continues to accept you, he will not be my betrothed much longer," Aurelia said.

"Oh?" Brutus set the tips of his fingers together, clearly pleased with himself. "The Mistress will be interested to know that."

"Their agreement has not changed," I said, eyeing Aurelia. "It *will not* change."

Aurelia's proud shoulders fell. For the first time, she seemed to understand at least this one reason why I had not offered marriage. As long as she was connected to Crispus, she was safe from the Mistress.

"If that is true," Brutus said, "then my only business here is with Nicolas. I have an offer for you."

"My answer is no," I said, which would be the response for whatever he wanted. Enough magic had returned to me that I could get both Aurelia and myself away from here if I chose to. But something had changed in this conversation. Brutus wanted to talk and not simply fight. I needed to stay and hear what he had to say.

Brutus arched a brow. "You answer quickly for someone who is in the process of losing everything."

I kept my expression even. I wasn't losing. I had the Malice and the bulla, the Mistress was trapped, and my mother and Livia were safely on their way to Britannia.

Yet at the same time, I knew I wasn't winning either. The greatest force of my magic had failed to destroy the Malice, which meant I was still a target and always would be. The Mistress was constantly in my head and would inevitably escape from the cave one day, with my name at the top of her list for revenge. And even if my family was safe, everyone else I cared about was still in terrible danger, Radulf most of all.

Maybe he was right. I really was in the process of losing everything.

"What is your offer?" I said to Brutus.

"Accept it." The Mistress's growl echoed within her cave. "Pledge loyalty to me, or face a battle such as you have never seen." Only I could hear her. I knew that, yet I shook my head to try to separate from her voice.

"Don't listen to him!" Aurelia said.

"Don't listen to *her*," Brutus said. "You have warred against me, Nicolas, as if I am the enemy. What if I'm not? What if I hold the only solution to the one thing you want most? Your freedom."

The beat of my heart quickened, but I still spoke with caution. "If you claim the power to give me freedom, then you must believe you have the power to take it back again. I will claim my own freedom instead."

"Then claim it while you stand at my side," Brutus said. "The price is less than you think, and the rewards are sweeter than you can imagine."

"What rewards?" I asked, taking a step toward him.

Brutus arched a brow. He liked that I was curious.

Aurelia was somewhat less enthusiastic. She grabbed my arm and gave it a tug. "Let's go."

I shook it off. "You want me to make a Jupiter Stone, is that it?"

"You would hold the full power of the gods. What finer reward could there be?"

"It wouldn't be my reward," I said. "The Mistress wants to use it, to use me."

"Yes, she does need you," Brutus said. "Imagine the greatness of what she offers. Perhaps she would give the orders, but you'd be the one holding the power."

"*Our* power," the Mistress whispered to me. "You would be the most powerful human in the lands, riding astride the most powerful of creatures. A dragon." She was laughing now, not from anger or a desire for revenge, but from hope. It was the first time I'd felt that emotion from her.

"He's lying to you, Nic!" Aurelia said. "The Mistress has no intention of sharing power with you."

"The Mistress needs his magic," Brutus said. "And this boy needs her strength."

"To destroy Rome?" Aurelia asked. "Why would he do that?"

Brutus casually waved her off. "Rome will fall sooner or later. Why not be the one to control the fall, to see that it falls in the best possible way? You can be part of raising a new and better empire!" He stepped toward me, and his eyes lit with anticipation. "Make us a Jupiter Stone. In exchange, I will return your treasonous grandfather, alive. I will give you more than freedom, I will give you power and protection for your family." He glanced at Aurelia and then back at me. "You would be free to live your life, even with a sewer girl, if you want that." He took yet another step and now was almost close enough to touch me. Almost. "Nicolas, give me the one thing I want, and I will give you everything you want."

I felt Aurelia tugging on my arm again, trying to pull me back with her, away from Brutus. I understood why and knew she was right to do so, but I still wasn't moving.

He took his chance to continue persuading me. "Release the Mistress. Set her free, and she will help you create the stone."

"Come with me," Aurelia said. "Don't listen —"

"How can the Mistress help me?" I asked.

Brutus stepped closer again, and now if he did reach out, he could easily touch me. Aurelia tried moving between us, but I grabbed her wrist and held it firmly, forcing her to remain where she was.

Brutus seemed to be weighing his answer to my question. "Vestals are sensitive to magic. Atroxia can help you find the stone. But the Mistress cannot be there when it's created — you can understand how dangerous it might be for a dragon created by Diana to find itself in the presence of Jupiter's magic."

"He won't create a storm for you!" Aurelia turned to me, her face almost as bright as the dragon's crimson scales. "Why are you listening to him?"

"Because someone is finally making sense!" I said. "Why shouldn't I have a chance at freedom? Why shouldn't I consider an offer that brings peace with the Praetors? Rome has done nothing for me — why should I care what happens to it?"

"You've said it's because what replaces a fallen empire is only darkness." Aurelia touched my arm as she added, "Or do you no longer believe that?"

"He believes that what replaces the empire is even better," Brutus said. "Imagine a world ruled by the Mistress, under control of the goddess Diana."

"He's not that foolish!" Aurelia tried to free herself from my grip, to no avail. Now she became even angrier, if that was possible. "Or maybe you are."

"The Mistress will help me find the stone," I said, repeating his earlier instructions. "But I have to create the storm alone. If she's caught up in Jupiter's lightning, it might break the curse."

"Yes." Brutus hadn't even finished speaking the word before he realized what he had done. When he did, he sucked in a large breath, as if trying to draw the word from the air.

I only smiled and moved to a safer distance. "Thank you for that information. Now I know."

Brutus didn't take kindly to being tricked. He muttered a string of curses and lunged for me, but I had already raised the shield between us. He could not touch us.

Beyond that, I had magic again and plenty of it. Releasing Aurelia's wrist, I immediately shot out a ball of magic aimed directly at Brutus. It caught him square in the chest and knocked him hard against the far wall. A nearby statue on a pedestal was knocked off balance in the fall, and the statue toppled onto the ground, barely missing his head.

The Praetors who had only been watching us a moment ago moved toward me again, waiting for my shield to fail. If they had seen my indifferent reaction to the broken statue, then they would've known it was the least of the damage I was about to cause.

"Get out of this home while you can," I warned, though I didn't much care if they listened. Then I crouched to the ground and put a hand flat on Radulf's floor, letting the magic travel away from me to shake the earth below us. Radulf's entire villa quaked, enough that any other statues still standing fell as well, crashing into pieces. The pool in the center of the atrium cracked, leaking out water along the floor, and with another larger shake of the home, the opening above the atrium became significantly wider than before. Even with the shield, it was still necessary for Aurelia and me to dodge some of the larger falling pieces of plaster.

I guessed most of the servants of the villa had left shortly after the Praetors arrived. If they hadn't, I figured the quake would encourage that decision. They had all better be gone.

Once the Praetors got back on their feet, they pulled out swords and advanced toward me.

"You can't hold that shield forever," one man said. "And we'll be here when you drop it!"

"I hope you are here," I said with a grin. "Because I'm not finished."

By now, the whole power of the Malice had returned, and I emptied it completely on Radulf's home, beginning with the doorway behind us. The opening crumbled to pieces as the villa walls shifted, leaving long cracks in the plaster. Some of the Praetors cried for help and raced to safety while I grabbed Aurelia's hand and led her on a race toward the back of the home, which was still intact, mostly. That wouldn't last for long.

She seemed to know where I was heading and soon ran ahead of me toward the rear entrance, where the stables were. Several Praetors had followed us, and now I used a bit of magic I hadn't tried in a while. I raised up the water from Radulf's baths until it all hung midair, floating in the room like a very, very wet cloud.

Aurelia grabbed my arm. "No more games." Apparently, she wasn't enjoying this as much as I was.

"The empire is fond of games." I couldn't help but chuckle. "Entertainment first, no?"

Once the Praetors had joined us, their eyes went to the water overhead. Wiser men would've run, but they only stopped as if mesmerized by how it could be floating there. Did it not occur to them that I was holding it in place with my upturned hand?

Aurelia pulled me with her to the rear door of the home. She went through first, and once she was safe, I rotated my palm, letting the water crash down upon the Praetors. It swept them off their feet where they were either carried into the pool or simply left upon the ground. I chuckled to see it and barely paid attention to the fact that I was almost as wet as all of them. It was the second time in two days that these waters had made me laugh.

"Nic!"

I glanced outside. Aurelia already had Callistus saddled and was on his back. I nodded at her and then heard Brutus run into the room.

"This is not over!" he cried.

"I agree," I said. "Consider this my rejection of your offer. Your power is coming to an end. Then all my family — my grandfather included — will leave the empire. Your days are numbered, Brutus."

"As are your grandfather's," Brutus said. "If you refuse me, by tomorrow night, he will leave the empire in a coffin. Then I will come for you."

"Your end might be sooner than that," I said. "At the count of three, I will collapse the rest of this home. Get out any way you can. One."

Most of the Praetors had already emptied the room by then, pushing their way past Brutus, who was still hurrying toward me, his hand outstretched. He meant to touch me and take my magic.

"Two."

Only Brutus and I remained in the room. I was protected by a shield and only steps away from the exit. Maybe he didn't know that.

Or maybe he knew that the magic to collapse this home would cause my shield to fail. He was on a full run toward me.

"Three." I raised both arms and exploded out the sides of the home. The ceiling shattered into a thousand pieces and began raining down on us both. Brutus lunged for me, but I was already out the door. Aurelia grabbed my outstretched hand, and as soon as we had climbed onto Callistus's back, we raced away from the stables and whatever was left of the home. I glanced backward and saw Brutus slowly get to his feet in the stables. I had to admit that he was a stronger man than most around him. Even if he had no magic himself, some of the blood within his veins came from the gods.

Safely away from the villa now, Callistus slowed to a steadier pace. From behind her, I brushed my hand against Aurelia's arm, and this time she was the one to shake it off. "Are you mad at me?" I asked.

"Of course."

"I found out how to remove the curse on the Mistress."

"How does that help anything? If you hit her with a bolt of lightning, what do you suppose that'll do to you?"

"It's either that, or I have to kill her. At least I know it's possible to break the curse. Besides, I did get us out of Radulf's home."

"Only because his home no longer exists. You didn't have to explode it."

"True," I said, smiling. "But it did make for a fun escape."

FOURTEEN

It took at least a half hour to convince Aurelia that I had never seriously considered Brutus's offer. Or rather, it took five minutes to convince Aurelia, and the rest of the time to get her forgiveness for not including her in the deception. I didn't think she was truly angry, only that she had been afraid of the consequences if I had really intended to join him.

"When I believed you were listening to him, my only thought was that I couldn't follow you," she said. "That's still true. Even if you think you're doing the right thing, I will do whatever it takes to stop you from creating a Jupiter Stone."

"What if I'm doing it for you?" I asked. "To save your life?"

"Even then," she mumbled. "If necessary, I will become your enemy."

"We started out that way, more or less." Then I added, "At least we are friends now."

"More than friends." Aurelia shrugged. "I can say it, even if you can't."

"Neither of us can say that," I corrected her. "Or at least, neither of us should."

Still irritated with me, she groaned extra loudly. "Have you ever spoken to Crispus about our betrothal? Do you know how he feels?"

"How he *feels*?" I shook my head. "We're boys. We don't talk about —"

"That's the stupidest thing I've ever heard. Speak to Crispus. You might learn a thing or two."

"I don't have to speak to him. I know why he offered you marriage."

She harrumphed. "Really? Why is that?"

"You had just inherited your father's wealth," I said. "Or you would inherit it, if you were married. He made the offer to help save your inheritance."

"Do you think the money ever mattered to me?"

"If it did matter, I wouldn't think worse of you. I have nothing, Aurelia. I can't blame you for wanting to keep what is rightfully yours."

"So you won't blame me for anything I choose to do with my inheritance?"

I waved off that concern. "Whatever brings you the most happiness, that's all I care about."

My hand was loosely around her waist for balance. She brushed her fingers over mine and sighed. Hadn't I just said that I wanted her happiness? Why did she seem so sad?

"You must live," she murmured. "Of all the promises you've made, keep that one."

I looked down, unable to answer. When I did, for the first time I noticed a bracelet on her wrist, gold and in the shape of a coiled snake.

I gestured toward it and asked, "What is that?"

She shrugged. "A gift from Crispus, as an apology for trying to bargain me away last night."

Suddenly, I wondered if I should've gotten her a gift too, or at least if I should've apologized. Well, I wasn't going to. I hadn't done anything wrong, at least as far as I knew. Besides, I'd already apologized for tricking her in Radulf's home today. Couldn't that apology count for last night as well? Probably not. Anyway, that was Crispus's gift on her wrist, and not mine.

Luckily, Aurelia had already moved on to other thoughts. "So where will you go now?"

"What do you mean?"

Then I understood. An hour ago, exploding Radulf's home hadn't seemed like such a terrible idea. Livia and my mother were already on their way to Britannia. Once I got Radulf free, he'd immediately go to Britannia too. But I wasn't going to Britannia, which left me with the problem of a big hole in the ground where my bedroom used to be.

When I explained this to Aurelia, she said, "Let's go to my father's home, on the condition that you won't destroy it too."

"That depends," I warned. "Is Sal still there?"

Back when I had worked at the mines, Sal had been my

master, and my choice as the worst person ever to roam this earth. Making my life miserable had been a game for him. Making his life worse than mine had been my daily goal. However, shortly before Aurelia's father died, Sal had gotten himself named manager of her family's estate. According to her father's will, Aurelia would need to marry someone soon, or else she would lose her entire inheritance to Sal. Since she had already mentioned it, I figured that inheritance was our reason for going to her home.

"Sal is still there, and in fact, he's the one I need to see." She glanced back to look at me. The expression in her eyes wasn't quite disapproval, but it was close. Maybe she knew that I still relished the idea of ruining any day of Sal's life. "I don't think I can trust you. Stay outside. I won't be long."

"Has he taken your inheritance? Has he stolen from you?"

"No! And please don't ask me anything more. Just wait here."

The road in front of her home was relatively quiet today, but she still led me and Callistus through a back alleyway, out of sight. We weren't particularly worried about being attacked here — certainly I could fend off anyone who came along — but it also didn't seem wise to advertise the unicorn more than was necessary.

Once we were in that alley, Aurelia stood to face me, shifting the weight on her feet more than could possibly be necessary for her comfort.

Finally, she said, "You told me that none of what Brutus offered you was a temptation. Is that true?"

The tone of her voice confused me. Only minutes ago, she had been angry with me for listening to him. Now she seemed frustrated because I had not listened carefully enough.

"None of it tempted me," I told her, just as I had said several times before. "It was only a trick."

"None of it? There was nothing he offered that you want enough to have considered his offer, even for a moment?"

"Everything he offered was a lie," I said. "He can't give me anything I want."

"But if he could —"

"He can't! Making a Jupiter Stone —"

"That wasn't my question! I only wondered about what you really want for yourself." She flashed me a glare, daring me to answer her question.

"Freedom," I said. "That's all I want."

"Is it? That's all?"

"Maybe some food to eat, if you have anything here." I winked at her.

Instead of returning my joke with one of her own, her expression soured. "Wait for me. And don't explode anything."

Before I could ask her another question, she swerved on her heel and left me alone with Callistus. Still confused, I brushed a hand across his neck. "What was that about?"

Callistus snorted and tossed his head. If I could speak unicorn, there was probably meaning in that snort. Of course, I'd learn to speak unicorn years before I ever learned to speak girl.

"Nicolas Calva!"

I stiffened, recognizing that voice. Magic immediately filled my arms and hands, uninvited and unwelcome. Aurelia had warned me twice not to destroy her home, so I had to assume she'd meant what she said.

"Go away, Sal," I muttered.

"You're giving the orders now?" He *tsk*ed with his tongue. "I suppose I might've expected that from someone who's become so famous in Rome." He moved closer. I knew because his rancid breath always arrived sooner than he did. "Or are you infamous, perhaps? I've heard that our new emperor views you as an enemy."

"If I were an enemy, Rome would know it," I said, still unwilling to turn and face him.

The narrow alleyway widened behind Aurelia's home, enough for Sal to pass me while still keeping what he considered a safe distance. If only he knew how far he'd have to go before it was safe between us.

As he walked past me, Sal took in the unicorn and my finer tunic and sandals. I'd always been barefoot while a slave and had always worn shredded tunics with more holes than thread. Beneath those rags, I was mostly skin and bone, whereas I looked much healthier than ever before. For that matter, he'd never seen me as clean as I now was.

"I always knew you'd make something of your life," he said. "And I don't say that only because of what your magic could do to me. I say that because it's true. You were always different. I thought maybe, if you survived the mines, one day you'd become a supervisor. I didn't expect this, I admit."

Despite the tension in every muscle of my body, I couldn't help but snort out a laugh. "I never expected this either."

He scratched at a balding patch on his scalp. "Late last night, Aurelia sent a message asking me, as the head of her household, to do a service for her. It's against my better judgment, but I have no power to stop her." Sal's bloated face somehow widened ever further. "Trust me, I tried."

"Nobody ever changes Aurelia's mind. What was her request?"

"Two requests, actually. For the first, I want you to know she paid me very well, but not as much as I could have demanded."

I sighed, growing impatient. "What did she ask, Sal?"

"I went to the magistrate this morning and paid the tax to have you and your sister officially freed. You're no longer a runaway slave, or any slave at all. You are free and a citizen of the empire. You are a Roman now."

He said the words so casually that I almost didn't pay them any attention. Now I stood frozen in place, replaying his words in my mind, trying to figure out where I had heard him wrong.

Finally, I turned to him, unsure of what to say. This didn't seem like a trick, but I couldn't imagine why he would've agreed to Aurelia's request. He said he did it for less than he could have demanded.

"You freed us?" I finally mumbled. "Why?"

"When we were in the amphitheater together, you saved my life." He shrugged. "Why?"

Maybe asking the question was all either of us would ever get from the other. Maybe that had to be enough. I nodded at him and stretched out my hand.

"Nic, don't!" Aurelia yelled.

Sal and I both turned, and from the panicked expression on her face, I thought she believed I was about to attack him. But instead, when Sal looked at me again, I placed my hand on his shoulder. He did the same to mine.

"I hear people talk about you," Sal said. "I know that none of what they say is true."

For once, I felt no need to lower my eyes when I spoke to him. "Thank you, Sal."

"That was unexpected." Aurelia walked forward, holding a satchel in her hands. It was made of thick gray cloth and bundled with a rope at the top. She swung the loose half of the rope over her shoulder but kept it close to her body.

"What's in there?" I asked. "Is it your other request to Sal?"

I looked to him for confirmation of the answer. He merely nodded and then disappeared back within the home.

"I'll tell you what's in here later. For now, let's go." She started toward Callistus, but I called her name and she stopped.

"Sal just told me I've been freed." I still couldn't believe it. "Is that what you meant, about how you'd use your inheritance?"

Her feet shifted again beneath her. "He paid the tax from his own savings. He told me a while ago that he wanted to do it ever since you rescued him in the arena. I just paid him enough to be sure he got it done today."

"I can't repay you for this," I said. "Not yet, at least, but I will."

She shook her head. "I don't care about that."

"Then how do I thank you?"

She stared at me a moment, biting on her lip as she did. Finally, she said, "Thank Sal if you must. You owe me nothing. Now take this. You said you were hungry." In her hands was a pear. A little underripe, but still good enough to eat. I placed it in the pocket of my tunic for later.

Then she backed away to Callistus and swung into the saddle, placing the satchel in front of her. Something was still bothering her, which concerned me, but I didn't know what it was and she clearly had no intention of telling me.

"Now where do we go?" I asked, climbing up behind her. It was equally obvious that Aurelia had a firm plan in place, and that I was only being allowed to come along since I had nowhere else to go.

"Crispus's home. He's planning a special supper tonight and wants me there."

I shrugged. "Am I invited too? He hasn't said anything to me about it."

She gave Callistus a pat on his shoulder, mostly ignoring me. "We'll see."

And this was what I'd meant by thinking that I did not speak girl. Her words had some sort of meaning. I just had no idea what it was.

FIFTEEN

We were welcomed into Crispus's home by his mother, who informed us that Crispus still hadn't returned from his business for the day. We already knew his business — doing whatever was necessary to rescue Radulf from the courts. However, if he had a supper planned for the evening, then he should arrive soon.

Crispus's mother was a proper, nervous sort of woman who I'd noticed often held something between her fingers for distraction. Right now, it was an ivory comb that probably belonged in her hair. She glanced over my tunic with mild disapproval. Except for the tears in it from my explosion outside Radulf's home, and then the explosion *of* Radulf's home, there was nothing wrong with it, but it clearly wasn't fancy enough for whoever was coming to the supper. For that, I'd need a toga.

"Crispus's father had several," she said. "You can use one of his, if you don't mind wearing the clothes of someone who's died."

I did mind. Something in her expression blamed me for Valerius's death. Maybe I deserved that. I stared back at her while my heart pounded in my chest. Should I apologize to her? How could any apology possibly compensate for my failure to save him?

"Thank you," Aurelia said on my behalf. "Perhaps a servant can bring that toga to his room? I'd better go get ready too."

After Crispus's mother had left, I asked, "Who is coming tonight?"

Aurelia was making herself busy with anything that kept her from looking at me. "A friend of Crispus's family and nobody you'll know." Then she drew in a deep breath. "It'd be better if you weren't even here tonight, but since I know you won't sit quietly in your room, will you at least agree to sit quietly at the supper?"

"Can you tell me what this supper is for?"

She huffed, then said, "Crispus arranged this last night after he found out the Praetors' plans for Radulf. Crispus has always intended to do everything he could to clear him of the charges but knew it probably wouldn't work — Brutus is far too powerful. So this is our other plan."

I pointed at the satchel in her hands. "What's in there?"

She shook her head, refusing to answer. "I don't want you trying to talk me out of this plan. Crispus already tried that, and you won't have any more success. You'll find out after everything is settled, not before." Then she disappeared deeper into the home, I assumed to the room that had been given to her whenever she stayed here. I suspected she had stayed fairly often.

She'd never want to be in the same home as Sal, and besides, with her betrothal to Crispus, it wouldn't be unusual to see her here.

After an hour in my room, a knock came at the door. I opened it, expecting to see a servant with one of Valerius's old togas. I didn't have the first clue for how to wrap it around myself, but figured I'd be laughed at if I asked. Not nearly as much laughter if I didn't ask, I supposed. I needed help.

Except that it wasn't a servant, and I was horrified to see who had come. Livia.

Once I recovered from the shock of seeing her, I pulled her into my room and shut the door. "What are you doing here? You're supposed to be on the carriage with Mother!"

Livia's eyes darted away, then back to me. "Don't be angry —"

"I am angry. Livia, you're not safe here!"

"Are you safe here? Did you consider how it felt to be told I was leaving the empire, then told I would have to leave you behind? Back at the mines, I protected *you*! When did I become so useless?"

My heart softened, as it always did with Livia. "You have never been useless. But when a million Romans decided they wanted my magic, and when an entire army of Praetors realized if they can capture you, they can get anything they want from me, things changed." I drew in a deep breath. "Things have changed, Livia."

She pointed to the Malice on my wrist. "I retrieved that for you. I kept it safe from all those Praetors, and from the Mistress! I can still help you win."

"No, you can't." Frustrated, I ran a hand through my hair. "I can't destroy the Malice, which means this magic will always be a part of me, which means I'll always be a target. I've got to find a way to save Radulf. After I do, I'll send you both up to Britannia, and this time you will go."

Her delicate eyes softened. "What about you?"

"That's what I need everyone to understand." I shrugged. Despite all that I could do, or maybe because of it, my choices were limited. "I can't go to Britannia. Not ever."

"If you defeat the Praetors, and the Mistress —"

"There are only two ways to break the curse upon her. Neither of them is good."

Tears that she'd kept welled up began to slide down her cheeks. "You can't fight this war forever."

"No, but I can keep it from following me to Britannia."

She brushed away the tears, but more appeared in their place. "Then where will you go?"

I had no answer to that, and even if I did, it would only give her more sadness. So instead, I pulled her into an embrace and let her cry, while fighting against my own emotions. "This is for the best," I whispered. "Trust me."

She shook her head, even as it was buried in my shoulder. "You have to find a way. At least try."

"I will." Saying the words was the easy part. Everything that came next seemed impossible.

Another knock came at the door. "Nic?" That was Aurelia's voice.

Livia stood back from me and wiped her tears.

"Don't tell her any of this," I said. "Aurelia needs to go to Britannia too." With Crispus.

Livia nodded, and I asked Aurelia to enter. Her eyes instantly went to Livia.

"What is this?" she asked. "I thought you'd left!"

"I learned from you." Livia faked her happiness well, I had to admit that. "My choices belong to me."

Aurelia smiled, making sure I saw it. "As they should! Well, you must join us for supper. Crispus will be thrilled to know you're still here."

"He won't be angry?" Livia said. "He was the one who told me to stay in the carriage this morning."

"He won't be angry . . . with you." Aurelia also made sure I heard that last word, which was unnecessary. No one could stay angry with Livia for long. And besides, Crispus had only sent her away because I had asked him to. It shouldn't matter to him whether Livia stayed or left.

Aurelia handed me the toga that was in her arms. "I picked this one out myself. The blue fabric will look nice with your eyes. It will also blend in well with the background, which is your only job tonight."

Though there was a lightness in her tone, she wasn't teasing. She was clearly anxious about whatever the plan was for the supper, and she didn't want me interfering. That was fine. I had no intentions of causing any trouble until after it was dark and I left this home to go rescue Radulf. That would be more than enough interference for one day.

Aurelia put an arm around Livia. "We need to get you cleaned up for tonight." As they started to leave the room, she turned to me and added, "If you need help with that, just call out and someone will come."

"I don't need help," I said. The truth was, I didn't even know where to start with all this fabric.

She giggled and Livia joined in, but before they left, Livia looked back one last time, fighting away more tears.

I was glad they left when they did. Because the truth was, so was I.

SIXTEEN

Crispus arrived home only a few minutes before the supper was meant to begin. A servant outside my door told him I was here, and immediately he asked to come in my room.

"How is Radulf?" I asked as he adjusted the toga's knot on my shoulder.

Crispus's tight expression didn't offer much hope. "It's bad, Nic. His prison is damp and likely infested with disease. I brought him a little food, but if I gave him too much, he'd be attacked by the other prisoners for it. As weak as Radulf was when they put him in, he'll be worse when he comes out."

"And when will that be?"

"Tomorrow. They'll hold a trial in the Basilica Julia because they say his crimes originated with Caesar himself." Crispus licked his lips. "I'm only one of a hundred judges to hear his case. My vote will matter little. And the chairman of the trial will be Decimas Brutus."

Aurelia had explained it earlier when we rode together.

At the trial, some orators would speak in favor of Radulf's conviction, and others would speak in his defense. The chairman's job was to ensure fairness during those speeches, though I hardly believed fairness was ever a priority for Brutus. In the end, Crispus and the other judges would cast their votes upon wax tablets. The votes were supposed to be secret, but again, I thought it was likely that Brutus would do everything he could to influence the outcome. After all he'd done to get Radulf arrested, he would not risk losing now.

"Are there any ways to avoid the trial?" I asked.

"Not unless Brutus drops the charges, and you can guess how likely that is." Crispus motioned for a servant to bring him a braided gold rope to tie around my waist. "Honestly, don't you know how to wear a toga?"

"No." Nor did I much care about it at the moment.

"You weren't supposed to be here," he muttered. "Listen, what's about to happen is not my idea. It's Aurelia's, and she wants to do this."

"To do what?" I asked. I did care about this a great deal, and if it took a properly belted toga to learn her plans, then I would gladly cooperate.

A servant opened my door and poked his head in, addressing Crispus. "Master, your guest has arrived."

"Aurelia's plan obviously involves Radulf's trial tomorrow," I said. When Crispus didn't answer, I added, "Is your guest tonight another judge?"

Crispus nodded. "A very influential judge. After the trial, others will watch his vote before casting their own."

Suddenly, I knew exactly what was in Aurelia's satchel, her reasons for inviting a judge to this supper. And I didn't like any of it.

Considering the food preparations under way when I'd passed by the *culina* earlier, I had expected a large group in attendance at supper, but Crispus's guest came alone. His name was announced as Manius Cornelius Nasica. I suppressed a smile when I heard it. *Nasica* meant "pointed nose," and this man certainly fit the description. Caela's beak was less sharp than his. The thin band most Praetors wore wasn't around his arm, which was a relief, though it hardly made me trust him.

By the time we entered the triclinium, Nasica was already reclined on a couch with Aurelia on a second couch. She had the satchel at her feet, and they appeared to be in quiet conversation. Aurelia eyed me as if she were displeased that we had come so soon, and then shook her head in a quiet reminder for me to not interfere.

"Welcome, my friend." Crispus was quickly growing into his role as master of this home. He seemed comfortable with greeting a man who was twice his age and at least twice his girth.

Nasica stood and gave a polite nod of his head to Crispus, but his eyes quickly rested on me. "This is the slave that does magic?"

"He's a freeman and a citizen." Aurelia spoke the words as if nothing more needed to be said.

"This is Nicolas Calva," Crispus added. "Our friend."

Nasica looked at me from over the top of his pointed nose, his lips pursed together in disapproval. That was fine by me. He didn't need to consider me a friend. I was in no hurry to befriend this fool of a man either.

After exchanging curt nods, Crispus sat beside Aurelia while I took the third couch. We had only just been seated when Livia entered the room, looking impossibly lovely considering that she'd only had a few minutes to prepare herself. I noted, also, that her toga had been correctly tied. Hers came up over one shoulder but was pulled beneath the other arm and was fitted with two gold bands, one at the lower waist and the other higher up. She looked natural in such fine clothes, unlike me, who looked as if I'd become tangled up in a bedsheet. This was the way Livia had always been meant to dress.

It was also the way Aurelia would dress once she was in Britannia, if people dressed in togas up north. Crispus would be good to her, provide her with a life I never could. If I truly cared for her, I should be happy to know that with him, all of life's comforts awaited her.

"Sit down, Nic," Livia hissed.

I hadn't realized she had moved from the entrance and was already on the couch beside me. Had Crispus introduced her to Nasica, or was he waiting for me to do it?

Livia giggled. "Really, Nic. Sit down."

Aurelia was giggling too, but I avoided looking at her. And before I could sit, Crispus's mother entered the room, elegantly dressed in the darker colors of someone in mourning. There was nowhere for her to sit except beside Nasica, and she did so, looking very uncomfortable. I considered offering to exchange places with her, but I had promised not to interfere tonight, and settling myself between Aurelia and Nasica seemed like a definite interference.

The supper was as extravagant as any meal I'd ever eaten. We began with radishes, boiled eggs, and a warm drink sweetened with honey. Then a variety of fish and carved meats were served, some of which I'd never tasted before, since Radulf preferred simpler meals. I ate a great deal because I was as hungry as usual, but also because the conversation was rather dull.

Nasica was a dim-witted sort of man who seemed to find amusement in sharing the details of trade routes to Africa, the exact shade of purple on plums as compared to grapes, his extensive family history, and other facts determined to put me to sleep. He must be very wealthy because nothing in his conversation helped me understand why anyone might follow his lead. In her kindness, Livia encouraged him by asking questions, though I knew she couldn't have held any actual interest in his dusty stories. Crispus and Aurelia paid polite attention, but I knew they were waiting for the main meal to end so they could get to the actual business of why Nasica had been invited here. And I was quickly losing patience with the entire ordeal.

Why didn't Aurelia just open that satchel at her feet and show him what was inside? How much of her inheritance did she intend to use as a bribe for Nasica? I doubted it would take much. If anything, Nasica owed us money as an apology for being forced to endure his stories all evening.

Once the meats were taken away, the servant announced a short break before he would bring out the fruit and cakes. Crispus's mother used the opportunity to stand and say she had a headache and would retire for the evening.

Crispus stood, offering to escort her to her room, but she nodded instead to me. "Perhaps Nicolas can walk me there."

I stood as well, but I didn't want to leave, not now. Had Aurelia prearranged for Crispus's mother to get me out of the room, or was it just a coincidence? I looked to Aurelia for an answer, but her head was still down as if suddenly fascinated by the tile floor.

"Will you escort her?" Crispus asked me.

What else could I say?

"Of course." I held out my arm to his mother, but as I led her from the room I gave one glance back at Aurelia. Her hands were wrapped so tightly around the satchel that her knuckles were white. Yes, they were going to discuss the bribe without me there. I hated this.

We walked most of the way to his mother's room in silence.

I barely knew her and couldn't think of what I might say. Again I wondered, should I apologize for not being able to save Valerius in that battle? For bringing the battle to her property in the first place? For being here now? How could I possibly apologize for one fault without making myself even more guilty of the rest?

As we neared the door, his mother stopped, released my arm, and said, "Do you know why I asked you to walk with me?"

Because Aurelia asked you to? Because she and your son have a plan and all I can do is frustrate them? Because I was never supposed to be here in the first place?

Those were the things I did not say. I'd learned many times that speaking usually led to greater problems in my life. So instead, I only shook my head at her.

His mother's eyes darted from left to right and she licked her lips. "I must be honest with you. I don't understand my son's friendship with you, just as I never understood my husband's interest in your . . . in the things you can do."

What did she expect me to say to that? Crispus had always been a loyal friend, but that was not true of Valerius. The help he had given me was only because he wanted some control over my magic.

She continued, "However, it's obvious that you have a significant role to play in the future of Rome, so Crispus says we must do all we can to help you succeed."

"Thank you," I mumbled, not sure of what exactly I was

thanking her for. More than anything, I wished I could just leave this conversation, and possibly leave this home.

"But in return for our kindness, I have a request. You must not let anything happen to my son. He's all I have left."

I scuffed my sandal against the floor. "Crispus offered us your family's home up in Britannia. Would you consider coming too?"

"If Crispus stays in Rome, I will stay. If he goes to Britannia, I will go," she said. "My husband always believed Crispus could be made into a politician in time. I know his interests lay elsewhere."

"He's a good person," I told her. "And as you say, a great friend."

"He values your friendship as well," she said. "So much that he has risked everything to protect you: our family's honor, our fortune, his very life." She drew in a sharp breath, and I stood facing her, feeling worse than ever. "My husband is gone, Nic. You couldn't save him, I know, but do you not care that my son is in danger too?"

Almost unable to breathe, I stepped back. If she were speaking in anger, I could have countered in anger, telling her that Valerius had involved his family with me, and not the other way around. But she wasn't angry. She was a mother as terrified for her family's future as my mother was afraid for Livia and me. I couldn't blame her for those feelings, nor could I escape my own faults for the reason she felt this way. I had no idea what to say to her.

She reached out and put a hand on my shoulder. "Promise that my son will live. You gave Radulf his life back, but not my husband. When the time is right, will you promise to give Crispus his life back?"

I had promised Radulf to destroy the amulets.

Promised Aurelia that I would live.

And promised nearly everyone I'd ever known that I would never make a Jupiter Stone.

In the end, I would likely break all those promises. But I fully intended to keep this one.

"Crispus will get his life back," I said. "He deserves that much."

"In every possible way, Nic. Give him his life back."

I understood her full meaning. If Crispus became seriously injured, I had just promised to heal him, which of course I would do if it was at all within my power. But there was more. She was asking me to allow Crispus to continue on with his life, as it would have been if I had never entered it. She was asking me to leave and not return.

I bowed politely to her as she left for her room, then hurried back to the triclinium to find Crispus, Aurelia, and Livia huddled in close around Nasica. Even Livia was allowed to stay?

Crispus looked up when I entered, eyes widened in alarm, as if I were a soldier here to arrest them for bribery, rather than a friend.

He shook his head in a warning to stay out of their

negotiations, and Livia motioned me over toward her. Aurelia didn't seem to have noticed me at all. When I stood behind her, I saw the contents of her satchel, opened and spread out on the table. It was a thick papyrus scroll, rolled out, and from what I could tell, detailed the entirety of her family's inheritance.

"A year's wages is more than fair," Aurelia was saying. "You see that I can pay it."

"General Radulf is a traitor to Rome," Nasica replied. "It's an insult to think I can overlook that on only a year's wage."

Aurelia glanced sideways at Crispus, then said to Nasica, "Sir, my inheritance is not as large as you may think. There are some debts, and wages that must be paid to the servants of the home."

"Crispus will vote to free the general," Nasica said. "Perhaps some of the other judges will see his weakened condition and show mercy. But only a few."

"He should go free." Crispus straightened his back. "The general has made threats against Rome, but has not carried out any of them. Instead, he has fought valiantly in war, expanding our territories and bringing glory to this empire."

That was only half-true. Radulf did fight on Rome's side, but he did it to expand his own power. It was never about the empire's glory.

"As chairman, Decimas Brutus will tilt the trial against the general," Nasica said, completely indifferent to Crispus's argument. "He has already ordered himself a new toga, to be worn at Radulf's execution."

My right fist tightened with the feeling of magic. I shook it away, but my hand filled again. As I'd suspected, there was no chance of Radulf receiving a fair trial. If Nasica knew that too, then he was more clever than I had thought.

He continued, "Radulf needs fifty-one votes to set him free. If I make it known early how I intend to vote, I can save him from execution. What is that worth to you?"

Aurelia leaned forward. "What is that worth to *you*?"

He waved a hand toward the scrolls. "All of this."

Livia glanced up at me, licking her lips with worry. She and I had nothing to offer — even the clothes on my back were not my own. But if she agreed to this bribe, Aurelia would have nothing either. She had come from a life in the sewers; she knew as well as I did what poverty meant. I couldn't allow her to do this.

Yet I also understood why she had asked me not to interfere tonight. She did not want me to influence her decision.

I would not influence her decision — nothing could ever make Aurelia change her mind. How many times had I learned that?

But I could stop the decision from happening in the first place.

I marched forward. "Leave this home, Nasica. How dare you sit there demanding so much!"

Aurelia stood, hands on her hips. "Nic!"

"If he would sell his vote with so little integrity, how can you trust that he won't sell his promise again if Brutus offers him more? Don't do this!"

Now Nasica stood, as beads of sweat broke out on his forehead. "Give me that scroll, and General Radulf will not face the executioner."

"He's lying," I said. "Do not trust him."

"We have to trust him." Crispus was also on his feet. "I know you think you can rescue Radulf alone, but your grandfather is well guarded in his prison. You won't get past them all, and even if you did, they'd only come after him again. And when Radulf is put to trial tomorrow, he will lose unless we have Nasica's vote."

"Give me the scroll." Nasica spoke more urgently now.

Aurelia looked over to me. "What I've always told you is true. I never cared about my father's money, except for who I could help with it. Today I'm helping you."

She rolled up the scroll and put it in Nasica's hands. The moment she did, I turned on my heel and stomped out of the triclinium, slamming shut the door to my room. It felt childish, but I didn't care. I was furious with them and humbled by Crispus's mother. But even more, I was embarrassed that for as far as I had come since the mines, and for all the magic that flowed through my body, I still needed help in so many ways. Aurelia had just given up everything to save Radulf, and I had stood by, completely useless.

Several minutes later, someone knocked at my door. I didn't know whether it was Livia, Crispus, Aurelia, or all three of them together. Nor did I care.

I rolled over on my bed, ignoring the knock until it finally went away.

SEVENTEEN

I wasn't in Crispus's home when they awoke the next day. Instead, I had left early in the morning to find the *carcer* where Radulf was being held. It wasn't hard to figure out where he was — the building where they were keeping him was surrounded with so many Praetors and Roman soldiers, they were practically standing on top of one another. I wished they had been — it would've been entertaining to knock them all over.

The temptation to attack was strong. From my hiding place behind a column in front of the Senate building, I could easily bury most of these men in an avalanche of ruins, letting them become part of the same rot they created everywhere they went. However, that would also bury Radulf, who no doubt had been lowered into the deep prison hole beneath the building.

But as the birds began to awaken, I knew what I could do instead of an attack. For all the strength the Malice gave me, I needed the bulla, which allowed me some communication with animals.

I whistled softly, calling their attention, then whispered through the morning breeze what I needed.

And the birds responded to my call by diving at the Praetors with their sharp beaks and claws. They weren't as sharp as Nasica's nose, perhaps, but they'd still do. The men cried out, attempting to wave off the birds, but found themselves pecked mercilessly in the process. With another whisper from me, several of the birds responded by leaving their droppings on the heads of the men as they scattered. I doubted birds had any sense of humor, but if they did, then I hoped they were enjoying this scene as much as I was. Each time droppings landed on someone's heads, the groans became louder. Weapons clattered to the ground as the Praetors ran in every direction, more than one yelling about bird droppings in either his mouth or eye.

For my part, the scene was so funny, I nearly lost my hiding place behind the Senate columns, bracing my side against the ache from holding in so much laughter.

Once the prison entrance was abandoned, I peeked out from around the column, ensuring that I was alone.

At first I thought I was. The Praetors were all gone, and to avoid the cries of prisoners, few citizens ever wandered this way. Then somewhere in the background, laughter rang out, startling me. I glanced back and saw it was only a handful of senators in the distance, the first arrivals of a new workday. I adjusted my hiding place around the column to avoid them and then checked the area one last time.

Before anyone else came, I ran forward. Compared to the other elaborate buildings in the forum, the carcer was square and rather plain. Of course it would be. No one needed to be impressed by the place Rome held and executed her prisoners.

Or at least, the lesser prisoners were executed here. That would not be Radulf's fate. Brutus would ensure his execution was as brutal and public as possible. A public beheading in the center of the forum perhaps. I had little faith in Aurelia's bribe to do anything beyond make Nasica wealthier than he already was. Saving Radulf was up to me.

The carcer appeared to be empty when I entered. All the guards had been with the Praetors outside, probably warned to watch for me. The prison was just as simple on the inside, with no frescoes or statues, or anything as grand as the other forum buildings. Overall, the room appeared to be little more than aged layers of stone and brick with a single altar toward the back.

I followed the sound of water toward that altar. But before I got there, I saw a metal grate on the floor with a nearby rope attached to an anchor in the floor. Below me came the sounds of moans and cries, maybe from other prisoners below, not too different from Atroxia's constant cries. Maybe from Radulf too, I didn't know.

I glanced around again, just to be cautious. I could defend myself from anyone who might come, but now that I was so close, I didn't want to risk anything happening to Radulf. The floor beneath my feet could easily cave in if I became careless in a fight.

Once I was certain I was alone, I studied the grate again. Nearby was a long metal bar the prison guards must use to pry the grate up, and even then it probably took at least two men to do the job. Thankfully, I wouldn't need the bar, or anyone's help. Well, I'd need the Malice, but that was different. I leaned over and picked up the grate, then tossed it aside.

Then I quickly lowered the rope into the hole, and while doing so lay on my belly and called out, "Radulf, I'm here to get you!"

The moans went quiet, and from the silence, a voice squeaked, "Nic?"

"Take the rope."

More silence. Then the voice said, "I can't hold on to it."

I had never known anything from my grandfather but strength and power. This weakened, sickly man was a stranger to me. No doubt it had cost him dearly to lose his magic, but I also had to remind myself he had been within a whisper of death only two days ago. Though I had brought him back from the edge, he still needed time to regain his strength. A sewage-infested hole was hardly the place for that.

"Livia is expecting me to return with a grandfather," I teased. "So if you can't hold on, then get me another old man to pull up instead. Preferably one a little stronger than you."

He grunted in annoyance, which I took as a good sign. A moment later, I felt his weight attach to the end of the rope, and he told me to hurry, which was definitely my plan too. I stood and began pulling, one tug at a time. Thanks to my years in the mines, I was already strong, but with the combined magic of the Malice and the bulla, I might as well have been lifting a feather out of that hole.

When he was about halfway up, I stopped lifting. Dozens of footsteps were rushing into the carcer. They weren't heavy, as the footsteps of soldiers or Praetors, and the sounds were accompanied by some laughter. Young voices.

Even if they were no threat, this was a bad position to be in. If I lowered Radulf to the ground, he might not have the strength to take the rope again. If I kept him suspended below, then my hands weren't free to use magic — they were still holding the rope. So I whispered to Radulf to hold on and readied myself for whoever might come. However, I never could have prepared myself for the faces I saw. In some ways, they were my own.

Twenty or thirty boys about my age had come into the carcer, all barefoot and in rags similar to those I had worn for years. These were Roman slaves. They were who I had been only months ago, maybe who I still was on the inside.

One boy was pushed to the front of the group, licking his lips like they were coated in the sweetest honey. He was nervous, and probably afraid of me. He looked at me, then his eye traveled down the rope into the open grate. It was obvious what I was attempting to do, one of my more serious crimes thus far. Maybe at the moment, I was more afraid of him.

"You're Nicolas Calva," he said. "Your family is from Gaul. I'm Donnan. My family was brought here from Gaul a year ago."

I stared at him, still cautious. Did Donnan think that fact

would make us friends? Or that I'd be less likely to defend myself against him and these other boys simply because we'd been born within the same defeated borders?

That was ridiculous. None of that mattered to me. And yet my awareness that I could have been standing where he now did mattered a great deal. I could defend myself, and I would if necessary. But I would not attack.

Keeping my eye on Donnan, I began pulling on the rope again. Radulf wouldn't be able to hold on much longer. "What do you want?" I asked.

Donnan's eyes darted toward the hole, and he licked his lips again. "Our masters sent us here to fetch the general."

"Go tell your masters they'll be crusty old corpses before I let the general return to them."

Donnan nodded. "They told us that's what you'd say, more or less. Our masters said that if we leave this building without General Radulf, we will all go to the games this afternoon."

I knew what that meant. They wouldn't go to the games as audience members in the amphitheater. They'd go there as entertainment for the people, and as supper for the animals of the *venatio*.

Sincerely hoping to help, I turned to Donnan. "Once I have the general up here, then you can come out with us. I will defend you from your masters. I will help you escape."

Donnan shook his head. "We have families. I don't even know where my parents are. I have a sister who works in the mines. What happens to her if I rebel?"

My heart pounded. Sending these boys in here was as cruel as anything the Praetors had ever done to me.

"I have a sister too," I said. "And General Radulf is her grandfather. If I give him to you, the empire will have him executed."

"If you don't," Donnan said, gesturing to the boys around him, "then we are executed."

Radulf was almost high enough now that I could reach him. He called up, "I'll go with the boys. I'll face the charges against me."

I stopped pulling, unwilling to bring him to the surface only to see him carried away to trial. "We can disappear."

Radulf looked up at me, with little more than blackness and the sound of running water below him. He was straining so hard just to keep hold of the rope that veins were bulging on his face. "Where would we go?" he asked. "Take me away and they'll only come after me again, with higher stakes next time."

I shook my head, almost angry with him. "You're my family, Radulf. You can't just give up!"

"If I am family, then let me care about you as a grandfather should. Let me go."

He stared at his hand holding on the rope, clenching his fist in a way that I knew trouble was coming. I immediately dropped to my belly and reached into the hole, grabbing his wrist just as he let go of the rope. My other hand was clenched around the bolt in the floor to which the rope was tied. It was all that kept me from sliding into the hole with Radulf.

"If you fall back into that hole, it'll kill you!" I shouted.

"If I go to trial, the empire will kill me," he replied.

"I can save you!"

"But at our expense," Donnan said. "We have to take the general!"

"No, you won't!" I flexed my arm to pull myself away from the hole, bringing Radulf upward. Once I got him to the surface, we could work out a plan to save ourselves without sacrificing the slave boys, though I really didn't know how to do it.

Below me, Radulf only shook his head. "I was not happy when my son chose your mother for his wife. I was never as kind to her as I should have been. I wish for you to make an apology for me. Tell her I'm sorry I did not help her when I could have done it. I could have saved you all from the mines, and I should have. I've been so wrong for such a very long time, but perhaps I can repent here, if forgiveness is possible for crimes such as mine."

"There is no forgiveness for traitors," a voice said. Brutus. Immediately, a hand clamped down on my back, directly over the Divine Star, and I gasped with the pain of it.

I lost my grip on the bolt in the floor and would've gone over the edge with Radulf had Brutus not been holding me. Bright lights seemed to flash in my vision, enough that I had to close my eyes to keep them away. All that mattered was keeping hold of Radulf. I would not let him go, but I couldn't pull him up either. Not anymore.

Brutus laughed and pressed his hand deeper into my back. "Some of the Praetors thought you would wait until the trial to attempt a rescue, but I know you better than that, Nicolas. I knew you'd come here."

His knee was on my back as well, pinning me to the floor. In this position, all I could do was keep hold of Radulf's hand for as long as possible. Without magic, I felt the sweat on my palm. He was slipping.

Brutus called for Donnan and a few of the other slaves to come forward. "Get this man to the surface before he's late for his trial."

"I'm sorry," Donnan whispered to me as he knelt on the other side of the hole. "Truly, I am, Nicolas. We wanted you to succeed. You're one of us."

"I never was," I replied between gasps for air. Echoing in my head was my own voice, "You're not a freeman either."

Three boys reached into the hole and took Radulf's arm, pulling it from my grasp and inching him out of the hole. All I could do was remain pinned on the floor, trying to breathe and silently communicate my apologies to Radulf. He came to the surface looking as sad and empty as any person could, swallowed up in his guilt and weakness, and the reality of what he was facing after he left this building.

"You are my grandfather," I told him. "My pater familias."

Radulf was pulled to his feet, but before the boys led him away, he said, "If I am, then you will obey this order, Nic. Break free from that pig kneeling on top of you, then fulfill your promise to me and destroy the Malice."

"Get him out!" Brutus snarled. "General Radulf, I promise that you will pay for those words at trial."

"I do not fear you," Radulf calmly replied. "But if you harm my grandson or any of my family, then you should fear me."

"You will be dead by the end of this day," Brutus said.

"And you will not last the week." Radulf smiled at me as the boys finally led him away. He walked with a limp, I noticed, probably from when he had been dumped into the carcer hole last night. And even if his smile was as fake as those chiseled onto the statues of Rome, it gave me courage for what was coming next.

Because even if I was very lucky — and I never was — this escape was going to hurt. A lot.

EIGHTEEN

Brutus had my left hand pinched behind my back, but it was the right arm he wanted, the one with the Malice on it. As soon as the boys had grabbed Radulf, I'd stuffed that arm beneath me, out of his reach. Brutus rolled off me and tried to twist my body enough to get hold of that arm.

"My grandfather just called you a pig," I said. "You are many things, Decimas Brutus, but not a pig."

He hesitated. "No, I am not. Thank you."

"After all," I added, "that comparison is a terrible insult to pigs."

Furious, he thrust his knee into the small of my back, pushing me even closer to the hole. I yelled out and kicked backward at him. His hand slipped from the Star, but I still wasn't free.

"I need help, you fools!" Brutus yelled. And only then did three other Praetors emerge from dark corners of the carcer, having waited all this time for their orders.

I searched within myself for any remaining magic — surely with the Malice, there had to be something. But within seconds, the Praetors had flipped me onto my back and were holding my legs and had my arms raised high over my head. Brutus pulled out his knife.

"This can be quick, or it can be slow," he said, bringing the knife near my chest. "Pledge your loyalty to the Mistress. Choose her or choose to die."

If I really did have a choice, it would be to melt that knife into putty. And that was only a start of what would happen if I had magic.

"Tell me where you hid the Mistress," he said. "She calls to me."

I struggled again, and when that failed, I spit in Brutus's face. That wasn't exactly the answer he wanted, but when he raised the knife, I immediately stopped fighting.

"Enough of this," Brutus said. "Let me see his arm. I'll take that Malice, then take the bulla. After that, it will be an easy thing to get his vow of loyalty."

The Praetor holding my arms started to raise the right one toward Brutus, but in the same second as he reached for it, I yanked my arm away and then crashed a fist into Brutus's jaw as he bent over me. He reeled backward, landing on the Praetors holding my legs.

I rolled one more time, wrenching my left arm free and almost falling into the dungeon hole.

"Get him under control!" Brutus yelled.

The Praetors lunged for me, but it was too late; I'd made my decision. Falling into a deep hole was sure to be a bad thing. It smelled awful, was sure to cause me any number of injuries, and would be full of prisoners who'd take pleasure in adding to those injuries.

On the other hand, there were Praetors up here. It wasn't a difficult choice.

With one more roll, the bulk of my weight went through the hole, sending me in almost a dive toward the dark ground below.

I crashed on my side onto solid rock, feeling shock waves course through my body as they encountered what was likely several broken bones. It had been at least a twelve-foot fall. Dizziness encompassed me. Even on the hard rock floor, I had trouble figuring out which way was up. My breath entered with sharp gasps, and failed to release until my body was forced into it. Something warm and wet was pooling beneath my head.

"Get the rope!" Brutus said. "Lower me down!"

I couldn't move. Magic was returning to me, but I wouldn't be able to heal myself before he got down here. The room echoed with dripping water. This dark dungeon was a cistern similar to where Aurelia had held me when I'd first been lost in the sewers. That had to be the source of the dripping water now.

The moans I'd heard before had stopped when I first crashed, but they had started again and were coming closer.

Barely within my field of vision, the end of the rope dropped to the floor, landing close to where my feet lay. I heard Brutus swing his weight inside the hole.

I closed my eyes, exhausted, and in so much pain it hurt to breathe. What was this place?

The dripping water, the horrid smell — it reminded me of the Cloaca Maxima. At the moment, it was the only place I could visualize with any clarity. How many times had it saved my life in the past? It would have to do so one more time.

"He might not have survived the fall," Brutus called up to his men. "I'll check."

He released the rope and jumped the remaining distance to the ground. My eyes were still closed, and though I heard the slap of his sandals onto the rock floor, I wasn't a part of the dungeon anymore, not really.

Instead, I was focused on the sound of the water, on the stench of the sewers, which was already thick around me. But I'd been in places far worse than this before, where it was impossible to keep the noxious odor from clinging to your skin. As soon as I had a clear picture of that place, I was there.

Brutus had probably tried to put a hand on me within the same second as I had vanished from the dungeon. I'd reappeared here, somewhere in the Cloaca Maxima, as lost as I ever was in this place. At least when I'd come here before, I'd had some orientation as to where I entered. Now that was impossible. I could be anywhere within the maze. I was lying on the narrow walkway only inches above where the sewage flowed, which was disgusting, but it was enough for now. I needed to heal.

Without magic, I never could've survived that fall, and even with magic, I knew how damaged my body was. I lay there for almost an hour just to regain enough strength to begin healing myself.

The process was slow, but I worked in order of places that hurt the most, or that seemed the most vital to be healed. My chest and ribs first. My leg nearer the end. Even after I was healed, it was at least another hour before I could do anything more than sit up. And that was with the help of magic. No wonder it was taking Radulf so long to regain his strength.

Once I was on my feet again, I debated what might be the best next step. Brutus was the chairman of Radulf's trial, and I suspected once he lost me, he had gone directly to the trial. It was probably over already, and maybe had ended a long time ago. I doubted Brutus would make it any longer than it had to be. He wasn't interested in fairness or justice. He wanted Radulf's execution. I had to find out where it would be and stop it.

Aurelia and Livia would know. They would have been at the trial and would follow Radulf as far as they could to his end. I still wasn't as strong as I could've been, but time was not on my side and so I only hoped I was not about to send myself to a place where a fight was already under way. The way I felt, I wouldn't do much good there.

I closed my eyes and pictured Aurelia in my head. Her smile, the gentle curls of her hair. The way her eyes had looked the first time I saw her, in a field outside of Rome. It was so easy to picture her, and suddenly, I saw that image moving. She was in a crowded place. And I was there with her.

As it turned out, I did arrive at a place where there was fighting, though it fortunately wouldn't involve me.

Aurelia was headed out of a tunnel of the amphitheater,

toward the seats. Below her, the crowd cheered. A bulky gladiator was already in the arena, his arms raised in victory while slaves carried a still body out of the west gate, known as the Gate of Death. The gladiator pumped his arms in victory, calling for even more cheers and admiration. The slave boy Donnan had told me there were games today.

"Nic? Where did you come from?" Aurelia grabbed me and pressed me against the wall, blocking my body with hers in case others had seen the unexpected mode of my arrival. "How did you know I was here?"

"I didn't. I just —" I searched for the right words, and failed. "Why are you here?" There was only one reason Aurelia would've come to the amphitheater today.

Her eyes darted sideways. No one was paying us any special attention, at least not right now. "Radulf's trial is over."

"And this is his sentence?" I stepped out of the tunnels where I could see into the arena better. "He's to be executed in the games?"

"It's not an outright execution," Aurelia said, following me. "He has a chance, but not a good one." She pulled me aside again, out of the main flow of the crowd. "The trial didn't go well at all. Radulf put up no defense for himself. He barely spoke a word the entire time. I think he's so lost without his magic that he really doesn't care what happens to him. Because of that, nobody could vote for his innocence."

"What about Nasica?" I asked. "The bribe?"

She nodded at the bracelet on her wrist, the one that had

been a gift from Crispus. "This is the only thing I have left of any value. You were right not to trust Nasica." Her sigh that followed was filled with regret. "He accepted money from Brutus as well, more than what I had to give him. Crispus did suggest to the other judges that Radulf should be shown mercy, given that Radulf is a war hero and has been popular with the people. Nasica wasn't convinced until he thought about the games today and realized maybe *he* would be more popular if he could donate another fight to the mob."

"Brutus allowed this?" I had expected he'd prefer a more certain execution.

"He was furious, but he had no choice. The judges had spoken. Radulf was taken immediately here, where they are preparing him for one of the upcoming fights."

"He can't save himself." My heart was already pounding in anticipation of what was coming. "I saw him before they took him away for the trial. He won't last a minute in there."

"I know," Aurelia said. "But until you came just now, nothing more could be done for him."

"Is Livia here?" I asked. "And Crispus?"

Aurelia took my hand and led me back into the crowd of onlookers. "Although Radulf lost at trial, Crispus made a passionate speech to save him, which impressed the emperor. You should've heard it, he was amazing! Because of that, he's been invited to sit near the emperor for the games, which is a great honor."

I scanned the lower seats until I saw the imperial box. Our new emperor was named Marcus Aurelius Probus. He was standing in his box and had just waved his arms, permitting a new fight to begin. Emperor Probus was tall with short brown hair and a long, narrow face. He was said to have been a skilled military commander who was tough but also fair. I hoped that was still true. If Probus was fair, we at least had some chance today.

Crispus sat tall behind Probus, clearly proud to have been invited into the imperial box. Usually, that was reserved only for the emperor's family and his closest counselors, but his family didn't seem to have come and the counselors were pushed to upper rows. Crispus's speech must've been as impressive as Aurelia said, though it had failed to win Radulf's freedom. That was all I really cared about. As I watched, Probus said something to Crispus, who nodded and replied. I wanted to think Crispus was still trying to win mercy for Radulf.

And perhaps he might've been successful, if another man had not entered the imperial box as well. Decimas Brutus had come, though he was in an expensive yellow toga now, not in the dark tunic in which I had last seen him. He bowed low to Probus, at first kissing the hem of his purple robes, then kissing his hand as well. Once he rose, he seemed to offer a greeting to Crispus. Crispus looked at Brutus, then, without a word or even a nod of acknowledgment, turned away.

My heart sank. Whatever argument Crispus might make in Radulf's favor, Brutus would be there to immediately counter it.

Aurelia released my hand to point out where my sister was sitting. "People have begun staring at you, Nic, and not in a good way. Let's go sit down. Livia is in the upper tier, waiting for me. She'll be relieved to see you too."

Their seats were high in the amphitheater stands, where only the poorest of citizens could afford to sit. That certainly described me and Livia, and Aurelia now as well.

The sounds from the arena still carried up here, but we were so far from the action on the floor that I'd have only a vague idea of how Radulf was doing. Not that the outcome was in any doubt. Radulf was strong and a good fighter, but his many victories as a gladiator had come because of magic. Now, weakened, out of practice, and with little enthusiasm for his own life, he had no chance at all.

Aurelia looked back at me as we climbed. "No offense, but you smell awful. Almost like you were in the sewers again." As I remained quiet, her smile fell. "Nic, you weren't."

At least the sewage waters had washed the blood from my tunic, though the fabric was cut where Brutus's knife had been. I hoped she wouldn't think too much about the cut.

"I had a hard time finding fresh water before I left," I said.

Aurelia shook her head. "I don't want to know why you were there. I'm just happy you finally got out without me needing to come in and help."

Livia waved when she saw us approaching and started to offer me a hug, until she sniffed and then pushed away. I took no offense at that. If it was possible, I'd get away from myself too.

Rather than ask about why I smelled like something that had crawled out from the underworld, Livia merely crouched down to a sack at her feet and pulled out some olives and crackers. "I'm sure you're hungry. You probably haven't eaten yet today."

I was hungry and was even more grateful to not have to answer any questions. I'd already swallowed most of the olives and several crackers before Livia also found some cheese that she said was meant to go with those crackers.

"They'll meet up in my stomach," I told her as I reached for the cheese.

The gladiator who had claimed victory until now wore a helmet and chain mail almost to his knees, and was armed with a long sword he clearly knew how to use. His new opponent was a red-haired man who was armed with a crescent blade, and for the most part, they had been equally matched against each other. But that changed when the gladiator swiped the man across the leg with his sword, leaving a deep wound. He could still walk, but barely, and the gladiator took the opportunity to heighten his attack. It was only a few clashes of their swords later when the man fell and the crowd cheered.

It disgusted me. Despite my love for this great city, and even my admiration for the greatness of the empire, I wished to leave all of it behind. At its finest, Rome was unconquerable on the battlefield. But here, where blood was entertainment, Rome deserved to fall. They were no better than the bands of thieves and murderers who used to stalk the streets of Gaul.

Aurelia elbowed me. "I think Radulf will be coming out soon. Look — the emperor is standing again."

While slaves cleared the arena, Probus waved his arms to get the crowd's attention. When it had quieted down, he called out, "Our next match returns to us an old favorite of the games. Years ago, I watched him myself, fascinated by his unique style and reputation for never losing a match. For that reason, his popularity grew, so much that he eventually became a general within the empire, one of our finest generals. However, my friends, power corrupted him. Or perhaps the escaped slave with magic, Nicolas Calva, corrupted him."

"Put your head down," Aurelia hissed at me. Some people around us had already recognized me. I'd heard their whispers of my name.

I should've done as she suggested, but I was still looking at Crispus and Brutus, now sitting on opposite sides of the emperor. Brutus was casually reclined, smug and certain all was in his favor. Crispus was the very opposite. He looked as nervous as I felt.

The emperor continued, "So we will let the gods decide. Is General Flavius Radulf Avitus a hero to Rome? If so, may the gods favor him and give him one more victory." Cheers followed until he added, "But if General Radulf is a traitor to Rome, may the gods punish him with death. Release the general!"

The gladiator turned around in the arena until he heard the sound of a door opening in the floor. Doors sprang open from the sand. Radulf's head rose up from below as he was delivered to the battle.

His clothes had been changed from the toga in which he had gone to trial. Now he was in a simple white tunic with a thin rope belted at the waist. He had a mace in one hand, but only held it limply at his side. Even more disturbing was the way his head hung low, as if he had no will to even try to save himself.

"Look at him," Aurelia breathed as she clasped Livia's hand in her own. "He isn't going to fight."

"If he did, could he win this battle?" Livia asked.

I spoke the words under my breath, hoping that against the sound of the crowd's applause she would not be able to hear me.

"No. He cannot win."

NINETEEN

Radulf had barely gotten his footing on solid ground when the gladiator attacked him for the first time, swinging for a quick victory with the sword in his hand. Radulf dodged it, but made no reply with the mace he had been given. I wasn't sure how much experience Radulf had with a mace — probably not as much as with a sword. But Radulf had relied on his magic for so long, I doubted he really knew how to fight without it anymore.

I wondered if that would eventually happen to me. I loved the feel of magic, the strength and power it offered. But I didn't want to need it, to be useless without it.

The gladiator charged at Radulf again, his sword above his head, ready for a strike. Radulf stood as if welcoming the attack, then at the last moment stepped aside, leaving one leg in the gladiator's path, tripping him. The gladiator fell forward and Radulf hit him in the back with the blunt end of his mace. It would leave a bruise, but nothing else.

"Why didn't he do more?" Aurelia asked. "That was his moment."

The crowd had a mixed response to Radulf's non-attack. They half booed what they saw as his cowardice. And half cheered, expecting he was only toying with the gladiator before launching his real assault. Nobody cheered because Radulf had shown mercy. Nobody in Rome ever cheered for that.

Radulf limped away without noticing the gladiator jump to his feet, ready for revenge. He raised his sword again, and Radulf still hadn't turned around. It would be an easy defeat . . . unless I helped. With a little swipe of my fingers, the gladiator fell forward, as if his sandals had been laced together.

Laughter erupted throughout the audience as the crowd shouted out insults about the gladiator's clumsiness. Embarrassed and ready to redeem himself, the gladiator got to his feet again, this time lunging toward Radulf with his sword outstretched.

Unfortunately for him, he tripped on those invisibly laced sandals a second time. I shouldn't have been grinning to see it, but I couldn't help it. The audience roared with laughter, and the gladiator remained seated, clearly confused. He checked his feet to see what the problem might be, and looked even more confused when he couldn't see any problem at all.

Radulf knew what had happened. He stopped walking and began scanning the stands with his hand over his eyes to block the sun.

"He's looking for you," Livia said, glancing sideways at me.

Maybe he was, but he'd never see me up here, almost high enough in the stands to reach the clouds, and only one of fifty thousand other Romans in attendance. Since I wasn't close enough to see his expression, I chose to believe he wasn't entirely annoyed with me.

Cautiously this time, the gladiator got to his feet, testing his balance before taking his first step forward. I allowed that and instead focused on his sword, pouring heat into the metal until the gladiator's fingers began twitching. When the metal itself began to smoke, he threw it onto the sand and then gently rubbed his burned hand.

Livia giggled. "What's next?"

"A terrible fit of hiccups, I think." I smiled over at her, though I doubted that trick was within my abilities. It would be fun to see.

Aurelia tugged at my arm. "What is Brutus doing?"

Brutus had leaned in toward Emperor Probus and was speaking to him while gesturing down at the gladiator fight. After a moment, Crispus noticed the conversation and spoke too, though the emperor was looking only at Brutus.

"I don't like this," Livia said.

I didn't either. From this distance, it was difficult to see anyone's expressions, but Crispus's body was rigid, and Brutus was clearly angry. Probus nodded, and then Brutus stood at the edge of the imperial box and raised his arms for the attention of the crowd. Everyone grew silent, and the gladiator stood with one arm across his chest, in respect of the emperor.

"Nicolas Calva!" Brutus yelled. "The emperor demands you show yourself at once."

Livia gripped my arm, her nails digging into the flesh.

Beside me, Aurelia gasped and whispered, "You shouldn't have heated that sword."

"Do you really think the sword is the problem?" I scowled. "It's the reason Brutus and I are not friends — that's what you think?"

"This is what I warned you about before," Aurelia said. "You take the wolf by the ears and expect it won't try to bite!"

"The wolf down there is already biting!" I said. "Better me than Radulf!"

"Show yourself, Nicolas," Brutus repeated. "Or I will order this match to end."

Just beyond the arena wall, I saw archers positioned with arrows already nocked in their bows. All it would take was an order to fire. I could shield Radulf from their arrows, and even from the gladiator's blows, but not permanently.

To make his point, Brutus nodded, and the gladiator suddenly lunged at Radulf, knocking him down onto his back. Along with most of the crowd, I stood, trying to see better, and realized the gladiator was fighting Radulf for the mace. They exchanged a few blows, though Radulf was in the much weaker position and received far more hits than he gave.

Livia cried, "Help him, Nic!"

By the time I had a clear look at what was happening, the gladiator had the mace in his hands and had already used it to take at least one hard swing at Radulf, who still lay on his back, either unconscious or close to it. I used magic to take control of the mace and raise it high in the air. The gladiator had been holding it so tightly that he rose with the mace and dangled midair. He wouldn't dare let go now.

"Do you think I won't let the gladiator die?" Brutus yelled. "Do you think I won't sacrifice as many people as it takes until you kneel before me in this arena?"

Crispus was on his feet, speaking to Probus, and this time he had the emperor's attention. But whatever he said clearly wasn't going well, because when Probus stood, Crispus went to his knees and was shaking his head.

Brutus signaled to his archers, who raised their bows to the gladiator. I didn't want him killed for my actions. This was between me and Brutus, not someone who was probably as much a slave of the empire as I had once been. So I lowered him to the ground, then raised a shield around Radulf.

Surprisingly then, Probus said something to his guards, who shouted an order into the arena that I couldn't hear.

Livia gripped my arm. "What's happening?"

Before I could answer, the gladiator bowed to the emperor, dropped his weapon, and was escorted out of the arena. Radulf remained in there alone. He was also on his knees now, though I suspected that had more to do with the injuries he had just received than with his respect for the emperor.

A hush fell over the crowd as they waited for what Probus would do next. Had Radulf been pardoned — would he go free? It certainly looked that way.

"This is your chance," Livia said. "Go down there and disappear with him."

"Don't go down there," Aurelia said. "It's a trap, but I can't see how, and that worries me."

"He has the Malice," Livia said. "Even if it's a trap, Nic can win!"

"No, I can't." My heart sank. Those same guards brought Crispus to his feet and thrust a bow into his hands, then walked him beside Decimas Brutus at the front of the imperial box. They stood behind him with swords raised, communicating a very clear message. Should Crispus refuse the orders he had obviously just been given, the swords would fall on him. Crispus was supposed to shoot the arrow to end Radulf's life. They were making Crispus do it.

The shield I'd placed around Radulf would protect him for several minutes, but what would happen to Crispus if he failed to shoot, or if he tried and missed? Radulf was not the only one in danger now.

Seeing the arrow raise toward him, Radulf only stood and called up something to Crispus that I couldn't hear. Based on what I'd seen of Radulf since he'd come back from the Mistress, I suspected Radulf was telling him everything was all right and that he didn't blame Crispus for what was about to happen. But Crispus still shook his head and brushed at his eyes with the back of one hand.

"The emperor offers a trade, Nicolas," Brutus called. "Show yourself. Save the general."

"This will never end," I said, more to myself than for anyone else. "All they want is me."

Aurelia's eyes locked with mine, and in hers I saw fear and sorrow and the same dread that went to the core of my own body too. She wanted to say something — I felt that urgency in her, but in the end, there were no words to be spoken.

I couldn't let Radulf die.

I couldn't let Crispus be the one to do it.

And I couldn't pretend there was any reason this was all happening, except for one reason alone: They wanted control of me.

"I'm afraid, Nic," Livia said.

Aurelia reached across me to take her hand. And though Aurelia whispered words of comfort, I saw Aurelia's fingers shaking too.

I closed my eyes long enough to call out a request to Caela. I needed her help and hoped she would come. Then I held out my right arm to Livia.

"Unlace the Malice."

Her eyes widened. "No! Use it to stop what's happening."

"Magic is not the solution," I said. "Every time I try it, the Praetors counter it with a trick of their own, and every single time, I end up in worse trouble."

Brutus called out again, "Nicolas, do you think you can stop this arrow by shielding the general? It's costing you strength you will need very soon."

This was true, and it worried me.

"Hurry, Livia," I said. "I will solve this, I promise. But not with the amulets."

With my other arm, I removed the bulla from around my neck. I immediately felt the change in the weight. Soon I would feel the loss of its power too.

I gave the bulla to Aurelia, who shook her head at me. "You're going down there without magic?"

"I have two choices left. One is to stop the Praetors, permanently."

"You're going to kill Brutus?" Livia asked. "Don't do that, Nic. Even for Brutus, it's wrong!"

"The second is to make them believe these amulets are destroyed, that I have no magic to create a Jupiter Stone."

"If they think you have no magic, the punishment they will give you —" Aurelia drew in a sharp breath. "It will be awful."

"I can stop Brutus before that happens. And if I don't, then at least I can make him believe the amulets are destroyed."

With that, Livia finished removing the Malice. "What should we do with these?" she asked.

"Go find Callistus, in the stables of Aurelia's home. He'll carry you to a safe place to hide them."

Livia shook her head. "If people notice us leaving and follow us, what then?"

"Keep the amulets hidden in your robes while you leave. And if there's trouble, you have Aurelia. She'll keep you safe." I took my sister's hand and gave it a firm squeeze. "You must leave this arena immediately, no matter what happens below." In fact, I wanted her to leave before anything happened down there. Either way, it would be ugly.

She nodded and then I turned to Aurelia, who said, "Come back from this, Nic. Remember your promise to me."

I reached over and pulled Aurelia toward me, then kissed her lightly on the cheek. It wasn't much of an answer. It wasn't any answer at all, but it was the only thing I could do.

When she leaned away, she used the back of her hand to brush at a stray tear, then stood. "Let's go, Livia. I don't want to see this. I can't see it."

Livia gave my hand one last squeeze, then stood and followed Aurelia into the tunnels behind our seats.

Down on the arena floor, Radulf was still standing before Crispus, both of them waiting for my shield to fail. Blood ran down the left side of Radulf's face, and he had drawn one arm close to his chest, as if it were injured.

I focused on him so intently that when I closed my eyes, I could see him in my mind. Going into the arena would take nearly all the magic still left from the bulla. The Divine Star would continue to help me, but I wasn't as experienced in using its lesser magic. My time was now as limited as my options ever were. Hopefully, what I'd bring with me into the arena would be enough.

I felt my body leave the seats in the stand and the compression of traveling through nothingness to suddenly land on my feet on crunchy sand. The audience's loud gasps followed by almost total silence told me I was in the arena now.

I opened my eyes, a little disoriented at first. Thousands of faces were staring down at me, more than what they had appeared when I was in the stands. I was almost directly in front of the imperial box, standing between Crispus's arrow and Radulf. The emperor's soldiers immediately gathered in closer, ready to protect their emperor, if harming him was my intention. They were lucky I had other plans. Besides, standing by the emperor would only put them at risk too. My aim with magic was never as good as I wanted it.

Up close, Probus seemed more human than he had while at a distance. His eyes looked tired, and he bore visible scars from his past military battles. I was tired too, exhausted from so many fights, so much running. For all his power, the emperor was at risk of my magic. And for all my magic, I could still be brought to my knees by this empire.

Seeing me now, Brutus stood taller in the foreground, and a wicked smile widened across his face. He must've thought his plan to trap me had finally worked. But he never considered that I would've had my own ideas about coming here.

I turned in a circle, this time looking for the archers. They had been easy to spot when I was up high in the stands, but from here they were nearly invisible. Maybe I didn't need to see them. It was enough to know they were there, and had plenty of arrows if Crispus failed.

In a loud voice, Emperor Probus said, "Your name is Nicolas Calva. You are the escaped slave with magic stolen from the gods."

I faced him, hands down and palms open. "I came to accept your offer. Allow the general to leave this stadium, unharmed."

Radulf barely spoke, but I heard him. "Fool grandson, how many times must I order you not to save me?"

One corner of my mouth curved upward. "As many times as you wish to have your orders ignored, sir."

"He can leave the stadium," Brutus said. "If he can walk out on his own."

Probus didn't seem to enjoy the joke, but he didn't correct Brutus either.

With all eyes on him, Radulf nodded at the emperor, then took a step toward the nearest gate. His attempt failed, and Radulf immediately fell forward onto the sand floor. I heard his grunt of pain and hurried over to help him get up. There was no time to heal him here, nor did I have the magic for it. But I could help him stand in front of the emperor and face the citizens of Rome as an honored general, not a fallen victim of a second-rate gladiator.

"This is all wrong," Radulf mumbled. "I'm getting what I deserve."

"Forgiveness is real," I said. "You've suffered enough."

Above us, Crispus was talking to the emperor again. This time, Probus was nodding and looking at both me and Radulf.

Finally, Probus announced to the audience, "I have made my decision. It is one of justice balanced with mercy. The general cannot be allowed to remain in Rome, but in exchange for Nicolas Calva's arrival in the arena, I will let the general live. I sentence Radulf to be exiled from the empire, immediately."

That was exactly my plan. I scanned the skies for any sign of Caela, then said to Radulf, "You are going to Britannia and there will make a home with my mother, and soon with Livia and Aurelia."

Radulf put a hand on my shoulder. "What about you?"

I shrugged and let my eyes fall from his gaze. "You know what I have to do."

Radulf nodded, but before he could speak, Caela's caw echoed down into the amphitheater and her great form created a shadow upon us. Cheers erupted from the audience when they saw her, and I helped Radulf limp over to where she would land.

"I am so very sorry," Radulf said once he was on Caela's back. "My boy, you deserve none of what has come to you."

My shoulders straightened in grim determination. "I will come back from this, you'll see."

He reached for me, but by then Caela had already launched herself from the amphitheater floor. For as steep as she flew, I wondered how Radulf managed to remain on her back. She made one wide circle not far above the crowd's heads, and then the most amazing thing happened.

The audience stood, each with an arm crossed against his chest, just as Radulf's arm had been when I came down into the arena. They were giving tribute to their general, honoring his victories for them. Radulf had always been loved here in Rome. I hoped he saw their respect too.

After they finally flew away, the crowd seated themselves, and Brutus said to me, "You know what must happen, slave boy.

Kneel before Caesar, acknowledge your humility before the empire. And accept Caesar's judgment upon you."

To refer to the emperor as Caesar was a title of respect, one of the highest ways to honor him. I knelt as ordered, but not to accept any judgment. Instead, it put my hand within easy reach of the sword the gladiator had dropped. The weapon looked heavy and would cost me far more strength than an arrow. But I had to use what I was given.

When I rose again to my feet, the sword came with me.

"I will accept any judgment that comes to me," I shouted to Brutus. Raising the sword, I added, "But you must accept your judgment too!"

TWENTY

I raised the sword into the air, aimed toward Brutus. As I'd expected, the cost to my magic was high, but I had enough in the Divine Star to do this and perhaps to defend myself afterward. At least, I hoped I did. Once this sword found its target, the reaction would be swift and fierce.

If I was wrong, however, and didn't have the magic, then at least I'd fall knowing that Brutus would come to the Elysian Fields with me. Or in his case, he'd go to Tartarus, where evil men were sent deep into the darkest pit guarded by a monster with fifty sharp-toothed jaws. I liked the idea of him spending some time there, though it was hardly fair to the monster to have to deal with a venomous man like Brutus.

Both my palms were turned to the sky, fingers inward, keeping the sword in place. All it would take was to rotate them toward the emperor's box and the sword would fly at Brutus. My heart pounded with the realization of what I was about to do. *If* I could do it.

Threatening the Praetors, or even giving them a few bruises and broken bones, was one thing. They had started this war, and whatever I'd done to them had been meant only to save my life and the lives of those I cared about. I tried telling myself that killing Brutus was no different. He would continue on with this war until either my defeat or my death. If I were to have any chance of one day living a normal life, this was the right thing to do. Maybe it was the only thing to do.

And yet I wasn't sure that I could do it. The look in Livia's eyes when I'd told her my plans still haunted me.

My hands began to shake, and with it, the sword quivered too. I closed my eyes, attempting to summon a depth of courage that I knew I did not possess.

Seeing my hesitation, Brutus took the moment to grab Crispus and pull him directly in front of his body. Crispus cried out, and when I opened my eyes, I saw him struggling to move away, but Brutus was keeping him in place.

"What if the sword misses?" Brutus shouted. "Now will you do it?"

No, of course I wouldn't. Immediately, I rotated my palms downward, and the sword fell with it, near my feet.

"Arrest the slave boy!" Probus ordered his guards.

"Wait!" Brutus thrust Crispus aside and spoke to the emperor, muttering words I couldn't hear. Crispus was kept on the outside of their close conversation, though I noticed him trying to speak as well. At one point, Brutus pointed back to Crispus, who shook his head and said a few more things, but the emperor nodded, obviously in favor of Brutus's proposal.

The guards surrounding Probus kept their place, but Crispus's curly blond head disappeared from my sight, so I gathered he had just been given orders to come through the tunnels into the arena where I stood. They wouldn't send guards to arrest me, wouldn't even send Praetors. Or at least, not the Praetors who were my enemies. They would send someone I had just proved I would never attack. I didn't have much time.

I raised the sword again, this time determined to do the thing I had come here to do. Brutus had to die. It was awful, yes, and I hated to be the one to do it, but he wasn't giving me any other choice.

Behind me, I heard the archers rise into position, ready to shoot me upon the emperor's orders. They worried me, but less than before. Brutus wanted me alive, and from his gestures, I knew he was trying to persuade the emperor to hold off on any orders until Crispus entered the arena. At that point, the arrows could be trained upon Crispus. They would tell me to lower the sword and save Crispus's life.

And I would give in, because I always gave in under such threats. So if I was going to use the sword, I had to do it now, then immediately get Crispus and myself out of here. I had to do this.

I couldn't do this.

But I had to.

Brutus was still in the imperial box, facing me with a smug, taunting grin. Either he believed he was safe, or he knew running would be futile. Both of us were about to find out which was true.

My upturned hands were shaking again, but not as much as before. I would just do it. Do what I had come here to do, and know that whatever burden of guilt and punishment followed this crime, at least Brutus would be dead.

Before I did, Crispus burst through a gate to my left, the same one in which gladiators usually made their entrances before the games. He waved at the archers behind us. "Do not shoot! I'm here."

He was here already? Had he somehow flown here or mastered the art of disappearing? Crispus gave a quick bow to the emperor, signaling his respect, and then faced me. His chest was visibly rising and falling. If he was out of breath, that could be explained by the speed with which he had entered the arena. It could also be that he was nervous to approach me now. He was here to carry out Brutus's plans, and we both knew it.

I took a step back. "Do not lay a hand on me. Not yet."

"Lower the sword, Nic. The archers are only waiting on orders to fire. You can't block all the arrows."

"I know that. Go back into the tunnels. You'll be safe there."

He inched closer and in a quieter voice said, "If you can disappear from here, then do it. I'll make it look like I'm trying to reach you but didn't get to you in time."

"What will happen to you if I do that?"

He shrugged without answering, but he didn't need to. I already knew. If Crispus let me escape in front of these fifty thousand Romans, embarrassing Brutus and the emperor, he would pay a terrible price. I turned my attention again to the sword.

"Disappear," Crispus said again. "If you use that sword, it will prove to this entire crowd that you are a traitor to Rome. The emperor will have no choice but to order your death."

"And what are his orders if I don't use the sword?"

"Maybe there is another way." Crispus addressed the emperor with another bow. "Look carefully," he said, loud enough to be heard in the imperial box. "The amulets you seek are no longer on his wrist or around his neck. Nicolas Calva has no value to the empire."

"This is a great idea," I muttered. "Convince the emperor to kill me. Can I at least use the sword first?"

Brutus hadn't seemed to notice the Malice and bulla were missing. Now he leaned over the emperor's balcony to study me more closely, his face reddening as he realized Crispus had spoken the truth.

"Where are they?" he shouted. "What have you done with them?"

"They're gone," I said. "Out of your reach." Which was only true in the sense that Livia and Aurelia were currently physically out of reach of Brutus's arm length.

"If there is any way to retrieve the amulets, you will find that out only if you allow Nic to live," Crispus said.

"Do not encourage him to find those amulets," I hissed. "Let them remain in hiding."

Crispus looked at me and then his eyes widened as he realized what I must have done with them. "How else can I save you?" He nearly mouthed the words, but I understood his meaning.

"You cannot." I felt the full weight of my words, and the consequences that seemed inevitable now. "Leave this arena, please. I can't shield us both." By now I probably couldn't even shield myself.

Crispus licked his lips, then started to back away. Not as far as I wanted, though, and he wasn't leaving the arena as he should have.

"I'm giving you your life back," I said to Crispus. "Go away!"

"I'm your friend," Crispus said. "I'll stay with you." He had no idea what his mother had asked of me.

Brutus was furious beyond reason. "Kill the slave boy! Send in the lions to rip his flesh, and that of his friend!"

I raised the sword higher, my eyes focused squarely on Brutus. He stared back at me, smug in his belief that I wouldn't do it. But I had good reason now. With Crispus in the arena, I had to protect his life before Brutus released those lions. I would carry no guilt away with me.

The instant the sword struck, I'd try to at least shield Crispus before the arrows flew. It was beyond foolish, but that was my plan. Brutus could duck, run, or try to protect himself. None of it would work. All I needed was a simple rotation of my hands.

Except that someone else caught my eye. Directly behind the emperor's box were the seats reserved for the vestals of Rome. All six women were there now, of varying age, and all of them dressed in the same white robes. But one woman was standing. It was the vestalis who had allowed Aurelia and me to take sanctuary in Caesar's temple, and the one who had helped me find the rock for the Jupiter Stone outside Diana's temple.

She was staring intently at me, her face etched with sadness and concern. The sword was in my control, and I was finally ready to use it. But under the stern gaze of the vestalis, I began to have doubts again. My hands had been raised, but now I lowered them for good, and the sword lowered too. She shook her head at me, a clear warning not to carry out my plans.

My heart pounded, and I was vaguely aware of Crispus moving toward me again, although I didn't hear anything he was saying.

"You're wrong!" I wanted to yell at her. Maybe she didn't know how evil Brutus was and how terrible things would get if I abandoned this plan. I wanted to believe that if I explained everything to her, I would make her understand why I was right, why killing Brutus was necessary.

But I'd never shout at someone like her, in anger or for any other reason. And I'd be a fool to believe I could ever be right and she wrong. But that didn't mean I had to be happy about the consequences of her being right.

The vestalis shook her head again, and I felt the magic fade from within me. The sword dropped back to the sand, as useless now as a limp reed. I would not kill Brutus. I would not end this war. And I probably would not live long enough to regret either of those decisions.

"Listen carefully," I quietly said to Crispus. "Please get Livia and Aurelia safely to Britannia. They must bring the amulets with them and hide them there, burying them so deep they will never again be found. They cannot remain here in the empire."

"Disappear!" Crispus hissed. "You must leave or they will take you."

I glanced back at the vestalis, who had continued staring intently at me. I sighed, hoping I had not misread her thoughts. "Even if I could, that's not what I'm supposed to do."

Crispus cursed under his breath, then stepped forward again. "Emperor Probus, you have seen for yourself only the smallest part of Nicolas Calva's powers. If he had wanted to bring harm to Rome, he could've done it. But he has only added to the entertainment at these games. Reward him with his freedom."

Brutus leaned over and said something to the emperor that I could not hear. Probus shook his head, then gave a reply that Brutus clearly disliked. Finally, Probus waved his hand, gesturing that his decision was final.

Brutus turned, and though he was spitting out the words in his reluctance to have to say them, he announced to the crowd. "Tomorrow, Nicolas Calva will be tried for treason against the empire. He has been freed as a slave, but the emperor does not recognize his citizenship of Rome and the rights that would come with it. Yet in his mercy, Emperor Probus himself will sit in judgment of the boy. I will prosecute his case." His eyes darkened as he glared at me. "And I will see him executed."

"I will defend him!" Crispus shouted.

I looked at Crispus, trying not to let my fear show. "What experience do you have in criminal defense?"

"None." Crispus shrugged. "But it's better than nothing at all."

"Is it?" I asked. Somehow it seemed about the same as nothing at all.

Brutus looked at Crispus. "Caesar ordered you to put a hand on that boy. Do it, or I will."

Crispus turned to me, his eyes full of sadness. "Better me than him."

"It's all right," I said, stretching out my arm. "There isn't much magic left in me anyway."

"Whatever happens once they take you, don't fight," Crispus said. "Don't make this any worse for yourself."

"How could it be worse?" I asked. "Seriously, how could it get worse than this?"

"It will get worse," Crispus said. "What's coming is awful. I'm so sorry, Nic."

He put his hand on my arm, and though his touch had none of the anger or hatred in it that I usually felt from the Praetors, it had all their power. Magic emptied from my body, and with it the added strength and energy that I had become so dependent upon.

Other Praetors were headed toward us now. I readied myself for them as best as I could, but my heart was already pounding.

"Don't be sorry," I said to Crispus. "I did this to myself."

"I am sorry," he said. "I will do everything I can for you tomorrow, but I doubt it will be enough."

I already understood that, far more than I wished I did. He would do his best tomorrow to defend me at trial, but he would lose.

And I would die.

Right or wrong, I never should've listened to the vestalis.

TWENTY-ONE

The arrest happened quickly and, considering that I was not fighting back, seemed unnecessarily harsh. The Praetors surrounded me, pushing Crispus away from their circle. Everyone who could get a hand on me had done so, just to ensure I remained in their control. As they pulled me from the arena, I did everything I could to keep up, but so many feet were near mine, I eventually tripped and they took to dragging me, which was what they had clearly wanted in the first place.

The audience rained down their disapproval with loud boos, and some took to throwing loaves of bread or even rocks into the arena. At first I thought it was because they'd have rather seen me fight, rather seen more of what I could do with magic. But their chants were growing louder: "Free the slave, free the slave." Their demanding shouts followed me long after we had left the arena gates. Rome was a mob, perhaps, but they were a powerless mob today.

Crispus was somewhere behind us — I heard him calling

my name and shouting orders for the men to slow down, but he was entirely ignored.

The street was filling too — those who had been in the stands were following us into the forum, wanting to see what happened to me there. I had expected they would take me into the same prison where Radulf had awaited his trial, but for better or worse, their plans were far more public.

They dragged me into the center of the forum, into the *comitium*, where the public sometimes gathered to vote or hear speeches delivered from the *rostra*. The rostra was a curved platform up seven or eight steps, and the speaker could address an audience from either side, depending on the size of the crowd. Marcus Antonius had eulogized Caesar's death from there, igniting the people's anger against his murder, a crime for which Atroxia had paid the price.

The senators met in the Curia Julia on my left, and Radulf's carcer was across from it. Other statues and columns decorated the area, a dense crowd of self-congratulatory trophies Rome built to itself.

Least of all to one side of the comitium was a fig tree, raised from the ground level and behind a short sitting wall. It must have had some significance, since they'd allowed it to remain here amongst the temples and marble floors, but I didn't know its story, nor did I care. All I knew was they were dragging me toward the tree very quickly, and someone was calling for chains to be brought. The Praetors pulled me face-first to the trunk, wrapping my arms around it and tying them with some rough cords. I didn't bother with fighting to get free; there were still far too many men for it to do any good. Beyond that, I was terrified by what was about to happen here. Brutus had threatened to expose me to the lions, letting them do with me as they wanted until I confessed where the amulets were. He would be no more merciful now. And I could never tell him where the amulets were. Never.

Crispus pushed forward through the crowd of Praetors and put his back to mine to stop anyone else from coming closer. "Nobody will harm him!" he shouted. "He's a Roman citizen now. Decimas Brutus has no authority to order any punishment until after a trial!"

"But I do." The entire crowd immediately fell to their knees, including Crispus. At least one Praetor behind the tree still kept a hand on my arm, but at least they had gone quiet. Because of how my arms were tied, I couldn't kneel and could only barely turn enough to see Emperor Probus. It wasn't worth the effort, though. He had just claimed authority to punish me any way he wanted. And I had no doubt that Decimas Brutus was whispering into his ear the very nature of that punishment.

Crispus was no longer at my back, and I craned my neck enough to see him fall again to his knees at Probus's feet. He kissed the hem of the emperor's purple toga, then said, "Hail Caesar."

"You've already stated your arguments on behalf of this boy." Probus spoke to Crispus in a respectful tone, but without yielding any authority. "And tomorrow you will have the chance to present them at trial."

"Tomorrow, I will argue for his innocence," Crispus said. "If you find him guilty, punish him then. But today, I ask for both your mercy and justice — he's not yet been tried."

Standing beside the emperor, Brutus showed less respect in the tone of his voice. "Whatever treatment Nicolas receives now is not a punishment. It is to force him to reveal the location of two amulets that belong to the gods. They must be given to the empire."

"If I did, how would you use them?" I asked. "Tell the emperor why you want my magic!"

Only a moment passed before Brutus said, "For the glory of Rome, and for the gods we serve, naturally."

His lies were coated in honey, smooth enough to make Probus swallow them whole. Brutus only served Diana, and her intentions for the empire had nothing to do with its glory. But I also knew that Brutus wouldn't volunteer that information to the emperor.

I heard footsteps on the grass and turned again enough to see Probus behind me. I lowered my eyes in respect, but looked up, sooner than I should have, curious as to what would happen next.

He pulled my tunic down enough to look at the Divine Star on my shoulder. His finger ran along the scar. I felt the touch and flinched, but he gave me none of the pain that Brutus did. This man had no hatred of me or wish to control me. But I did sense his concern for what harm I might bring to the empire.

"This is what gives you the ability to do magic?" he asked.

I nodded.

"The bulla, and the Malice of Mars, these contain the magic of the gods, yes? More powerful than what this scar alone can do?"

Again, I nodded.

"Where are they? I wish to examine these amulets."

I stared forward without responding. My heart was pounding, though, as if it wanted to scream out the answers. I would be screaming soon, no doubt.

Probus raised his voice, just to be sure I had heard. "Where are the amulets, Nicolas? If you truly intend no harm against the empire, then you should be glad to show them to me."

Should I be glad? Knowing full well that Brutus wanted those amulets in his hands so he could force me to use them in service of the Mistress and Diana. If I confessed their whereabouts, within the hour, Aurelia and Livia would be arrested on charges of treason, just as I was now charged. With all of that on my mind, did he really think I should be glad to obey any of his orders?

I only shook my head at his request. Now they could add refusing a direct command of the emperor to my list of crimes. I would pay for this.

The emperor made some sort of gesture that I couldn't see, and then walked away. Other footsteps echoed behind me, and this time I made no effort to turn and look. I lacked the courage to do it and only knotted my fingers together, hoping to stay strong for as long as I could.

A whip snapped in the air, echoing against the many marble walls in the forum. Brutus chuckled and said, "Hear that, Nicolas? The sound will be even worse when it hits your back. Unless you tell the emperor where you've hidden the amulets."

"I threw them to the bottom of the Tiber River." I scowled. "Why don't you go dive for them? Don't come up for air until you've found them."

With that, Brutus's whip hit, cutting like a blade into my back. I cried out and my legs crumpled, but the Praetors holding my arms on the other side of the tree refused to let me fall.

With the second lashing, I collapsed against the tree. My face scraped against the bark, though that was nothing compared to the sting on my back.

The next lash struck behind my knees, which hurt far worse, and forced a cry of pain from me that surely even the gods could hear. Why would they leave me to this fate? Was I not protecting their amulets from Brutus, from a goddess who had declared war against them? Were my crimes awful enough to deserve their abandonment?

Or had I been abandoned since the moment I escaped the

mines? Maybe the gods had not forgiven me for taking the bulla, regardless of what I had tried to do for Rome since then.

"Where are the amulets?" Brutus said, accompanying his question with another strike to my back. It was a reminder that this was only about getting the amulets. The greater punishment for my crimes was still to come and would no doubt be worse, if that was possible.

"He won't tell you anything!" Crispus yelled. "Don't you see this is useless? He'll never tell."

No, I wouldn't. I couldn't tell, no matter what they did. Nor did I intend to die this way, with Brutus taking my life one lash at a time. But it was becoming easier to believe that no matter what I intended, this whipping would continue until he had succeeded.

Brutus struck again, cutting deeper into the wound already behind my knees. This time, I collapsed with so much force that the Praetors could not keep me up. For the briefest of moments, they let go of me, and the magic in my shoulder attempted to give me a spark. I felt it, and then Praetors had my hands once more. The spark disappeared, leaving me more hopeless than ever.

"Tell me where the amulets are, and this will end," Brutus said. "Tell me what I want to know, and it will go better for you at trial tomorrow. You might even hope to earn a little mercy."

"I won't beg mercy from you!" My teeth were clenched so tightly together that he might not have heard me.

The snap of his whip said otherwise. "You were too weak to kill me when you had the chance, but I am not so weak in dealing with you. Tell me where those amulets are, or I will end your life."

"Do it!" I shouted. "The amulets will disappear forever, as will the only person who can make them work. I dare you to do it!"

And a growing part of me wished he would. Without magic to sustain me and heal me, I would not last much longer anyway.

I clenched my fists as the whip snapped again.

TWENTY-TWO

This time, the whip didn't touch me, but I felt Brutus's anger just as if it had. He knew I was right in the threat I had made. Without me, even if he found the amulets, they would be useless.

"Fire!" someone yelled. "On Aventine Hill!"

I leaned sideways just enough to see smoke rising over the temples and basilicas.

Crispus ran up the rostra steps, where he could have a better look. He called back to the crowd, "The fire is near Laverna's gate." Then he faced the emperor directly. "Laverna, goddess of thieves. This is a sign, no doubt. She demands that Nicolas be allowed a fair trial before anything else is done to him."

Brutus didn't strike me again, so maybe the emperor had gestured for him to stop while he considered Crispus's warning. All I could do was remain on my knees, clinging to the familiarity of Crispus's voice and reminding myself to keep breathing.

Since he already had the rostra from which to speak, Crispus continued, still addressing the emperor. "Caesar must know that to offend even a minor god like Laverna can have serious consequences for Rome. I propose we use the rest of the evening to give proper worship to the gods, then conduct Nicolas's trial tomorrow morning."

"If you let me continue, I will get the boy to talk," Brutus said. "Perhaps Nicolas cannot be persuaded when it's his own pain. But if Caesar will allow me to put the senator's son beside him, Nicolas will tell us what we want to know."

I looked over at Crispus with panic in my eyes. Surely they wouldn't do that. His eyes had widened too, and I could almost see his heart beating from here. He had just witnessed my lashing, so it must be far worse for him, wondering if he would be next and if he could endure it. Which forced me to ask myself how long I could let it happen before telling them about the amulets.

I couldn't tell, not even for Crispus. I hoped he would understand that and forgive me.

However, Probus said, "Crispus is a respected citizen of Rome, accused of nothing more than being a loyal friend." His tone became angry. "How dare you suggest such a thing, Brutus? This is finished. You have disappointed me with your failure and your cruelty. Crispus is right. Tonight we shall pay proper respect to the gods in their temples, and tomorrow the boy will receive a fair trial. And someone put out the fire on that hill! I will not sit by as Nero did and allow this empire to burn! Everyone go back to your homes, now!"

The crowd that had surrounded me immediately began to disperse, and Probus disappeared with his soldiers too. But Brutus walked forward and crouched beside me. I suspected he would have liked to touch my shoulder and inflict whatever last bit of pain he could, but with the blood on my back, he only stared at me, red-faced and sputtering with anger.

"How did you start the fire on that hill, so close to Laverna's gate?" he asked. "You should not have any magic."

"I didn't start it," I mumbled. Nor did I know how the fire had started, whether it was a warning from the gods or merely a natural coincidence that benefited me.

He continued staring until he decided either I was telling the truth or that he'd get no confession. Then he motioned toward someone on the other side of the tree, who began replacing the ropes that had bound me with chains. When that was finished, the Praetor pulled at my right arm. Whatever he was doing, I didn't resist. I couldn't, but I did wonder what was happening.

Brutus answered my unspoken question. "It's the same armband all Praetors wear, though there's a lock on yours to keep it from coming apart. With that on your arm, it'll be no different than our touch. You won't feel any magic."

That didn't matter. The only thing I felt was the pain on my back and behind my knees. I doubted there was room within me to feel anything else.

Now Brutus leaned forward and said, "You may feel proud

for refusing to answer me today, but this only puts you in a worse situation for the trial. If you had cooperated and told me where the amulets are, I could've saved your life. But when the emperor finds you guilty, your execution will follow. You will have fought for nothing, protected nothing, and given your family nothing but memories of your failure. The pain you're in is nothing compared to your fate tomorrow. I am offering you one last chance. If you give me the amulets and promise to help me use them, you will not die tomorrow. That is your only chance."

"I have no intention of dying tomorrow," I mumbled. "Nor of giving you those amulets."

"You think this stubbornness is a strength, but it is a weakness that will destroy you in the end." Brutus frowned. "Think on my words tonight. You may feel differently when the sun rises again."

Then he patted my head until I pulled it away. He stood and gave me a light kick before leaving. As soon as he was gone, Crispus rushed forward. He braced me with his arm and said, "I'll call for someone to tend to those wounds."

"For what purpose?" I asked. "We both know how my trial will end. Let them be."

"You shouldn't be here right now. Back in the amphitheater, they gave me a bow and ordered me to shoot Radulf. I know you came to the arena to protect him, but I never would've done it."

"Then they'd have killed you too. Your mother . . ." I had to swallow before I could finish. "I promised her . . ."

"If you kept the amulets, you could've gotten all of us out alive."

"Until they come again." A brush of cool air flowed over my back, and I clenched my teeth until it passed. "Fighting always makes things worse, with more people paying for my crimes. The war has to end, with either my defeat or theirs." This time I paused to consider my own words. "I think it'll end with mine."

"If I could break the lock on your armband —"

"Someone would see what you're doing and report you, and you'd end up here in chains beside me." I barely had the strength to shake my head, so maybe it didn't move at all. "Besides, the Divine Star isn't strong enough to heal me now. I'd need the bulla."

"It's worth trying. If you saw your back, if you knew how bad it looks —"

"I can feel it; I have some idea." I forced out something close to a smile. "I'd rather you just . . . stay with me. Please just stay here."

He nodded and sat against the tree trunk near me. I remained on my knees, which were beginning to ache, but the idea of moving to a new position seemed worse, so I stayed as I was. Everywhere the whip had touched stung like lines of fire burned there, but at least the worst was over.

Or maybe it wasn't. Brutus wanted those amulets. He would do whatever it took to force me to use them. I didn't want to think about what was coming for me tomorrow.

So rather than keep my thoughts there, I said to Crispus, "Aurelia wants me to ask about your . . . feelings."

He looked up. "My what?"

"Feelings. I don't understand the point of it either, but she thought it was important."

"My feelings about what?"

I would've shrugged, except that simple act would've left me gasping in pain, so instead I sighed and said, "About Aurelia, I suppose. Do you love her? Do you still want to marry her?"

"I never *wanted* to marry her." He quickly followed that up with "At first I offered because my father suggested I should. Then I offered because someone had to protect her inheritance. Then I offered because it was the only way to protect her from the Mistress." He was silent for a few beats. "I never offered because I loved her."

"Your father is gone," I said. "And so is Aurelia's inheritance. And the Mistress is trapped far beneath Lake Nemi. Will you still marry her?"

"I'm an honorable person. So I will keep my promise, for as long as she asks it, but I will not ask that she keeps her promise." Crispus looked sideways at me. "Not if she wishes to promise herself to someone else." He paused, as if waiting for me to say something, and when I didn't, he added, "Nic, why haven't you told her how you feel?"

I snorted. "Looking at my situation now, is that really such a hard thing to understand?"

"No." Something tugged at the corner of his mouth. In any other situation, it would've been a smile. "I've always understood your reluctance to offer marriage. But I wish you would. Because although I'm not in love with Aurelia, there is a girl I want to talk to you about."

A glimmer sparked in his eyes, one I should've noticed before whenever he was with me and Livia.

Livia.

I thought back to shortly after his father's death. While I had stared dumbly at him, completely unsure of what to do next, Livia had embraced him, attempting to share his pain and, in that way, ease it a bit. She was beautiful and kind and more of the proper sort of girl who would be a fine match for him. She had seemed genuinely interested in hearing more about what he hoped to do with his life, and believed those dreams were possible.

Of course he loved her.

And though in my opinion she was still too young for marriage, there were others who had married at her age. It wasn't impossible to consider giving her permission to do the same.

"Does my sister know how you feel?" I asked.

He shrugged. "I've said nothing to her, and I won't say anything, ever, if necessary. But I must confess that when I offered to take your family to our home in Britannia, I did have a dream of settling there with Livia eventually becoming my wife, and seeing you and Aurelia together as well."

I chuckled lightly. "It's a good dream, Crispus. I wish I'd be alive to see it happen."

"So the question is, how long you will remain alive." He drew in a deep breath. "When I was in the imperial box, Brutus kept arguing for your arrest. Probus didn't see the point of it. He's afraid of your powers and wants you killed as soon as possible."

"Thanks, Crispus." I cocked my head. "That's really good to hear."

"I'm not saying anything you don't already know," he said. "But you do need to know how serious things are."

"That's been made perfectly clear." Tired of this conversation, I said, "Perhaps you can find me some water?"

He got to his feet. "Will you be here when I get back?"

My answer came with a jangle of my chains, gaining a sheepish nod from him. Once he had left, I leaned forward, resting my head against the fig tree.

If Crispus did remove the armband, how long would it take to gather enough magic to heal my wounds? Hours, probably. After that, with only the Divine Star, it would take all night before I was strong enough to defend myself. Radulf had earned much of his magic by taking it from others. I'd never done that, and thus, my Divine Star was weaker. Still, it was a mistake not to have practiced with what I did have.

One of many mistakes. It was a miracle that I had lasted this long. At least Livia would not have to see me now, or Aurelia.

I didn't want Aurelia to see me this way, that was definite. But I did want her to see me, especially now that I had spoken to Crispus and understood his feelings. I wished I had spoken to him sooner. I wished I had let her know my feelings, even if my situation had not changed.

I wished she were here.

TWENTY-THREE

I must have fallen asleep at some point or passed out. It was impossible to be sure. Either way, I awoke with a start when a woman said, "This might be your last chance to save me."

It wasn't just any woman's voice. Atroxia was inside my head again. Her crying had ended, but her voice was more desperate than before. She knew time was running out for me and, thus, for her.

"I owe you nothing," I mumbled. There was a bitter edge to my voice. "Go beg help from Diana and leave me alone!"

"Diana serves only her own interests, and the Mistress serves only Diana." Atroxia went quiet for a moment before adding, "I was wrong before, wrong about everything, including my loyalties. I was arrogant in my situation, believing that no harm could come to a vestalis. But I have to believe there is forgiveness for my crimes."

"Get your forgiveness somewhere else."

"You must ask the empire to forgive me, please!"

I snorted. "If the empire listened to me, do you think I'd be here right now?"

"Who are you talking to?" someone asked with a touch to my shoulder. Expecting Praetors, I jerked my arms toward me, but they were still bound in chains around the tree, so all I felt instead were the bruises that had settled into the muscles of my back. I cringed from the movement, and then in the darkness a face emerged.

Aurelia knelt beside me. "It's all right. It's only us."

Crispus was with her and had a large pitcher in his hands. When I had asked him for water, a cup would've been enough. He must have been gone for at least a couple of hours. I really was thirsty now.

"Atroxia?" That was all Aurelia needed to ask, and she didn't need my nod to know she was right. Even before she spoke, she had already begun digging into the same satchel that had once held her father's inheritance. I didn't know what was in it now.

"You shouldn't have come," I mumbled. Though I was glad she had.

"Hush." Crispus took the sliced edges of my tunic and ripped a larger hole into it, fully exposing my back.

Aurelia stifled a small cry when she saw the worst of my injuries, though she immediately began working with whatever items she had pulled from her satchel. I smelled something sweet, but that was as far as my curiosity went.

Beside her, Crispus poured me a cup of water. "I hope this takes care of your thirst. The rest of the pitcher is to get you washed." He helped me to drink, which cooled the burn in my throat that still remained from my screams during the lashing.

"Eat this." Aurelia handed me a cracker sprinkled with some powder over some honey. The sweetness I'd smelled. "It's willow. It'll help with the pain."

I took it, as glad for something to eat as I was for the medicine.

"I'm sorry not to have anything better," she continued. "It's all we could get in a hurry."

"Where's Livia?" I asked. "Is she safe?"

"I used to have some hiding places for children trying to stay out of slavery. I hid her in one of those places. Both she and the amulets are safe."

"Thank you." I wanted to apologize for giving her the amulets in the first place, for putting her in so much danger. But an apology wasn't enough. Not unless it could include apologizing for our friendship, for my broken promises, and for all the heartbreak I'd caused her. She didn't deserve this. Nor did Crispus, whose mother had asked me not to be his friend any longer.

But before I could say anything, Aurelia hushed me and told me to lean forward.

I let my weight fall against the tree, keeping my back as straight as possible. Aurelia started by washing away the blood. Although I knew she was being gentle, it still hurt. I tried not to let it show, but finally, I could hold my breath no longer and I released a gasp.

"I'm sorry," she said. "It's so bad, Nic."

"It could've been worse." I turned my head a little so that I could almost see her. I caught only a wisp of her hair, which was folded over one shoulder and hanging in soft waves from an undone braid. "You lit the fire on Aventine Hill, the one at Laverna's gate."

She sighed. "I can take credit for the act, but not the idea. That was Radulf's."

"Radulf?"

"Caela brought him from the arena to find me and Livia. Setting that fire was the first thing he asked me to do."

I closed my eyes and whispered a thanks to him, though I knew he'd never hear it. He also couldn't have known that at the point the fire had been spotted, I had almost given up entirely. He'd saved me.

"Where is Radulf?"

"Livia is caring for his injuries, but Crispus arranged for them to leave Rome at dawn tomorrow. Under the terms of his banishment, he must leave as soon as possible." She drew a breath. "Crispus thought it'd be best if Livia left too . . . before your trial."

Before the outcome of my trial. That's what Aurelia meant to say. Still, I nodded in agreement, then added, "What about you?"

"I'm staying here."

"I want you to go with Livia and Radulf."

"I'm sure you do," she said. "But I won't leave without you."

"You know I'll never —"

Her response came swiftly, though her voice seemed to break a little. "Don't say it, Nic, just don't! We will find a way to get you to Britannia, alive and well."

I was glad she believed that, for what little good it did any of us.

Aurelia noticed the somber change in my mood and quickly added, "Radulf's leg was injured even before the arena, but it will heal eventually. Livia bound up his wrist, but it wasn't as bad as it could've been. He'll be all right, thanks to you." Her hand accidentally brushed against one of the wounds higher on my shoulder, and I gasped again. "Oh, sorry!"

"There's no point in this," I said. "By tomorrow, it won't matter."

Crispus leaned toward me. "I'm defending you, remember?"

Yes, with his long history of having defended exactly zero other people before. My confidence in him was not great. "Have they listed any charges?" I asked. "Or am I on trial simply for existing?"

He shrugged. "The charges aren't hard to guess. They'll accuse you of attacking your master and the soldiers at the mines, escaping as a slave, causing the destruction of the amphitheater — I'm not sure anyone's ever done that before, but it's got to be a crime. They'll also try you for the theft of the bulla, which they will claim is the property of Rome, and will probably accuse you of the same with the Malice."

When he went silent, I asked, "Is that all?"

He missed the sarcasm. "Well, they might try to connect you to the deaths of the two previous emperors, but I'm fairly sure I can save you from that accusation."

"Only that one?" I asked.

"I can defend you of everything where you're innocent."

"I had nothing to do with the emperors' deaths," I said. "But for the rest of the charges, I'm guilty. Make whatever fancy speech you want — nothing will change the fact that I took the bulla from Caesar's cave. Every crime I've committed began there."

"If I had any money left, I'd bribe them all," Aurelia said.

"And I can't bribe them," Crispus said. "Not as a judge of these courts. It would be dishonorable."

"Bribery wouldn't save me anyway," I said. "There isn't enough gold in Rome to persuade the emperor to let me go. We all know that."

Aurelia touched Crispus's arm. "He needs more bandages than I've brought. Can you find some?"

"The markets are closed already," he said, getting to his feet. "But if I find anything that can be used, I'll bring it here."

Once he had gone, Aurelia began applying the medicines to my back. The honey was warm and sticky, but it soothed the worst of the sting, even beneath her touch. As she worked, I couldn't clear from my mind the conversation I'd had earlier with Crispus. He didn't love Aurelia and was only marrying her out of a sense of duty. But he'd release her from her promise if she wanted that, if there were someone else she'd rather marry — and hadn't she all but said those very words to me?

"Does this hurt?" she asked.

"No."

"Are you sure? Your breath is shallow."

Yes, it was. I turned to her, lowering my voice as much as possible in case anyone passed by. "That's because I've got to talk to you. And maybe it's better that I can't really see you because I think if I could, I would lose what little is left of my courage."

She stopped working on my back, lowered the medicine jar she'd been holding, and leaned around to where I could see her. As I had suspected, my courage faltered, but I was still determined to say what needed to be said.

"Crispus wants to marry Livia." I spoke the words slowly, watching for Aurelia's response. Did she already know this? Was she in favor of the idea? Or was I revealing a secret that might wound her for years to come?

Aurelia immediately calmed any of those concerns. "Livia would like that too. It's one of the reasons she refused to travel to Britannia with your mother. She wouldn't leave tomorrow either if Radulf didn't need her help. She doesn't want to leave you behind, of course. But she's also worried for Crispus."

"Oh." Back at the mines, no one had been closer to Livia than I had. It made me sad to think that I had become distant from her, that she might have thoughts and feelings she kept to herself or, at least, kept from me. Though perhaps by the end of tomorrow, that distance would protect her emotions.

"She would want to know they have your blessing," Aurelia said. "She loves him and hopes you will understand."

"I'm not sure I understand love," I said. "Not the way I want to. When the Romans invaded Gaul, my father attempted to make a Jupiter Stone, knowing it would probably kill him, but believing it was his last chance to save my family. Was that love or foolishness?"

"Love can be foolish," Aurelia said.

"At the mines, my mother got herself traded away from me and Livia, believing that through her, they'd find me, knowing magic is drawn to my family. For five years, we had to make it on our own, without our mother. Was that love or her faith in us to survive?"

"Love does require faith." Aurelia moved closer to me.

"Radulf traded himself for me, knowing the Mistress would torture him. Possibly even knowing she would take his magic."

"Then love requires courage as well," Aurelia said.

"Why are you here?" I asked. "Why do you always come back, knowing the danger that has followed me since the first day we met?"

Her whole face seemed to glow. "You know why."

My breathing had become shallow again. "If my situation were different, or if I were anyone else, I would've confessed my feelings long ago." I paused a moment to lick my lips and to catch what little breath I still had left. "I'm in love with you, Aurelia. The kind of love where at first I couldn't get you out of my head, and after that, I never wanted to. The kind of love where I would take a thousand more whippings if it meant I'd have you at the end of it." Now my gaze fell. "But it's also the kind of love where asking for marriage would be cruel because we both know how tomorrow will go, and I won't obligate you to that."

"If you ask," she whispered, "I would still say yes."

Tears filled my eyes, and I had to look away. "Livia will eventually find someone else to love. I want you to keep your promise to Crispus. That will save you from the Mistress, from her revenge when she gets free one day. And after tomorrow's trial, I need to face my punishment knowing that he will always take care of you."

"I don't need someone to take care of me!" Aurelia's temper was stirring.

"If you marry him —"

"You say that you love me and then ask me to marry someone else?"

"For good reasons!"

"Nothing that's good would hurt like this," she said. "We can fix this. I'll go find tools that can get those chains off your wrists. Or fire off as many arrows as it takes tomorrow until you can run."

"You won't do either of those things. And you can't succeed here, even if you tried. We both know that." I drew in a slow breath. "Don't come to the trial tomorrow. Stay in hiding with the amulets, protect them with as much force as you'd protect me. After the trial, when Crispus comes to find you, leave immediately for Britannia, and catch up to Radulf and Livia if you can, for everyone's safety. My mother will be there — tell her I love her too. Promise me you'll go."

She shook her head, letting tears fall onto her cheeks. "I won't promise that."

"Aurelia —"

"Haven't you already promised that you would live? If you keep that promise, then there's no reason for me to leave tomorrow."

"I made that promise when I had enough magic to defend myself."

"And is that all you are? Back at the mines, before you had magic, weren't you fighting every single day? Maybe with your wit and intelligence, and maybe even your fists, if necessary, but you did fight. Use all of that now. Fight back and survive this, and then you will come and find me and ask me to marry you, and if you ask nicely enough, I might consider forgiving you for putting me through all of this and decide whether you deserve me."

I smiled. "Then you love me too?"

"I'm angry with you! If you want to hear anything more, you'll just have to live." She stood and then drew in a sharp breath.

"What is it?" I asked. Not that I could do anything about it.

"That stag we saw on Radulf's property a few nights ago; it's back."

I rotated my body until I could see it, passing between the columns of the Senate House. Its black eyes studied me a moment, and then Aurelia.

"This is no coincidence," Aurelia murmured.

Obviously not, though it was hardly at the top of my concerns. Only a moment later, Crispus called out that he had found bandages. The stag startled and darted around the corner of the basilica to the back of the building.

By the time Crispus placed the bandages in Aurelia's hands, she had forgotten about the stag. "Just hold still and let me bandage this," she said. "The wounds need to heal before you come with us to Britannia. Which I still believe you are going to do."

She returned to working on my back, which should've hurt. But it didn't. Instead, all I felt was the touch of a girl who expected me to survive so that I could marry her. With that thought floating in my head, suddenly I didn't hurt at all.

TWENTY-FOUR

My trial was to take place in the same open forum where they had kept me chained up all night. Crispus was at my side when they released me from the fig tree and had a new green tunic with an embroidered gold border waiting to replace the one the whip had shredded yesterday. Aurelia wasn't with us anymore. Once Crispus had agreed with me that it was more important for her to keep watch over the amulets, she finally left. That was only an excuse to keep her away from the trial, of course, and she knew it. But she also knew Livia was leaving and someone had to stay with the amulets.

Crispus seemed to know that some sort of conversation had taken place between me and Aurelia, but he didn't ask and neither of us offered any information. I appreciated that. I had enough on my mind already, and I hoped he did too, namely what sort of clever excuses for my crimes he intended to offer.

He did appear to be deep in thought while the emperor's soldiers unchained me and led me to the front of a gathering crowd. Emperor Probus would sit on the rostra while I was made to kneel on the ground before him. Crispus stood to my right, so nervous he kept clearing his throat with the same urgency as if trying to swallow a cucumber whole. Brutus was on my left, and I was sure the temptation to kick me was bothering him. That was fine. The temptation to trip him as he paced back and forth was bothering me too.

"How's your back?" Crispus asked.

I noticed Brutus staring down at me. It still hurt to shrug, especially now that my back was wrapped in tight bandages held in place with honey. So instead, I flicked apart my fingers and said, "Whoever whipped me hits like a grandmother."

Crispus chuckled at the insult but became distracted by a passing official asking him a question. While they talked, Brutus crouched beside me, gripping my arm so tight that my jaw clenched in response. "This is your last chance. Tell me where the amulets are, promise to help me use them, and I will save your life in this trial. Otherwise, the emperor will order several times worse than what happened yesterday. If he does not recognize your citizenship, then Probus can order almost whatever he wants for your execution."

"I have no intention of dying today." I tried to pull my arm away, but failed.

"Do you think your intentions can save you?" Brutus asked. "Look up beside you at the *boy* who is providing your defense.

By his own admission, he is no politician, no orator. He has never defended anyone before and has the unfortunate task of defending crimes everyone knows you have committed. If all your hope is left to Crispus, then you are doomed."

I looked him directly in the eyes. "It's not so much my faith in Crispus as my confidence in your ability to fail." Now I freed my arm. "Why has the Mistress put so much faith in a Praetor who has failed time and again to help her? Have you succeeded at anything she has asked? Once again, she is held in captivity, and you don't even know where she is."

"But you know," Atroxia said into my head. "If you die today, I am just as doomed as you are. I deserved my punishment, as you deserve yours. But neither of us deserves our curse, or our death. Please, Nicolas, obtain my forgiveness."

Brutus had flinched at my words, but then I had flinched at the Mistress too. Brutus quickly recovered, saying, "Where are the amulets, Nicolas? Where is the Mistress? Tell me so that I can ask for mercy upon you."

"What sort of mercy? Yours?" The idea of it nearly made me laugh. "Why would I agree to save my life only to have it placed in your hands? Is there anything you won't do to force my cooperation, anyone I care about who you will not touch? Once you have killed everyone who stands between you and my amulets, you will force me to create a Jupiter Stone, an act which will still get me killed." My eyes narrowed. "Is that your idea of mercy?"

He tapped the side of my cheek, playfully but still harder than I liked. "Yes, that is my mercy. And trust me, it would be better than this. Sit up straight, the emperor is coming. You're out of time."

When Emperor Probus entered the comitium, everyone who had gathered fell to their knees, then rose again upon his order. With chains still forcing me to stay down, all I could do was look up the marble steps at the emperor, cloaked once again in purple robes, but this time with a gold leaf crown on his head. Despite what he had allowed to happen yesterday, I still believed him to be a good man, not a madman like Caligula or evil like Nero, or even weak like the two emperors prior to him had been.

But Brutus was also correct that as a new emperor, Probus needed to prove his strength to the people. I was guilty of nearly all the crimes of which I'd been accused, any one of which was punishable in the most severe way. Even if I tried to claim innocence, at least half the population of Rome had seen enough of my crimes to speak against me and seal my fate.

"Nicolas Calva," the emperor boomed, "you were brought here from Gaul as a slave of the empire and assigned to work in the mines. Is that where you found Julius Caesar's bulla?"

"Yes."

"Surely you knew its value and knew it did not belong to you. Why didn't you give it to the empire?"

"I tried to warn the empire about it, and about the threats

that would come if they ignored the power of this amulet. Their response was a promise to kill me."

Crispus cast me a glare. In hindsight, it might've been unwise to remind Probus that the empire already had a verdict pronounced upon me.

"The empire's decision was correct." Probus leaned forward in his seat. "You were a slave, and a runaway slave at that. There's never been any value in your life."

"My life is important to me." I heard chuckles in the crowd and sat taller. "It's important to my sister, who needed me for her survival. And to my mother, who had my promise that I would bring our family together again. The Roman Empire is magnificent, and I have tried my best to protect it. But my first loyalty is to my family, to those I love."

The crowd seemed to have softened at that, but Probus did not. "Rome is the family!" he said. "Once you were sold to us, the empire became your only family."

No, for me, that was never true. I arched my neck. "My freedom has been purchased. I'm a citizen of Rome now."

"*If* I recognize your citizenship," Probus said. "Why would I do that for someone who thinks so little of the empire?"

Crispus stepped forward, saying, "He admits to having great powers, Caesar, but he used them only for the love of his family. If he wanted to destroy the empire, it would already be destroyed. If he wanted to use his magic for harm, he would have done it."

"Hasn't he done harm?" Brutus's voice was thick with righteous anger. "The amphitheater still has some damage from what Nicolas did the first time he entered it. Homes were also flooded and set on fire near the baths on the Appian Way. Throughout the city, strips of land have collapsed beneath his touch. And an ancient temple on Senator Valerius's land was completely destroyed thanks to this boy's magic, not to mention most of General Radulf's property. If you set this boy free, what will he do next?"

Explode Brutus's home. That was my current plan. But I didn't say that. It seemed unwise to offer up such an answer.

"Allow him to leave the empire," Crispus said. "Acting with strength and wisdom, Caesar gave mercy to General Radulf, granting him his life but banishing him from the empire. Give this boy the same consequences. For any crimes he may have committed, he was thoroughly punished yesterday. That was the strong arm of Rome. Let the people see that Rome has mercy too. Banish this boy from the empire, but give him back his life."

"Give *me* his life instead." Brutus looked down his nose at me, as if I were already in his control. "This boy came to Rome as a slave. What message does it send if Caesar releases him from Rome in freedom? Make him a slave again, and I will use his magic to serve Rome."

"Or destroy it," I muttered. "Praetors are the enemy here, not me."

"What was that?" Probus asked. "Speak up, boy."

"Don't," Crispus hissed at me. "Look at who is helping the emperor judge this trial. Praetors! What do you think will happen if you accuse them?"

"I ordered you to speak!" Probus clearly didn't appreciate being ignored.

Crispus turned to the emperor, becoming desperate in his gestures. "Caesar must forgive him. My friend is uneducated, and weakened from yesterday."

"I said that if you turn me over to Brutus, he will use me to destroy the empire." This time, I made sure I was loud enough to be heard by as many of the crowd as possible. Including the Praetors.

Crispus touched my arm. "Nic, don't —"

"Caesar, I ask to speak for myself." Crispus wouldn't like this, but I didn't particularly like being described as uneducated and weakened, even if it was true.

"It is not a wise request," Probus said. "But it is allowed."

Crispus shook his head. "No offense, Nic, but speaking for yourself has never been your biggest strength. You don't know the law, or how to speak to these men. There's nothing you can say to get yourself out of trouble."

"Be honest," I said. "Can your words get me out of trouble either?" When he failed to answer, I said, "Then let me speak."

Under Probus's order, soldiers came forward and lifted me

to my feet, though they remained on either side of me. I didn't know why. I was still in chains and still wore the Praetors' armband to keep me from doing magic. I couldn't swat at a fly, much less render any attack.

When I shuffled forward to address the emperor, I became aware of the many people watching me. It wasn't the first time I'd experienced this. Only yesterday when I'd appeared inside the arena of the amphitheater, the eyes of fifty thousand Romans were suddenly on me. But this was different. Here I was expected to speak, to say something intelligent enough to save my life.

The words I intended weren't nearly as eloquent as Crispus used, and certainly wouldn't be what he wanted to hear. But I would speak them anyway.

"All that I am accused of, I have done," I said. "And if you only wish to convict me based on my actions, then no defense can save me. But I hope you will hear my reasons and decide my fate based on those reasons."

"He will lie to Caesar," Brutus said. "The boy admits to his crimes, what more is needed?"

"I will hear his reasons," Probus said.

"I have seen the might and power of Rome. Nothing has ever existed in this world so great as this empire, and perhaps nothing again will ever equal it. If Rome falls, it will not come from the enemy at the city gates. If Rome falls, it will come from within." I grunted a little as I gestured at Brutus. "I am here to tell you that the enemy is already within your gates."

Probus leaned forward. "Oh?"

"Your Praetors have betrayed this empire. They are sworn to a power much higher than yours."

"Lies!" Brutus exclaimed. "The Praetors are bound to serve Rome, as am I."

I turned from Brutus back to Probus. "If you don't believe me, then turn me over to Decimas Brutus, as he asks. Then you will see for yourself his full intentions for Rome, if you are still here to see the end of his plans."

"That sounds like a threat against me." Probus's voice raised in pitch.

"It is a threat, if you give me to Brutus."

Probus arched a brow. "Why do you think Brutus has asked for you?"

"Because he needs my magic. No one in the whole of this empire can do the things I can do, and if you sentence me to death, you will rob your Praetor of my abilities."

"You're convincing him to give you that sentence!" Crispus hissed.

"Hush!" I replied.

"I only want the boy for the glory of Rome," Brutus said. "Nothing more —"

"Close your mouth, or my soldiers will do it for you!" Probus snapped. "Nicolas, why does Decimas Brutus want your magic?"

"He is a descendent of Marcus Brutus, the man who killed Julius Caesar. Marcus descended from the goddess Diana and served her will, as does the man beside me now."

"Don't we all serve the gods?" Probus asked. "It is good for Decimas Brutus to serve Diana, if he has blood ties to her."

"Then it is good for him to use my magic to do her bidding, no?" I smiled over at Brutus. "Tell the emperor what Diana wants. Be sure to include the part about bringing down the empire."

Probus leaned forward. "Speak to me, Brutus."

Brutus stared down at me, feeling the same loss for words that I usually did. But this time, I knew exactly what I wanted to say. I gave my attention back to the emperor.

"He would use my magic to create something called the Jupiter Stone, with powers that will rival those of the gods. Then he will turn it over to a dragon whose only desire is to see the destruction of Rome."

"Save me, destroy the dragon," Atroxia whispered. "Obtain my forgiveness."

In the quietness of her voice, I heard her in a way I never had before. Maybe she was telling me how to destroy the dragon. If I got Probus to forgive her crimes, it might be a step in removing the curse. I was her last chance, her only chance.

I hesitated a moment, then shook her out of my head. Once I'd pulled my thoughts together again, I stared Probus directly in the eyes, something no one should ever do, especially an uneducated former slave of Rome. "If you give me to Brutus, he will bring Rome to its knees. But if you set me free, I can stop him."

Probus looked back at me. "And what if I order your execution? Then he cannot use your magic."

I hesitated. This was what Crispus had warned me about, and now he stepped forward, a last effort to save me from myself. "If those are your orders, then Diana will find another way to get what she wants. And you will have executed the one person capable of stopping the Praetors. Nic can destroy this empire, but he is also the only one who can save it."

"That's what I'm afraid of," Probus said. "Has he not already told us he values his family more than the empire?"

"If *you* value the empire, then listen to me," I said, still looking directly at the emperor. "I ask Caesar for only two things. The first is that you arrest Decimas Brutus. Stop him before he carries out his evil plans."

"Of course the slave boy accuses me!" Brutus sputtered. "He lies! He lies to Caesar!"

"Then he lies with conviction," Probus said. "He lies with the boldness of looking me in the eye." He nodded in the direction of his soldiers. "Guards, arrest Decimas Brutus. I have many questions for him."

"I am a descendent of Diana!" Brutus shouted. "I am a Praetor of Rome. You would not dare!"

Probus stood. "And who am I but your emperor? Fall on your knees to me!"

Brutus looked around him as the emperor's soldiers moved in closer. Finally, he went to his knees and lowered his head. "I only meant . . . Caesar, this slave boy is a criminal and an enemy to Rome. He is no hero."

"I will determine that." Probus's eyes darkened. "And determine who you are as well."

With a nod of the emperor's head, his soldiers surrounded Brutus. His body had stiffened almost to corpse stage, enough that they clearly had trouble getting his hands in front of him to bind them. But they did, and once they brought him back to his feet, he stared across at me, tears streaming down his face. "I will answer the emperor's questions until he is satisfied of my innocence," he said, softly enough that only I could hear him. "He will release me, and the moment he does, I will come after you with a vengeance you have never seen before. You will make that Jupiter Stone for me, Nicolas. You will kneel before the Mistress and pledge your loyalty to her every wish. Of course, that is only if you are still alive by the end of this hour, which I most sincerely doubt."

I smiled over at him. "My final memory of you will be the way you cried like a baby when the soldiers led you away."

He lunged for me, but the soldiers held him back and quickly steered him out of the comitium. I hoped they were taking him back to the carcer, this time for a more permanent stay inside the prison.

Once he was gone, Probus leaned in to me again. "You said you have two requests. I assume the second is for your freedom."

Crispus bowed again, perhaps hoping if he did it often enough, it would save my life. "Caesar can see that Nicolas Calva is concerned for the protection of Rome. He is not a slave anymore, but a freeman and a citizen of the empire. Reward him for his loyalty and his bravery."

Probus nodded and considered that before he looked at me again. "There is no need for the judgment of the Praetors here — considering they are probably not fair judges at this trial, I will decide your fate alone. Your reasons are honorable, Nicolas Calva, and I respect you for them."

Crispus nudged me with his elbow, and for the first time, I allowed myself to hope. Was it possible I would escape this trial, and what's more, with Brutus under arrest? It seemed like too much.

It was too much. The emperor continued, his face turning more grim, "If all the empire had to contend with were the reasons for your actions, I would release you at once. There is logic to the things you have done. From what I've been told, you have acted in defense only, never to attack the empire, but to stop the attacks upon you. I cannot fault you for defending your life, or the lives of those you love. And yet, I must convict you. Not for what you have done, but for what you are capable of doing. You cannot be allowed to live while having powers that may even rival the gods. Nicolas, my sentence upon you is not a punishment for any crimes of magic, only a consequence for having magic in the first place. I sentence you to death, with full expectation that you will rise up in the Elysian Fields. And from that place of peace, I hope you will forgive the choice I've had to make this day. Long live the empire of Rome!"

Soon die the boy who tried to save it.

TWENTY-FIVE

The emperor's guards still remaining in the area immediately laid hands on me, but I struggled against them and shouted, "I said I had two requests of Caesar. You have not heard my second!"

"It was for your release," Probus calmly replied. "I have ruled against you."

"That wasn't my other request," I said. "Please hear me."

Probus arched a brow, curious. But he nodded, and the guards let me continue standing to address him, though their grip on my arms remained just as firm.

I said, "For as long as she is condemned by Rome, the dragon I spoke of will seek her revenge. This dragon is no ordinary creature. She was a young vestal who fell in love with Marcus Brutus and assisted him in Julius Caesar's assassination. For his greater crime, Brutus went free. The vestal, named Atroxia, was buried alive and cursed by Diana to become what she is today." By now my heart was racing, yet I had to keep speaking. "I ask you to pardon her for the crime. She has been punished enough."

"Where is this dragon, Nicolas?"

I shook my head, not as a refusal to answer, but simply a refusal to answer as completely as he wanted. "For now she is trapped, but once she gets free, she will seek the destruction of this empire. Perhaps if she had your forgiveness, it would give her peace to move on to the next life. You will save her, but not only her. Allowing her to pass into the next life might also save Rome."

"They will not forgive me." The Mistress was speaking into my head now, her tone cold and bitter. "Just as they will not forgive you. The empire does not understand forgiveness."

Probus placed a finger against his jaw. "I will consider your request, but that still does not change my verdict. You must die today."

A desperate voice called out behind us. "No!" I couldn't see her, but that was Aurelia's cry. Pain and sorrow carried from her voice directly to my heart. I didn't want her to be here, not for this.

Probus only momentarily glanced in her direction before adding, "The executioner awaits you now."

Behind me, Crispus went to his knees. "Reconsider, Caesar, I beg you. He is innocent."

But I wasn't. And it didn't matter anyway. Probus had already turned his back on me. His orders would be carried out.

The crowd that had been behind me parted, and when it did, I first saw the platform that must've been brought here during my short trial. In contrast to the elegance and beauty of most other symbols of Rome, this was a simple raised wooden block, built for no other purpose but death. The executioner was already there, dressed in a simple long black tunic and with an ax balanced in both hands, waiting for me. Of course he was already here. The outcome of my trial had been settled before the first word was even spoken.

Aurelia pushed forward through the crowd. In her hands was the same satchel as before. I had a guess what was in there now, and it concerned me. Although Brutus had been taken away, dozens of other Praetors still surrounded her. I hoped she had not brought the amulets into the forum, even if they were meant to save me. It wouldn't matter anyway. As long as Diana's band remained locked on my arm, the bulla and the Malice were useless.

She got close enough to grab me around the shoulders but was quickly pushed away by one of the emperor's guards. "You cannot save him!" he shouted at her.

The look in her eyes told me otherwise. Saving me was obviously her plan. She definitely had the amulets with her. Even if she meant well, she could find herself in more trouble and still fail to do anything for me.

Even as the soldiers pulled me onward, I looked back at her and firmly shook my head. Revealing she had the amulets would endanger her life, and certainly she'd lose them before they ever got into my hands. It wasn't worth the risk.

Crispus caught up to me, and since he had defended me in the trial, he was allowed to continue walking at my side.

"You only need enough magic to break that armband," he whispered. "I know it's in you somewhere. Please just find it and use it!"

I was stumbling against the fierce hold of the soldiers and their insistent march forward. With my still injured back, and the exhaustion and hunger of the past two days, I found it hard enough simply to remain on my feet. The idea that I might summon magic where there wasn't any was an utter joke. But I wasn't angry with him for asking. We both knew it was my last chance.

Seeing my failure to do as he asked, Crispus said, "I will take care of both Livia and Aurelia. And your mother and Radulf too; they will all remain safe for as long as I live."

"Thank you." I didn't ask him to marry Aurelia or refuse him permission to marry Livia. As far as I was concerned, Crispus had done more than enough to prove himself my truest friend. Whatever path made him happiest, I couldn't refuse him. I only regretted that at the end of his decision, either Livia or Aurelia would end up alone.

Aurelia tore through the crowd again, and this time I followed her eye to the sword at the side of the soldier standing between us.

"Stop her," I whispered to Crispus. "For her sake."

Crispus left me and ran to her, closing her in his arms and pressing her back into the crowd. At first she fought him, attempting to cross past him and get to that sword. But he held her tight and whispered something to her; then she let the tears fall and embraced him. Her shoulders were shaking with sorrow as I passed them, and only in the last moment of my passing did she look up. Her eyes were red and already swollen.

I pulled back from the soldiers, long enough to say, "Don't tell my family what happened here. Tell them anything about this moment, except the truth."

She nodded, allowing more tears to fall, but didn't seem to trust herself with words and only embraced Crispus again, burying her head in his shoulder. This time, I didn't mind that. I wanted someone there to comfort her, and I was glad it could be him. In his own way, he loved her too.

The platform was accessed by three wooden steps. Here at the base, they seemed as tall as a mountain, one from which I would never descend. I hesitated for a moment, searching within myself for the courage to climb them so I would not have to be carried up there like a coward. A soldier nudged my back, and then I somehow made it to the first step. After that, it was easier to climb the rest.

The executioner waiting at the top was almost as still as a statue. His eyes staring back at me seemed lifeless, and I wondered, with every execution he had performed, if a bit of his own life had been taken too. Perhaps that was the reason the vestalis had not wanted me to kill Brutus in the arena. Perhaps she understood that no matter what it did to Brutus, what it would take from me was far worse.

Although if I was being honest, it didn't seem that way at the moment. Nothing seemed worse than where I now stood.

Crispus still stared at me from the crowd, and I could almost picture him telling me that of all the methods of execution Rome might have used, this was one of the more preferred. By whom? I wondered. Who would prefer this?

A flat stone was set in the center of the platform with a basket in the front of it. I knew how this would go. I would be made to kneel before the stone and lay my head upon it. The executioner's ax would fall upon my neck, separating two halves of my body that I would have preferred to keep in one piece. I hoped that at least I'd bleed all over the executioner and ruin his tunic. It wasn't much payback for what he was about to do, but it was the last thing I had left.

"Kneel," a soldier ordered.

I remained on my feet. "Before I do, I must hear Caesar's decision. Will he pardon Atroxia? She has been punished long enough." When that still failed to get the emperor's attention, even more loudly, I called, "Pardon her, Caesar! You must, because if you don't, after my death, nothing will save you from her revenge."

Far behind me, Probus gestured with his hands, an acknowledgment of what I had asked. A silent but clear pardon of Atroxia's crimes.

Inside my head, Atroxia's voice returned. "I am forgiven?" she asked. "It is over?"

It was better, but far from over. Diana's curse remained upon her, and there was nothing I could do about that, not anymore. I didn't know whether the pardon would allow Atroxia's soul to journey to the Elysian Fields, but I hoped so. I hoped that despite my crimes, I might wake up there too.

"Now you will kneel," the executioner said. "I can do this while on your feet, but if I miss, you pay the price for it."

"Remove the Praetor's armband first," Crispus said, stepping forward again. Aurelia remained back amongst the crowd, refusing to look at me. But he had Aurelia's satchel, which meant the amulets were only a few feet away from me. If the armband was removed, and if he could get an amulet into my hand, I had a chance.

To the executioner, Crispus added, "Give this boy that one dignity, of dying without the token of his enemy on his arm."

The executioner raised his blade and wedged it between the slit of the thin silver band. He angled the blade enough to separate the pieces until the lock broke, and he pulled it from my arm.

It was as if he had removed a thousand-pound weight from me, one that had affected my ability to think and even to breathe. I felt an immediate spark within the Divine Star, and Crispus grinned and nodded very slightly at the satchel. He loosened the string around it and moved as if to reach inside it. Already I could sense the magic he held, close enough to save my life.

But it was not to be. The soldiers who had dragged me here came down the steps and grabbed Crispus by the arms, forcing him back to the crowd that had surrounded this platform. They stood in front of him, preventing either him or Aurelia from darting forward with the amulets.

He still stood close enough that I could feel the yearning of the amulets to return to me. At the same time, they were so far away. Like a scent of fresh baked bread that I would never be allowed to taste.

Impatient with my slowness to kneel, the executioner pushed at my back, directly over the Divine Star. Enough magic was in me now to flinch when he did, but not enough to fight back, so I still fell to my knees. The Divine Star could not erase my hunger or exhaustion, and it was not coming back strong enough on its own. In the time I had left, there wouldn't be enough. Magic wouldn't save me this time.

"Lower your head," the executioner ordered.

The stone in front of me was cold and smooth. I stared at it and then looked into the audience once more for Aurelia. Crispus was holding her again, so her back was turned to me. I was glad for that. I couldn't bear the thought of her having to see this.

I looked again at the stone, and suddenly, I knew there was going to be a fight. Because I could not and would not put my head down upon it. Even if I lacked enough magic to save me from that blade, Aurelia had been right before. I still had two good legs and arms, and a strong enough heart to use them. It wouldn't change the way the next few minutes ended for me, but at least I would go down with honor.

Or would I? For the moment I started to rise back to my feet, a nearby soldier grabbed the chains that bound my arms and yanked them to the floor of the platform. My body went with it, and cold stone slammed against my cheek. The execution stone.

"Whichever god will still hear you, this is your time to call to him," the executioner said. Even without looking, I knew he had raised his blade.

TWENTY-SIX

My eyes were closed, so I didn't see exactly what happened next, but I did hear a voice, speaking out loudly and with perfect clarity to the executioner.

"Stop this!"

Silence fell amongst the crowd, and footsteps padded toward me, though the soldier still held my arms down and I could not raise my head. It was a woman's voice, but not Aurelia's. The crowd would never fall silent for her, and even in her gentlest moments, Aurelia's footsteps were never soft upon the ground.

The executioner lowered his blade, and I heard him kneel behind me. "*Domina,* this boy —"

"This boy will come with me."

I knew the voice now. It was the old vestalis I had last seen in the arena, warning me not to attack Brutus.

"He has been convicted," the executioner said. "Sentenced to death by Emperor Probus himself."

The vestalis's voice strengthened. "I am a holy woman of Rome, and you will honor me as such! If the gods have brought me here to save this boy, then you will respect my word. A vestalis can free any condemned prisoner. You know this, and you will not question me further. Release that boy!"

The soldier removed his hands from the chains at my wrists, allowing me to sit up. I did, slowly, but I could not look at her. If it had ever been difficult for me to find the proper words to speak, it was nothing compared to what was happening now. I wasn't sure if I had ever known how to speak at all.

"Break those chains," the vestalis told me. "You are strong enough to do that now."

I widened my arms, holding my wrists straight, and the bit of magic in me responded, snapping the chains. Perhaps in another few minutes I could separate the metal of the cuffs and be rid of the chains entirely. But not yet.

The executioner had backed away from me, so I felt no fear when I stood beside him. My attention was across the comitium to the rostra where Emperor Probus had been. He was still there, also standing. But he only shook his head and walked away. Not exactly a pardon from the empire, but he wasn't challenging the vestalis either. I doubted he could.

After he disappeared, I still remained on the platform. Not because I was particularly eager to be near a blade that only seconds ago had had my name on it, but because I knew my legs would likely crumble if I attempted to go down the stairs. Instead, I gave the vestalis a respectful bow and left my head down.

"Do you still speak?" she asked. "I trust the empire didn't take your tongue."

"What you've done for me . . . no words exist —"

"Of course they exist. The words are 'thank you,' and I accept them. Come down from that platform. We have things to discuss."

I obeyed her, vaguely aware that Crispus was still holding Aurelia back, and acutely aware that my legs were shaking. When she gave me the warning not to kill Brutus in the arena, maybe the vestalis had known how this would all end, but I didn't. In fact, I still didn't know how everything would end.

"Domina —"

"This is not the place for us to talk."

The mob allowed us to leave them behind. Even the Praetors let me walk away, which had everything to do with their respect for the vestalis's power, not mine. I looked back for Crispus and Aurelia, but they were gone. I hoped they would be safe. I hoped no one else had guessed the true contents of Aurelia's satchel.

The vestalis took my arm as we walked out of the forums, though I didn't think she really needed it. It felt more like a gesture of familiarity and perhaps even a sort of affection. I already understood what it was to have a grandfather, even if Radulf was far from an ordinary grandfather. But from the vestalis, I now understood what it must be like to have a grandmother. Impossible not to love.

"How soon until you can heal the injuries to your back?" she asked.

"Not yet." Magic was slowly returning to the Divine Star.

However, my first priority was to get the chains off my wrists. I hated them there.

"The lashing was worse than I'd expected," she said. "I underestimated Brutus's anger."

I didn't have any answer for that. So instead, I asked, "Where are we going?" We were walking away from the forum, which was perfectly fine by me. But that didn't mean other surprises weren't somewhere ahead.

"You'll see, soon enough."

It was all the answer I was going to get, which I understood. The streets were crowded today, and enough of the passersby knew my face, not to mention the fact that I was being escorted by a vestalis. We were already drawing enough attention our way. There was no need to complicate it by having a conversation that was certain to be dangerous.

We entered Trajan's Forum, full of treasures that had been taken from areas Rome had defeated. Once we passed through the basilica there, we entered a small square with libraries on either side of me, one full of Greek documents and the other with Roman documents.

I doubted whether I'd ever have enough education to read in Greek, but how I longed to enter the Roman library and absorb every last page there. I could read a little, which felt like a single taste of the sweetest fruit. All I wanted was more. What sort of person might I become if I were able to take in everything a library offered me?

But that was not my life and probably never would be. It

was foolish to forget that only minutes ago, my life was condemned. I reminded myself again who I was, and why the vestalis had brought me here. We had not come to discuss books. Nor the happy prospects for my future, I guessed.

Nestled between the libraries was a wide marble column that seemed almost to touch the heavens. Well, maybe not, but it was higher than any of the surrounding buildings and had a viewing platform on top, so I supposed there was a door on the other side that was meant to be entered. I walked around the column, and though I found the door in the square base, my attention had already been drawn upward to the detailed and intricate carvings that wound their way up the column, telling a story of war.

"This was built many years ago in honor of Emperor Trajan's military victories," the vestalis said. "What images do you see?"

I walked around it, picking out the carvings that represented the emperor and his soldiers. Women and children were depicted here, as well as whatever army Rome had fought in this war.

I described everything to her, but with each image, the vestalis only nodded and asked, "What else?"

I circled the column again, telling her of the carvings of river crossings, the slaves who assisted in the battles, and the armored horses Rome brought into battle.

"Do you think any of that is what I wanted you to see?" she asked. "Look carefully, Nicolas. The army defeated by Emperor

Trajan fell far too easily. They are not worth such a grand column. Look again and tell me who the true enemy is to Rome."

I walked around it again, and this time my eye instantly locked upon the image of a serpent's head, its jaw open and baring lines of sharp teeth and a forked tongue. Though the carving didn't show fire on its breath, I could almost picture it there. I had seen this same beast before.

"The dragon," I said. "They show the dragon as part of the enemy army. Yet although I can see the images for the army's loss to Rome, I do not see the dragon's defeat."

"Because it never was defeated," the vestalis said. "The dragon remains an enemy to this empire. She has had many names over the centuries: serpent, draco, dragon. But you know her as the Mistress. The only way to save Rome is to defeat the Mistress."

"Why would I save Rome now?" I asked. "After what they've done to me, do you think I care at all about this empire?"

"You must care! Imagine a forest, thick with tall and deep-rooted trees. If one of those trees happens to fall, does it land on empty ground?"

"I imagine it would land on other trees, causing them to fall as well." I shrugged that off. "You're telling me that if Rome falls, other civilizations around it will also come to ruin. Well, maybe they should. The Mistress might be doing the world a favor."

"You don't believe that," the vestalis said. "If you did, you would not have asked the emperor to pardon her past crimes."

"I didn't want to die with Atroxia's voice still in my head. That's all."

Her tone sharpened. "No, you did it because you felt compassion for Atroxia, despite her crimes against the empire, and her crimes against you. All I ask is that you show the same compassion for Rome."

"You want me to save the empire." I shook my head, even as I mumbled the words. "On the same day the empire sentenced me to die."

"I ask you to end the Praetor War, on the same day I saved your life!"

"If I kill the dragon, as you want, it will kill Atroxia too. The Mistress may be an enemy to Rome, but Atroxia is not. She bears a curse that has changed her. That curse has done far worse to her than the punishment ever could."

"Yes, I know." The vestalis took my hand and gave it a firm squeeze. "Which is why it was such an important first step to get her forgiven of her crimes."

The first step? Suddenly, I understood my role in the vestalis's plan. She had given me asylum shortly after I got magic, protecting me from the empire's soldiers. She had helped me find the rock meant to become the Jupiter Stone. She had saved me from the executioner. Now I knew why.

It was only ever about reclaiming Atroxia, about bringing back one of her own. The vestalis had not saved my life. She had only delayed my death. Nothing she had done was for me — it was only to use my power the same way everyone else wanted to use it.

"I won't do it!" I yanked my hand away. "This is not a fair request!"

"It's not a request at all, Nicolas. It's your fate, and you must accept it."

I shook my head. "I've done all that I can do for Atroxia. I thought if she received forgiveness for her crimes, it would end her punishment and allow her to die."

"The dragon must die. Atroxia must live."

"I can kill the dragon, maybe, but the only way Atroxia will live is if I free her from the curse. Do you know the price for that?"

"Lightning." The vestalis spoke calmly, as if she had accepted my death, so I should too. "You must bring in a storm."

I stepped back from her, unable to believe she had really said those words. "You're asking me to make a Jupiter Stone. It's the same thing the Praetors want, the same thing the Mistress wants." My eyes narrowed. "Maybe there's no difference between any of you."

"There is every difference!" the vestalis said. "Have I asked you for glory or power? Have I demanded anything for myself? My only desire is to right a wrong that was done centuries ago. If we correct that wrong, then we will save an empire."

"But it will not save me," I whispered.

"To become free, you must walk through the fire," the vestalis said. "Haven't you always known this was how things must end? Every move leads you closer to it. Every attempt to avoid it fails."

I shook my head again. "You want me to create a Jupiter Stone and break the curse. But if I fail, then the Mistress gets the Jupiter Stone."

The vestalis smiled. "Obviously, then, you cannot fail."

"I'll destroy the amulets instead. If there are no amulets, there can be no Praetor War."

"Yet the dragon would remain, carrying out her own revenge against this city. Besides, what power can destroy amulets made by the gods?"

"It doesn't matter anyway," I said. "The stone isn't where we left it. I believe the Mistress has it, and she won't give it to me if she believes I'll use it to destroy her."

Without looking away from me, the vestalis stretched out her hand, then rotated her wrist to reveal the white rock I instantly recognized as the one I had taken from Jupiter's eagle.

I took the rock, rolled it around on my palm, and said, "I used to think you were saying I'd have to walk through dragon fire. But I've done that and nothing happened. You're speaking of the fire that comes with lightning."

"You must face both fires. The one will refine your courage, and the other will test its limits."

"I know the limits. I know the price of bringing in lightning." My heart pounded, even as I folded my fingers around the rock. "Do not ask me to do this. I will lose everything."

"To win, you have to lose. That is what you must understand."

"Understand what? Your riddles? Your advice that sounds exactly like what my enemies would say? I was brought here as a slave, and if the world made any sense, I wouldn't even be here, not in one piece. By your mercy, I am still alive, and that is the way I hope to remain. I thank you for my life, Domina; please do not ask me for it now. I've promised never to make a Jupiter Stone. I must keep that promise."

I went to give the rock back to her, but she held up her hands to refuse it. "That rock is yours. You fought Jupiter's eagle to get it. Keep it or destroy it as you will."

"It is not my fate to end a war in the heavens," I said.

She frowned. "If that is true, then no one can do it."

Sounds of an approaching horse caught my attention for a moment. When I turned back to finish the conversation with the vestalis, she was already gone.

TWENTY-SEVEN

"Nic!"

Aurelia called my name while they were still at the far end of the square. She was riding Callistus, and Crispus was behind her in the saddle. Although I didn't think it was particularly wise to have brought Callistus so out in the open, it was hardly the biggest of my concerns.

Aurelia leapt from the saddle even before Callistus had fully stopped, and threw her arms around me. I tried to hold her too, but the pain of moving so swiftly stopped me. I gasped, and she immediately drew back.

"I'm sorry," she mumbled. "If I just hurt you, I'm sorry, but I wasn't thinking . . . I can't think . . . I can't believe . . ."

"I came back from it." I was safe now, and more important, I intended to remain that way. Before Aurelia could ask me any questions about the rock, I slipped it into a pocket of my tunic.

"Why are you here?" Aurelia asked, looking beyond us to the column. "Was the vestalis here with you?"

"It doesn't matter," I said. "I told her no."

She furrowed her brows, clearly concerned at why my answer was so vague. But instead of pressing the issue, she reached inside the satchel now looped over her arm, and handed me the bulla.

Eagerly, I put the strap over my head, burying it beneath my tunic. I felt its strength immediately and the warmth that accompanied its magic.

"Get the chains off your wrists," Aurelia said. "You were freed from the emperor's sentence of death, and you have been freed as a slave. If you won't remove those bands, then all of that is for nothing."

"I'll gladly do it." The bulla easily allowed me to break the locks, and I let both bands fall to my feet.

Next, I gave attention to the worst of my injuries, those where time had not lessened their sting. With each wound that closed, relief poured over me. And while I let the magic work, Aurelia took my hand and continued to stand close by me. She withdrew the Malice and cuffed it around my arm, bringing with it immense strength and bolstering my ability to heal every wound I had received yesterday.

My eyes were closed when Aurelia said, "Now what?"

I looked for the vestalis again, but she was still gone. From the corner of my eye, I did see Crispus approaching me, his expression remarkably somber considering what I had just escaped.

"I tried to save you in every way I could," he said, barely

able to look at me. "Had it not been for the vestalis, my failure would have been complete."

"What failure?" I asked. "My crimes were indefensible, and you defended me anyway. You have proven yourself the truest of friends." With the injuries to my back in far better condition now, I walked forward and embraced him. "Thank you."

He gave a firm pat to my back, and only then did I remember that Aurelia had treated the injuries with honey. I stepped back, embarrassed, and stickier than any person ought to be. "I, uh . . . this tunic."

"At least it can be washed and used again, but you do need another one." Crispus shared a knowing smile with Aurelia. "I'm sure you must be hungry as well."

"I'm starving, yes."

Crispus put his arm around my shoulders. "Well, I'm quite sure that the vestalis had a reason for bringing you here, and quite sure that whatever she wanted, it's nothing you feel like discussing out in the open. Can that conversation wait until you have eaten and bathed?"

That led me to smile as well. "I think it must wait. Rome surely does not want to be saved by someone smelling like the sewers beneath it."

Aurelia giggled. "Nor will I join you for supper smelling this way. If you two want to go to the baths, I'll meet you at Crispus's home tonight."

We agreed to the plan, and Aurelia led Callistus in one direction, while Crispus and I went to the baths.

Because Radulf's home was so fine, it hadn't been necessary for me to visit the public baths before. Thus, my only experience with the public baths was soon after I'd obtained magic, and it involved me pulling the water from them to put out fires on some nearby homes. Hardly their intended use.

The baths Crispus and I came to seemed crowded today, but Crispus said they were often this full and that was how most people liked it. After a small meal of apples and bread, we started in the *caldarium,* where the hot waters melted the honey from my back and soothed any aches the magic had not touched. There, I saw men making business deals and discussing their opinions of the new emperor.

By the time we went into the warm tepidarium, those men had begun to notice me. They cleared out rather quickly, despite Crispus's assurances that I had no intention of exploding anything for at least the rest of the day. Actually, that assurance might've been the exact reason they all left so quickly.

But when we went to enter the cold *frigidarium,* those same men stood shoulder to shoulder, blocking our entrance.

One of the men near the middle nodded at me. He was muscular and stern and, as far as I was concerned, completely unlikable. Maybe because he had one long eyebrow that went across his entire forehead. Or perhaps because he clearly did not like me. As if I were still only a slave, the man addressed

Crispus. "That boy is not welcome in the baths. He's not welcome in Rome."

"He's a citizen and has as much right as you to be here," Crispus said. "He was also pardoned from his crimes."

"No, he was convicted," another man said. "I was there this morning. He was meant for the executioner, until saved by a vestalis."

"Let's go," I said to Crispus.

But Crispus wasn't finished. "Why do you think the vestalis saved him? Because she knew he was innocent."

No, that wasn't why. I grabbed Crispus's arm, urging him to leave with me.

But another man stepped forward from the group. This time, he spoke directly to me. "You claim to use magic in defense of Rome, but all I ever see is the lives of those around you put at risk. Wherever you go, things are left in ruins. I've seen it for myself. How many people have died because of your magic, and will still die?"

"No more," I mumbled. Now I did walk out, with or without Crispus, though I was glad to see him follow me.

In my head, the Mistress laughed wickedly. "They will all die. Once I'm free, I will make sure of that. I will come for you last of all, Nicolas."

I stopped walking, just to close my eyes and clear my head. If I was the only one who could stop the Mistress, then once she was free, would I be responsible for the damage she caused? All the lives that would be lost, would those be my fault? If I had committed crimes to gain this magic, was it an even greater crime not to use it now?

Crispus caught up and nudged me toward the dressing rooms. "You do not owe the empire anything. Don't let his words bother you."

"Of course they bother me," I muttered. "Everything he said was true."

I was grateful to see one of Crispus's servants waiting in the dressing room with a new tunic for me, this one all white. I didn't know how Crispus had arranged to get it here, but I was glad for it and made sure to quietly slip the rock from the vestalis into the new tunic's pocket.

"I promise not to ruin this one," I said.

His attempt at a smile seemed forced. "Don't make any promises you cannot keep."

Such as my promise to Aurelia that I would survive? Or my promise never to make a Jupiter Stone? Did he know what the vestalis had asked of me, and my refusal?

"*I* know what she asked of you." This was Atroxia's voice in my head. "What good is the forgiveness of the empire if I must bear the anger of one of its gods?"

I understood Diana's anger too. I had felt it and fought it and tried in every way I could to defeat it. But even the Malice could not grant me victory over her.

"Victory means you end the Praetor War," Atroxia said. "Only you can do it."

At the highest possible price.

"Did you hear me, Nic?" Crispus asked. "I told you that we'd wait and see whether you destroyed this tunic too? I'm thinking about buying them for you ten at a time."

"What if I promise not to destroy this tunic *today*?" I asked.

"Even then, I'm not sure you will succeed." His laugh seemed as false as his smile had been. "I'm sorry about what happened back there with those men. You didn't deserve that."

"Yes, I did. We both know that." I put the tunic over my head and began belting it. When I'd finished, I checked again to be sure the rock was still with me. "We'd better get back to your home. Aurelia will be waiting for us there."

TWENTY-EIGHT

Considering how turbulent the past two days had been, the dinner at Crispus's home was remarkably unremarkable. None of us wanted to talk about the trial or any of the events surrounding it, and we all knew I would lie if they asked what the vestalis had wanted when she spoke to me alone. So there was no point in bringing that up.

"I've ordered another wagon for morning," Crispus announced. "Livia and Radulf have a good start on us, but with his injuries, they're probably traveling more slowly than usual. We should be able to catch up with them before they leave the empire."

"Are all of us going this time?" his mother asked.

"Yes," Crispus said. "All of us."

Aurelia was looking at me, so I looked anywhere else. She wanted a confirmation that I would join them tomorrow, and of course, that was impossible. Crispus didn't notice. He only said something about being relieved to finally go, and then instructed everyone to get their bags packed by morning.

I excused myself before the final meal course, complaining of exhaustion. That was true enough, but it wasn't the reason I left early. If I had been taught any manners when I was younger, then it would've been unpardonable for me to leave so abruptly. As it was, my ignorance of proper behavior served me tonight. Because if I did not leave now, before the end of the night Aurelia would surely corner me and ask the questions I could not answer. She had to be avoided.

She stood as I moved to leave the room. "Can we talk?" It was a demand, not a question.

"Can it wait until morning?" I casually replied. "Once we're in the wagon together?"

"It cannot wait," she said very deliberately. "And you know why it cannot." She knew everything, then, perhaps even more than I had yet admitted to myself.

I glanced at Crispus, who shrugged back at me, silently confessing that he had told Aurelia what had happened at the baths. I couldn't blame him for that. With enough pestering, Aurelia would've eventually gotten the truth out of him, just as she would get it out of me if we were alone together.

So I only faked a smile and shook off her concerns. "Well, it must wait. The last couple of days haven't been my best ever, and I'm tired. Tomorrow."

There was nothing more Aurelia could do, although I suspected she was considering whether to follow me toward my room and force me to talk to her. I hoped she wouldn't. I'd feel ridiculous running away from her while trying to think of an excuse for why I was doing so. But that was my plan if she tried to come.

She didn't. And as I thought about that in my room, a part of me was disappointed. Not because I wanted to run away from her, but because I liked the idea of her wanting to speak with me enough that she would go to that much trouble. How ridiculous it was to think this way, childish behavior at best, but I didn't know what else to do. The more complicated my feelings became about Aurelia, the more difficult it was to understand my thoughts and actions too. The Mistress said I did not understand what it was to love. The more I recognized how intense my love was for Aurelia, the more I had to agree with her. There was so much still to learn.

Soon after arriving at Crispus's home that evening, I had borrowed a wax tablet from his *tablinum*. It had taken me most of the supper to figure out how to say what I wanted, and even as I etched the letters into the tablet, I knew it wasn't coming out the right way. I was grateful Radulf had taken the trouble to teach me some basic writing skills. If he hadn't, my only choice would've been to speak these words aloud, and the way I felt now, I didn't know if I could.

The tablet wasn't large, leaving me only enough room to write what absolutely was the most important. I didn't address the note to anyone — it would obviously be for Aurelia.

When I finished, the note simply read, "If you love me back, you will go to Britannia. Do not look for me."

I stared at the tablet for a long time, considering the effect my words might have. Nothing would make Aurelia agree with my decision, but I figured this had as good a chance as anything to make her do what I wanted and leave with Crispus in the morning. The only thing that truly bothered me was that I would never really know her reaction to my note. Would she be sad? Angry? Understanding? I could live with every possible reaction, except one. I didn't want her last thoughts upon leaving to be regret at having known me.

Though I figured, if anything, that's exactly how she would feel.

Once I was sure everyone had gone to sleep, I left the tablet on my bed to be found in the morning. The carriage would arrive early, and someone would come to my room to see why I had missed the morning meal. By then it would be too late. I would've disappeared already, and no one would have any idea of where to begin searching for me.

Out in the quiet atrium, I had a last-minute thought to bring some food. Whatever awaited me from this point forward, I liked the idea of having something to eat as part of that journey.

I didn't take much. Perhaps more than ever before in my life, I was keenly aware of how many crimes I had already committed, and stealing food from a friend was not one I wanted added to the list. I doubted Crispus would see this as a theft. It was really no different from the meal he would've shared with me anyway in the morning. And yet it felt different, so I took no more than he would've fed me had I been eating alongside him.

Like Radulf's home, Crispus's home also had a rear exit that led to the stables. Callistus was there and would take me as far as we could ride together. Away from Britannia. Away from Rome, and the Praetors and the Mistress. Away from everything and everyone I had ever cared about.

Yet as I approached the door, I saw a wax tablet propped on a shelf beside a single lit candle. It was the same tablet I had just left on my bed. I knew because it had the same scratch in the upper corner of the frame.

Holding it against the light, I saw letters carved so deep they probably had threatened to break the tablet itself. They read, "We will talk now."

While I was gathering food, Aurelia had found my note. Of course she did.

I sighed and brought the tablet with me out into the courtyard, where I already knew Aurelia would be waiting. She had Callistus saddled and was mounted on his back. Her bow and a quiver of arrows were fastened to the saddle, ready for battle. Her arms were folded, and her red face betrayed a level of fury I didn't think even she was capable of.

"*If* I love you, I will go to Britannia without you?" Aurelia asked. "What was I supposed to do with a message like that? In the wagon tomorrow, should I have congratulated myself on truly loving you because I left you behind, to fight and die on your own? Is that your understanding of love?"

"Yes, if it means you would live!" Her anger would not affect me this time. I wouldn't give in on this.

"I will not leave you alone here!" she said. "How many times do I have to tell you that?"

"Tell me a thousand more times; it won't change my decision. Be as angry as you want when you leave this place, but you will leave."

"I won't!"

"People around me are threatened, or hurt; they even die!"

"Which is why you need my help — to stop that from happening."

"Unless it happens to you!" My voice was too loud. It'd wake Crispus and the rest of his household. More quietly, I added, "Can you give me the peace of knowing yours is not one of the lives I will have ruined? Please leave, Aurelia!"

She dismounted and came over to me. Now her tone softened. "Where were you going?"

"Away. Away from everyone who knows I have magic and wishes to control it. Away from those who want either my life or my death if it means they get what they want." I stopped pacing to stare at Aurelia. "Away from you. Because I care more for you than either life or death, and the Praetors know that. Don't you see how dangerous it is for me to love you this much?"

Aurelia placed a hand on my arm. "And don't you see how impossible it is for me to love you any less? Whatever the vestalis asked of you, we can do it together."

"You know what she asked." I met her eyes, conveying all the seriousness within my heart. "So you know why I must leave."

She shook her head, as if her determination and grit were enough to change my circumstances. "There are still other choices!"

"And all of them are bad. Let me at least make the choice that gives the greatest number of people a chance to survive." I stepped toward her. "Don't make our last conversation a fight. Let me go, Aurelia."

Tears filled her eyes, and her breathing became uneven. "If I could do that, don't you think I would have a long time ago?"

I widened my arms for a final embrace, and she closed the gap between us, holding me with a fierceness that conveyed her desperation and sadness and growing hopelessness. If anyone could change my mind, it was her. Yet I knew with absolute certainty that the bulla and Malice drew enemies to me like an eagle hunts its prey. The only way this war ended was with me making a Jupiter Stone. But I hoped for another option, one that even the vestalis had not considered. If I disappeared from Rome, taking the amulets so far away that even the gods could not find them, then the war would atrophy on its own. Maybe the rest of my life would be miserable, but at least I would stay alive, and so would Aurelia.

"What about me?" Atroxia asked. "Set me free."

"No," I mumbled. Aurelia leaned back, curious about why I'd said that. I pulled her close again and whispered, "Know this. My heart will always belong to you."

She wiped her tears on my shoulder, and looked up at me. "If that is true, we should leave together."

She was staring so intently at me that it was impossible to look away. If this was the last time I ever saw her, I wanted to memorize every detail of her face so that if I closed my eyes twenty years from now, I would still be able to recall the intense look of her eyes, the color of her cheeks, the soft smile of her lips.

My hand slid up her arm, then as it moved around to her back and neck, I pressed her closer to me. I kissed her with a strength different from what magic had ever given me. This power came from sharing and giving, not the taking of power from the bulla or the Malice. A kiss like this was its own sort of magic. Love was far more wonderful. And so much harder to leave behind.

She couldn't come with me, of course. But the memory of this kiss would carry me far into the night, and that would have to be enough. Maybe one more . . .

Instead, the Mistress interrupted with a gravelly laugh that filled my head and knotted my insides. Something was different from before, as if she had been waiting for a moment like this. I pushed away from Aurelia, simply out of a reflex to protect her. Aurelia reached for me, but I put up a hand, warning her to stand back.

"So the sewer girl loves you too," the Mistress said inside my head. "Her promise to marry the senator's son was only a trick. She no longer has my protection. I call upon the goddess Diana to deliver her to me. Let my revenge begin with this lying girl!"

Clearly alarmed by my wide eyes, Aurelia said, her voice tightening, "What's happening, Nic?"

I raised a shield around us and put her directly behind me. "Something is coming for you. Something I might not be able to stop."

TWENTY-NINE

The Mistress had gone quiet, though I faintly heard Atroxia crying again for help. I didn't think she was in her human form; rather, it seemed that Atroxia was fighting as hard as she could to separate herself from the dragon, and failing.

Though I heard no response from Diana, I also knew that she would respond. The Mistress had called upon Diana's powers with certainty, fully expecting an answer. It wasn't safe to leave Aurelia here, not anymore.

"Let's ride Callistus away from here," I said, taking Aurelia's hand in mine. "Whatever Diana sends after us, Callistus is our best hope to outrun it."

"If she sends anything, it'll be a stag." Aurelia's eyes widened. "A stag! That's Diana's animal!"

Such as the stag we had seen on Radulf's land, and again in the forum. Diana had been watching me for some time; I realized that now. She had been waiting until the moment her servant called upon her to act.

Aurelia put a hand on her bow attached to Callistus's saddle, though it would take a moment for her to undo the knots around it. I opened the stable gates, but hadn't yet turned back around when I heard her cry out with fear. My hands filled with magic as I saw that same stag already within the stables, its dark eyes fixed on Aurelia.

I whistled to draw the stag's attention to me, yet it didn't waver in its gaze. I tried again, throwing enough magic its way to get some reaction from the beast, but it only edged closer to Aurelia.

"No offense, Nic," Aurelia said, her voice rising with panic, "but I've become used to these strange things only happening to you."

So had I. It would've made sense for the stag to focus on me, but it didn't seem to even care I was here. Suddenly, my heart slammed against my chest. I'd been wrong before. The stag hadn't been watching me. All this time, it had been watching Aurelia. Diana, Goddess of the hunt and of the moon, was watching Aurelia. But why?

"You're shielded," I said, keeping my voice calm as I started to move between them. "Get on the unicorn, quickly. We can outrun it."

Aurelia put one foot into the saddle's stirrup. The stag immediately charged at her, hitting her in both legs and knocking her back to the ground. She rolled and scooted beneath Callistus for protection, but he was nervous and prancing around. She wouldn't be safe there for long and maybe wasn't safe at all. The shield that protected her came from the bulla, filled with Diana's powers. I was willing to bet that meant her stag could run right through it. My shields were useless.

I sent a fireball toward the stag, expecting the animal to retreat from its flames. But the fire only evaporated upon contact, leaving the stag perfectly unharmed. I could use the Malice, but its greater powers worried me. Both Callistus and Aurelia were ahead of me, and past them was Crispus's home filled with him, his mother, and their servants. I'd already exploded one home. A second home seemed like too many for one week.

The stag pawed at the ground, preparing to charge. It would crash directly into Callistus, if necessary. Anticipating that, Callistus ran, openly exposing Aurelia. She stood and raced toward me, but the stag immediately took aim at Aurelia.

I threw myself between them, this time using the Malice to repel the stag. It felt the magic and hesitated a moment, then collided against me with a fierceness that would've killed Aurelia, and possibly even Callistus. I landed hard on my back, and though I could scarcely draw a breath, that was the least of my problems.

For by the time I rose up, ready with more magic, the stag had already circled back to Aurelia. She was running for the villa, but tripped on her robes and fell. I sent harder magic to the stag, determined to stop it, but this too, only caused it a brief pause.

Just before it reached Aurelia, the stag dipped its head, and Aurelia cried out. The gold bracelet from Crispus had become hooked on one of the stag's antlers, and it was already speeding away with Aurelia, out of the stables and down the hill into open fields.

I leapt onto Callistus's back, immediately giving chase. The unicorn's speed was unequaled by any creature on land, and I hoped that was still true with a stag from the heavens.

It was too dark to see Aurelia ahead, but I occasionally heard a cry. I could only imagine what it was doing to her to be dragged alongside a stag's leaping strides.

"Faster, Callistus," I whispered, and the unicorn responded. The scenery rushed past me in a blur. Before I even realized something was in our path, it was already behind us.

The general direction we were going was no great surprise. We were headed south again, leaving the city. To Lake Nemi, no doubt. It was Diana's one refuge within any distance of Rome.

Once the hillside flattened out, I got a better view of the stag, racing beneath the moonlight. Aurelia's body wasn't being dragged, as I had expected. She had somehow managed to get astride the animal, though she was lying low upon its back, probably her only way of remaining balanced. I was grateful to see her there. It could've been so much worse for her.

Callistus pushed forward yet again, until we were close enough for me to use magic. While Aurelia was on its back, I wouldn't send anything too powerful, but there were other options that might work better.

If I could call up water from Radulf's baths, could I also call up water from the earth? It made sense. So I stretched out my hand, focused on the ground ahead of the stag, and called any moisture within the soil to bubble up to the surface.

In the darkness, I couldn't be sure if it had worked, and remained unsure until suddenly the stag slowed. It was still running, still leaping, but with much greater effort and more slowly than before. It wasn't slow enough for Aurelia to safely roll off its back, but as long as Callistus stayed to the side of the mud, we could easily catch up to them.

As we got closer, I noticed a glimmer in the moonlight along the stag's body, reminding me of something from early in my battles with Radulf. He had a trick with the Divine Star I'd never been able to quite learn, one that allowed him to fight in a place where he was not. That was exactly what this stag was doing. It was here in front of me, carrying Aurelia away, so its presence was very real. But it wasn't entirely here. Nothing of my magic could do anything more than bruise it.

If stopping it wasn't an option, then at least I could stop Aurelia from riding on it.

Not so long ago, Aurelia and I had been in a chariot race together, one where it was necessary for me to leap from my chariot into hers. I didn't see how this was too different. She'd make the jump this time, and onto Callistus's back rather than into a chariot, but I knew she could do it.

As soon as we were a half-length behind her, I stretched out my hand. "Maybe you'll ride with me instead?"

She lifted her head enough to look at me. The wrist that had been caught in the stag's antlers was unhooked, and she was using both arms to keep her balance, so she probably wasn't injured. But she made up for that in the fear on her face.

Her eyes went to my hand. "You can't be serious! Do you know how hard it was just to get on this animal's back?"

"We've done a jump like this before." It would work again. It *had* to work again.

"Not at this speed!"

I raised up more groundwater in front of the stag, forcing it to slow down even further. Callistus matched its pace and got us closer to Aurelia.

She frowned over at me, though I was sure that was only to hide a slight grin. "I expected our first kiss to turn out differently than this," she said.

I stretched out my hand again. "Just imagine how the second kiss will end!"

She scowled, but reached for me. Our fingers brushed against each other's at first. With only moonlight above, I couldn't see most of what was ahead of us, but this was no smooth track like in the circus. We needed to hurry.

Finally, she was close enough to get a firm grip on my hand, but her other hand was still holding on to the stag's antlers. "Are you sure?" she asked.

"I'll pull you to me, but you have to let go." My voice was calm at this point. It was going to work.

"There's something dark ahead. What is it?"

I didn't know. As far as I could tell, everything ahead was dark. But when I really looked, I saw what she meant. We were still racing toward Lake Nemi, but the stag had led us on a slightly different route, one I wasn't familiar with. And I didn't know what might suddenly cause so much darkness. The moon had gone behind the clouds, and all I saw was sky, as if the ground ahead just disappeared.

It was a cliff!

"Now, Aurelia!" I yelled. "Hurry!"

She nodded, and started to swing her far leg over the stag's back, but then the stag took a sharp right, pulling her entirely away from me. To keep her balance, she threw her weight back with its movement. By then they had reached the cliff's edge.

The stag jumped into the air, accompanied by a scream of terror from Aurelia, one that chilled my spine.

Callistus careened to a halt, so quickly that I crashed into his neck. Aurelia's cry ended midscream, cut off too suddenly for it simply to have faded into the night air.

I leapt off the unicorn's back and saw, to some relief, that it wasn't a sheer cliff, but instead a steep downward slope, too steep for Callistus to navigate. Lake Nemi was far below us, and now the moonlight peeked out again enough to illuminate the hillside.

I scanned the slope and called out for Aurelia, but there was no answer.

There was nothing. Where was she?

·THIRTY·

I closed my eyes, trying to find Aurelia with my mind. I could see her . . . almost. The stag wasn't running anymore, but everything was dark around her, darker than where I now stood. Wherever the stag had taken Aurelia, she was no longer in these hills, which meant Callistus had no chance to catch up to her.

The moon grew brighter, its light hitting the lake at the exact angle to make the water glow. Except where it should've had a white glow, the water seemed red, like the glow of fire. Dragon's fire.

The Mistress.

The stag must have delivered Aurelia to the Mistress.

I scurried down the hillside, hoping that if I got closer to the water, I'd get a better sense for where Aurelia was. If I could get to her exact location, before the Mistress knew I was there, I could make her disappear to as far away as I could imagine.

With the help of the moonlight, I was already getting close to the lake, spending the bulk of my energy searching for any feeling that connected me to Aurelia. Would Atroxia call to me here? If so, perhaps she would help.

Or were her cries part of a plot to get me back to the caves where the Mistress lay in wait? It was sometimes hard to separate Atroxia from the dragon, if there was any separation between them. Still, I continued running down the steep slope, dodging large oak trees and wading through thick brush, steadily getting closer to the lake.

Obviously, Diana wanted me to return to the dragon, a thought that filled me with dread, but if there were any chance Aurelia had been taken to the cave, I had to go. I knew what the Mistress had done to Radulf. If she attempted even the smallest amount of that harm to Aurelia, it would kill her.

Not if I killed the dragon first. The vestalis wouldn't want that, but I didn't care. It would break the curse, and now it would save Aurelia too.

"You wish to kill me?" That was the Mistress's voice now. "No, Nicolas. If you return to my cave, you will not leave until you have pledged to obey my will."

"Never!" I shouted.

"Then Diana will not allow you to come."

Cries suddenly rose up from near the shores of the lake, though they weren't human and weren't really even cries. The sounds below me came from animals. A lot of them.

I slowed my run, hoping to approach with caution, to be sure of what was waiting for me before I announced my presence, but Diana took care of that too.

A huge brown bear darted from the underbrush, almost directly in my path. It rose to its hind legs, making it at least twice my height, and growled with a fury that even the Mistress would respect. I swerved to miss it, but it raised a claw and swiped at me. I flew several feet before landing on the dirt, then slid face-first the rest of the way to the bottom of the hillside.

When I raised my head again, I was surrounded.

To my right were more brown bears, at least twenty of them, and all larger than the first bear had been. Some were standing on their hind claws, and others paced on all fours like the tigers beside them, of equal number. To my left were packs of wild dogs, crouching low but barking out warnings that they would attack anything in here, or anyone. Two elephants were behind me, blaring out anger through their trunks like trumpets. Ahead of me were dozens of lions, already staring at me and growling.

"Swear to obey me," the Mistress said. "Or Diana will force that vow from you."

She meant that I'd be trampled, bitten, or half-eaten until I finally pledged my loyalty. I preferred to avoid any of that, but I couldn't deny this threat was real. These animals looked hungry.

They weren't wild, though, or hadn't been wild for the last few months. Elephants and tigers didn't wander about the Roman countryside, nor did lions, at least not in these numbers. They must have escaped the venatio, but for all of them to escape, and all of them to come here, was no coincidence. As the goddess of wild animals, Diana had undoubtedly sent them here to do her bidding.

Perhaps Diana had made a mistake, though, because with the bulla, I had some of her powers too. I backed up against a tree, hoping another brown bear wasn't behind it, then put one hand on the bulla and shouted to the animals, "I am not your enemy, and I will not harm you. Go into the hills of Rome. You are free."

I looked around, waiting for whatever might happen next. Though I'd had some success before in communicating with animals, the truth was that I was never sure what they were saying, and I'd only ever guessed that my messages got through to them. That was hardly enough reason to believe they'd understand me now, or obey my command.

Indeed, they were all watching me, and their total silence was far more unnerving than their noise had been. Silence meant they had heard me and refused to obey.

Inside my head, the Mistress laughed. "Did you think they'd care about your words while Diana speaks to them? They are hers, as I am hers, and by the end of this night, you will be hers too."

My back straightened in defiance. "I'd rather pledge loyalty to these animals' droppings!"

Unamused by my joke, the animals closed in tighter around me, attempting to back me away from the lake. If this was Diana's grand plan to keep me away from the Mistress, it was remarkably foolish. There was only one way for me to get into the cave, and that was by making myself disappear there. She could add another thousand animals, and it wouldn't make a difference.

Surely, Diana knew this. Which meant there was something more.

She was sending me a message, a warning. She wanted me to know that at least part of my powers were stolen from her, and that ultimately, she was greater than I'd ever be. Well, that was obvious. She was goddess of the hunt, and of the moon, and of wild animals. I had come from the mines not far from here. Nothing about me could compete with her, but that didn't mean I had to obey her.

Nor did any of the other gods, and there was one other whose magic I could wield: Mars. His animal did not obey Diana either, but it would hear me.

I used the amulets to call through the hills around this lake. Diana might have her war in the heavens, but different rules applied here on earth. Namely, that some animals are very territorial and will defend their land.

The hills around Lake Nemi belonged to the wolf. The animal of Mars.

They were already collecting in every valley and lining every ridge. Hundreds of them had answered my call. They howled at the moon, at the goddess who controlled it, and gave honor to their god of war for the battle that lay ahead. A venatio the Romans would never see.

Even before the wolves came, the dogs had already run,

almost immediately disappearing into the night air. By the time the wolves arrived, they had the remaining animals surrounded. Their teeth were bared, and their growls were fierce.

"I'll grant you safe passage to go." I was still in the center of the animals with the wolves on the outside of us all, but this time when I spoke, I knew they were listening. "The amphitheater is your enemy, and those who hunt you within its arena. Out here you are free, if you leave now."

As the wolves moved in, the elephants trampled through their lines, though it nearly caused them to trip over the tigers that were also leaving. I hoped they were smart enough to stay out of the city gates. Even then, some poor traveler was likely to get an odd surprise very soon.

The bears joined the stampede away, crashing over themselves in their hurry. Mars had answered Diana's threat with a greater threat of his own.

Standing closest to the lake, only the lions remained in defiance of the wolves. They were greater in number and seemed very willing to fight. The remaining wolves were behind me, their backs arched and fur standing on end.

I held up my arms, having full respect for the fiercely courageous natures of both animals. Such beautiful creatures could not be allowed to harm one another.

"You are pawns in a great war of the heavens," I said. "But you are not the war itself. If you fight, you will both lose. Leave this place. There is enough room for both of you, but you cannot remain here."

Growls were exchanged, and for a moment, I thought they would ignore me again. Then the lions ran off in one direction while the wolves ran in the other.

And deep inside me, I felt the Mistress recoil as if the animals' refusal to fight was a defeat. I felt just the opposite. This was a victory. It was proof that Diana had not yet won her war.

And if it was up to me, she never would.

"You cannot run away so easily as these animals." My whisper to the Mistress was quiet, but would sound like thunder in her dragon ears. "I'm coming. This ends tonight."

THIRTY-ONE

I closed my eyes, this time focusing on the gold in the cave, on the dragon who had been locked in there for so many days, and on the eerie cold wind that blew through the tunnels, so deep beneath the earth that no air should've moved at all. It was no common breeze, of course. That was Caesar's ghost.

I felt that wind first. It caressed my arms and the skin of my face, and I shivered against it. Then I detected the change in darkness, now an absolute black. I opened my eyes, though it really didn't matter if I did. And I listened again for any hint of exactly where in the caves I might be and, more important, where Aurelia and the Mistress were.

The first time I'd ever entered these caves was on a rope lowering me into an outer room filled with the bones of others who had failed in their quests. Here was where I'd found the bulla and its animal guardian, Caela. I doubted the Mistress was in that room — the doorway was too small for her to pass through, and I had a vague memory of that doorway being mostly collapsed anyway. So I must be in the larger room.

I swiveled my foot slightly and heard a clink beneath it. Gold coins. Any move I made on top of this ever-shifting pile would give me away.

Or perhaps my presence was already known. Heavy footsteps rumbled the room, and then came a voice, angry and rough as bark. Normally, I'd have heard it in my head, which was bad enough, but this time it echoed in the cave around me.

"I expected to receive the girl," the Mistress said. "But in her wisdom, Diana gave me something better. She gave me Nicolas Calva instead."

"Instead?" I cried into the darkness. "Where is Aurelia?"

The Mistress laughed, and with it came a breath of fire. It singed the hairs of my arms before I got a shield up. The fire had been meant to cause more damage than it did, and was also a mistake since it revealed her location. Unfortunately, it also revealed mine.

I charged toward the Mistress, but slipped on the coins, creating a jingling chorus directly beneath me. It hadn't been so long ago when stealing this gold had been a great temptation. What I would have given then for even a single coin from this room. Now I cared nothing for the treasure here. It would feed me for a week or a year, or even a lifetime, but what could it offer of anything that mattered?

Wealth had failed to keep Valerius's heart beating. It had also darkened the hearts of the Praetors. Until his heart was healed through love, it had threatened the most basic humanity within Radulf. And although Aurelia had inherited a vast amount of wealth from her father, she had never valued it for any purpose other than how she might use it to help others. Now everything she once had was gone, and that had only made her more dear to me.

"I defeated you before," I shouted to the dragon. "Tell me where Aurelia is, or I will do it again!"

"The girl is very strong," the Mistress said. "Diana has come to admire her bravery."

Using the Malice, I shot a full wall of magic toward the Mistress, which would've knocked her entire body backward. I couldn't see it in the darkness, but I did hear a great crash against the cave wall, and the silence that followed. Dirt rained down on us from above.

"Let the cave collapse," I said. "I will get out. Your bones will join the others down here!"

"And what of the girl?" the Mistress countered. "Will you ever find her without my help?" She followed that up with another flame, brighter than before. I released magic of my own to repel the flame back to the dragon's belly, and this time I saw where it hit. She scorched herself and yelped before everything went dark again.

The Mistress rotated her body, letting her tail swipe across the stack of gold near me. My only warning that it was coming was the sound of moving coins. I started to duck, but still was caught across the chest by the tail, which threw me against the far wall; then I dropped to the ground.

"Let me speak to Aurelia!" I shouted.

"Make the Jupiter Stone, and I will give you the girl," the Mistress said.

"Give her to me, and I won't make you into roasted dragon," I countered.

That elicited more fire from her breath, but it only went around my shield, allowing me to get even closer to her.

With my magic, I raised every object of gold inside this cave, and used the wind to send it swirling around her. The strong current of air it created pulled the dragon's fire into itself, becoming a pillar of golden flame that stretched to the roof of the cave. With the heat from the fire, the gold melted and then cooled in streaks that rose from the ground like a gnarled, twisted golden cage.

"What is this?" the Mistress growled. "Am I not imprisoned enough within this cave?"

Apparently not.

The dragon crouched, giving itself as much room as possible within its golden cage, then reared up, letting its wings flail outward. The golden bars shattered, and the dragon fluttered to another end of the cave, then roared fire directly at me.

The vestalis had told me the end to my troubles would come through crossing through fire. This was part of what she meant. I would have to cross through the fires of this dragon. I wouldn't think about the other part of what she meant, of the other kind of fire I would have to face. I couldn't think about that right now.

So I lowered the shield, letting the flames lick my face

and hands. I felt the hunger of the fire to consume the air around me. I even felt the heat, yet it did not bother me. I could bear this.

With greater confidence, I walked forward. The fire grew hotter and stronger, as did the Mistress's anger.

"Your powers are growing," Atroxia whispered inside my head. "But if you kill her, you will kill me. You must break the curse and set me free that way."

"I have to set Aurelia free too," I said. "I won't risk her life."

There was more to it, things I didn't say. If the empire's forgiveness had not released the binds between her and the Mistress, then maybe they could not be separated. Atroxia was forever sealed to her fate.

Unless I accepted mine.

But not at Aurelia's expense. I continued walking forward, letting the flames move harmlessly around me.

"It's the Malice!" the Mistress screamed. "*My* Malice protects you! Once it is mine again, you will feel the worst of my powers!"

Her anger didn't affect me, no more than her flames did. "You have no powers, only a bad temper and a tail that ensures you will die alone and friendless. Tell me where Aurelia is, or I will use the full strength of the Malice against you."

"Please don't do it!" Those were Atroxia's words, ones spoken only in my head.

The flames brightened again. The Mistress heard me and

was resisting my requests, but deep within the dragon, the human was fighting for control.

Once I was close enough, the flames stopped, and the Mistress snapped at me. She caught my arm between her teeth, one of which clamped down on the Malice, no doubt saving that piece of my arm. When she lifted her head again with her mouth still closed, I came into the air with her.

She must've raised me almost to the roof of this massive cave, because in the reflection from her eyes, it seemed to be very close. She reared back her head, intending to throw me against the cave wall. Instead, I hit the remnants of one of the long gold bars and there got my idea. I took hold of the bar, then leapt from it onto the dragon's back, high on her neck. She arched her head and flayed her wings apart, but nothing she did forced me to let go.

I pressed my hand down on the scales of her back, just as Brutus always did on my shoulder, but though he drew magic out of me, I was pouring it directly into the dragon. I had suspected there might be a reaction, but never could've anticipated this.

The Mistress arched her long neck, almost spinning with rage as she fought against the magic. I could destroy the curse this way, by splitting the dragon apart from within.

"Please stop!" That was Atroxia's voice screaming at me. "Perhaps the dragon can survive so much. I cannot!"

But the Mistress had become stronger within this cave, as if Diana herself fed her powers. It would take the full powers of the Malice to stop the Mistress, and wasn't this the reason I had it — so that I could claim victory even in moments like this?

I was willing to use the Malice to destroy the dragon. Indeed, it was a victory that could save the empire. But was I equally willing to let Atroxia be the price for that victory?

"Please!" Atroxia cried again, echoes of my own screams from when Brutus had flogged my back. If I was causing her anywhere near that amount of pain, I couldn't pretend that this was the right thing to do.

I released my hand, and after the briefest moment of silence, the dragon reared up, slamming me backward against the wall of the cave. Even with the Malice, I nearly fell. Hopefully, the Divine Star would cure the headache that was sure to follow.

On the other hand, the Mistress could cause pain beyond what an entire empire could bear. I couldn't ignore that fact either.

I raised my hand again, preparing to press it back down on the dragon's scales. I could still stop the dragon. I could win this.

And Atroxia would lose.

"To win, you will have to lose." That's what the vestalis had told me.

This wasn't about the Mistress, or Atroxia. It was about me. I had to lose here, in this cave.

How I hated every single word the vestalis had ever spoken to me. They were cruel and merciless . . . and honest. I hated the words because I believed them.

I had to lose.

"Find me in this room!" I yelled to the Mistress. I rolled off her back, landing somewhere on the cave floor. I came down on solid ground, leaving a soft echo in the room that would make it easy for the Mistress to find me. She immediately knocked me over with one leg, then clamped a clawed foot on my chest, pressing down until I could barely breathe, much less speak. Another breath of fire rushed at me, so hot this time that though I could bear the flames, it burned enough of my tunic to render it unfit for a second use. Crispus had been right earlier: It was too much to hope even for a full day's use from it.

The Mistress's flame began focusing on my right forearm, where the Malice was. As she had done with the gold coins, she was attempting to melt the silver enough to pull it off my arm. And as hot as it was becoming, I feared she might succeed.

Perhaps what I hated most about the vestalis's cryptic messages were the double meanings they often contained. This one was perhaps worst of all.

Did the vestalis mean that I had to lose? Or was there something more in her words? What if the vestalis meant that to win this fight, I would have to lose . . . Aurelia? Where had the stag taken her?

When her next breath came at me even hotter, I immediately called out, "I offer you a bargain, Mistress, one I'm sure you will not refuse. Tell me where Aurelia is. Let me save her, and I'll do as you ask."

"You will free me from this cave? You will use the Malice to bring in a storm?"

"Yes," I said, feeling an entirely new weight press in on my chest. "After Aurelia is safe, I will bring in the storm."

"The girl can still be useful," the Mistress said. "She will watch as you make the stone. But she should not worry about you, Nicolas. You will be protected by the bulla and that Malice. You will survive the storm."

It was exactly what Radulf had warned me she would say. He also warned it was a lie.

Her great snout turned down to me next, and behind it, eyes like the brightest sunset shone through each smoky breath. "I order you to free us from this cave."

We wouldn't go through the water again. It was difficult enough to keep myself balanced on the back of a dragon while underwater — the only way I'd held on last time was because my arms were wrapped around her throat. This time, we would fly.

Once she had released me, I raised a shield and then shot magic directly overhead, piercing rocks and hard-packed dirt and roots embedded deeply in the ground. They fell near me, but thanks to the shield, I was protected.

After the last of the debris had fallen, I said, "I've obeyed your first order; now you obey mine. Tell me where Aurelia is."

Low-pitched laughter erupted from deep within the dragon's belly. "That was the purpose of releasing us from this cave. I'm going to take you to her."

"Where is she?"

"She is in the place where you will make the storm. She is waiting for you."

She gathered me into one claw, crouched low, and then shot upward toward the open skies. In normal circumstances, I'd have rather continued fighting her on the shores of Lake Nemi than wherever she was taking me. But nothing about this was normal. I had to get to wherever Aurelia was, and do whatever it took to protect her. Beyond that, it suddenly seemed like a very good idea to preserve my magic for what would be our ultimate battle over a storm I had just promised to create.

THIRTY-TWO

From the uncomfortable angle in which I was being held, I wasn't certain exactly where the Mistress was taking me, though I knew we were headed back to Rome.

Where would we go?

There would've been advantages to fighting on the shores of Lake Nemi. At least, no other people would be in danger around us, and there would be no one to see me fall in the end, to talk about how pathetic my last moments were. I could go into the history books as a myth, as someone who was once said to have had great powers, but which couldn't be real, considering how easily it all ended. That's what they'd say, if they remembered me at all. I preferred that.

It didn't matter anyway. We were clearly returning to Rome, and I started ticking off in my mind the possible locations the gods would choose for creating a storm. Either the amphitheater or the circus gave me the most space, and even if games had been held there earlier in the day, they were likely empty now.

I didn't want to go anywhere in the forums. There were too

many people, and too many obstacles for me to hope for a clean shot at taking hold of a lightning bolt.

Taking hold of a lightning bolt? The idea of such a thing turned my stomach. This was madness at its finest.

No, that wasn't the plan. I had to stick with what I had offered the Mistress, and do nothing more. I would only create a storm. I had safely done it before, and I could do it again.

Although this time, there would have to be lightning. It was foolish to pretend otherwise. No, it was foolish to be in this position in the first place. My stomach leapt into my throat.

"How far will you go to save the girl?" Was that Atroxia's voice, or the Mistress's?

"Let me speak to Atroxia," I said.

"Atroxia is weak," the Mistress said. "She is flawed and fearful. Without me, she would have died long ago."

Without magic, I would've died too. Nothing was particularly special about either of us. We were simply two humans in extraordinary circumstances, who both had committed more than our share of crimes.

"I hate her weakness," the Mistress added.

I'd never heard weakness in Atroxia before. There was fear, yes, but who wouldn't be afraid in her situation? She must've been very young when she fell in love with Marcus Brutus, probably not much older than me, and I knew how my feelings for Aurelia often shifted everything upside down in my head.

Atroxia's terrible decisions had resulted in the death of Julius Caesar. My decisions had resulted in the death of Aurelia's father, and Valerius's death, and had nearly done the same to others I cared so deeply about.

And for as often as Atroxia had begged for my help, I had refused, claiming that she deserved her punishment.

Had I deserved the sentence the emperor delivered upon me? If the vestalis had not saved me, I would've met my end yesterday. I should never have been saved, but I was. And there would be a price for it.

Diana's curse upon Atroxia saved her too, though it also asked her to pay a heavy price. Even if the dragon swore revenge upon Rome, Atroxia had only ever wanted the empire's forgiveness.

Just as I wanted forgiveness.

I wondered again about where Aurelia was, if she was truly at the place where we were going, and if she was still safe. Depending on the answers to those questions, then I also hoped she would forgive me for getting her into this situation in the first place.

She might, considering that she had already forgiven me for other offenses just as awful.

I'd never fully understood how both Aurelia and Crispus could have forgiven me for what had happened to their fathers. I should've been stronger or faster or smart enough to help them before it was too late. Yet not only had they forgiven me, they had continued standing at my side.

Livia had forgiven me for upending our comparatively simple lives in the mine. My mother had forgiven me for refusing to obey her orders. So had Radulf.

Yet I was still carrying the guilt with me, like a constant burden chained to my back. Maybe it was no different from the dragon Atroxia carried everywhere with her. Atroxia's problem wasn't getting forgiveness from the empire — that's why the vestalis said it was only the first step in removing her curse. Atroxia's problem was that she needed to forgive herself for her crimes.

As I needed to forgive myself. Because very soon I would bring in a terrible storm, igniting a battle that I might not win. I didn't want to go into the next life still chained to my guilt.

That was what I had not understood about love. What the Mistress had to teach me. Forgiveness was real, and with it came love. The vestalis had been right again.

Which was why I knew she was right about the biggest question of all. I had to break Diana's curse. It didn't work for me to try killing the dragon; that would've killed Atroxia too. Only one other choice remained. I stuck my free hand into the pocket of my tunic and brushed my finger across the smooth stone. It was only a small white rock now, but its purpose was to become the most powerful amulet in existence.

If I made it happen.

Because what I was about to do would prove to be the greatest test of my life. The test of how close I could get to the edge of a cliff before I fell into nothingness.

The problem was, the only way to know that the edge is too close is after you've already fallen.

THIRTY-THREE

After we crossed over Rome's city gates, we flew northward between the circus and the amphitheater, and fortunately crossed over the forums before the dragon angled downward. At first I thought the Mistress intended to land near the Tiber River, a place I dreaded for the upcoming battle. The storm would cause enough trouble without adding floodwaters to a wide river I probably still couldn't swim.

Except we weren't going as far as the river. Instead, we circled over a building with a square entrance and arched roof, but the temple portion behind it was entirely circular with a rounded roof and a large opening in the top called an oculus. This was the Pantheon, completely unique among other buildings in Rome in both design and its equal dedication to all the gods. Of course Diana would want the storm created here. She had no interest in the equality of the gods.

When we were directly overhead, the dragon suddenly dove toward the earth, sharp enough that for a moment I was sure she intended to drop me, which would've been a problem, even with the use of magic.

We entered the Pantheon through its oculus, though it was only barely wide enough for the dragon when its wings were drawn close to its body. Radulf had brought me here once before, though of course we'd come and gone through the large bronze doors like normal people. On that day, I'd stared up at the oculus for a very long time, trying to understand its purpose. Radulf told me that nobody fully understood why the oculus was created. I had thought it was an eye for the gods, a window for them to look in on their people. Now I wondered if it was something different. Maybe the entire Pantheon had only one purpose, and maybe I was the one meant to fulfill it.

Although every temple was beautiful, no other place I had ever seen was so magnificent on the inside. The Pantheon ceiling had rings of coffers inlaid with bronze sheeting. Its walls were painted in bright frescoes and decorated with red, purple, and yellow gems. A marble altar sat in the center of the room, directly beneath the oculus. It was surrounded by seven alcoves along the circular floor, each with a different statue of a god in it.

When I'd come before, I'd studied Jupiter's statue for a long time, wondering if the Jupiter Stone was real, if a person could truly survive after creating it. If the Mistress had her way, I would have the answer to that question tonight.

Apollo's statue was in another alcove, and next to him Mars and then Mercury, Saturn, and Venus. I had only strolled past Diana's statue before, refusing to pay any respect to it. Now I wished I had, for Diana controlled the moon, which shone brightly into the building. She would be watching this place tonight, knowing that, by the end, she would either have her amulet to defeat the gods or her rebellion would be over.

It likely wasn't a common occurrence for a dragon to make an appearance within the walls of the Pantheon, so as we entered, I'd expected cries from temple worshippers as they scattered from the building.

If not that, then I expected to hear Aurelia's cries. The Mistress had promised to take me to her. She had to be here. Why was it so silent?

The Mistress released me as soon as we landed on the floor of the Pantheon, then flew back into the dome, digging into the cement coffers with her claws to give herself balance.

I immediately rose to my feet and looked around for Aurelia.

"Where is she?" I asked. "You promised —"

"She's here with me." Brutus emerged from behind the statue of Jupiter, holding Aurelia by the arm. She was bound with a rag tied over her mouth, and shook her head when she saw me. It was a message, that much was clear, but I had no idea what she meant by it.

"I hope she'll forgive me for tying her this way," Brutus said. "You cannot imagine how loud that girl gets when she's angry."

"And have you forgotten what I can do when I'm angry?" I said. Because I was plenty angry.

"How could I forget?" He smiled as he spoke. "What you can do is the reason we're all here tonight."

Not fully trusting my own eyes, I squinted back at him. "How did you get here? The emperor had you arrested."

Brutus widened his arms, showing his arrogance. "I told you that I'd give him the answers he wanted." His eyes darkened. "Not everything was to the emperor's satisfaction, unfortunately. I've been stripped of my Praetorship, my wealth, my social status." Then he nodded toward his arm. "Luckily for me, the emperor does not know the significance of this armband. By the time he figures it out, I will have forced you to make the Jupiter Stone and will have turned it over to the Mistress."

Aurelia yelled into the rag and shook her head again.

"Yes, girl." From above us, the dragon gave a deep laugh. "Use your anger. Diana admires that about you, just as she does in me."

"See what I mean?" Brutus shook Aurelia's arm until she quieted down. "Just imagine what she was like before I bound up her mouth."

"Make the storm, and we'll release her afterward," the Mistress said. "You promised to make me a Jupiter Stone!"

"With what rock?" I smiled, which I knew would irritate her. "Do you have one? Or did you forget about that?"

An irritated growl erupted from one side of her mouth. Her tail swished in the air a few times as she considered her options.

Would one of the fallen concrete chunks work, or a rock from the ground outside? Or was a special rock required for me to be successful?

Finally, Brutus said, "Diana will provide the rock. Then you can make it!"

"Even if I can, I still won't, not until you let me talk to Aurelia."

Brutus pulled Aurelia even closer to him. "You are thinking that if I refuse, you can throw a little magic at me and have your way. Well, I can do plenty of damage before that magic comes. You won't risk the sewer girl's safety."

"If you want my cooperation, *you* won't risk her safety either," I warned.

There was something about my words that Aurelia particularly didn't like. She leapt forward, yelling something again, until Brutus pulled her back.

"Give me the amulets," Brutus said. "For them, I will trade five minutes to speak with the girl, if you are foolish enough to remove the rag. Then when you return her to my control, I will return your magic and you will make the storm."

It was a ridiculous proposal. "Even you cannot be stupid enough to think I'd give you the amulets!" I raised a hand, intending to get Aurelia away from him, but he moved her body directly in front of his.

The tall bronze doors to the Pantheon opened, and we all turned to see who had come. I saw the shiny golden horn of a unicorn first. Callistus's hooves clattered on the marble floor, but he wasn't alone. Aurelia's bow and arrow were still fixed to his saddle, though when I saw the rider, I figured the bow would never get used. The old vestalis sat there, commanding and calm. Her white robes were nearly the same color as Callistus's fur, giving them a look of being as one.

However, when she saw me, every part of her face pointed downward in disapproval. Her eye roamed to the Mistress, then went to Brutus and Aurelia, ending again with me. She let out a heavy sigh. "If you had done as I asked in the first place, things would not be nearly so complicated now."

"How did you know I was here?" I asked.

The old woman smiled. "When you see a dragon flying over the streets of Rome with someone in its grasp, it's not hard to figure out what is happening. I called on your unicorn for help."

She surveyed the room again as if trying to orient herself to what was happening between Brutus and me. "Ah, yes," she murmured, then held out her hand. "I will hold the amulets."

If it were anyone else, I would wonder how she could know what our conversation had been. But somehow with the vestalis, I'd have been more surprised if she hadn't known.

With her hand still held out to me, she looked at Decimas Brutus. "Surely you trust a vestalis?"

From the pinch on his face, his answer was no, but he couldn't say that directly to a holy woman, so Brutus only said, "If you give your word to hold them until the girl is returned to me, then I must believe you."

Her intense expression asked me to trust her. "Nicolas, give me the amulets."

Aurelia shook her head and tried to speak. I kept a watchful eye on her as I unlaced the Malice, then pulled the bulla off from around my neck and handed them to the vestalis, letting my hand brush against Callistus as I lowered my arm.

It was an odd thing to see the vestalis holding the amulets, respectfully, but with no awareness of the magic within them. She didn't respond to their weight or warmth, or react any differently than she would if I had given her a child's bulla and a tin armband. Yet although she seemed unaware, I was not. All I could feel within me was the loss of magic, like a hole had opened inside me.

Well, there was one other feeling, and that was the desire to speak to Aurelia.

Once I'd backed away from the vestalis, Brutus pushed Aurelia toward me. "Five minutes."

Five minutes. That wasn't enough time.

THIRTY-FOUR

Gently, I took Aurelia's arm and led her to the alcove where the statue of Saturn stood. He was the god of agriculture, which I figured meant he was largely uninterested in the Praetor War. And if he did care, then it was because he was also the god of liberation, so if anything, he was on my side. We went behind his statue where we had at least a small measure of privacy.

I first removed the rag from her mouth, fully expecting a lecture to follow. Instead, all she said was "Why did you say you'd cooperate with them?"

I took Aurelia's bound hands in mine and immediately began to untie them. "In just a few minutes, there will be a distraction. Use that chance to get out of here."

"You didn't answer my question, Nic!"

"There's a reason I didn't."

Aurelia's eyes blazed. "We are not cooperating with them!"

"And you are not cooperating with me! You have to leave, Aurelia."

"*You* have to leave. Why are you doing this? You promised you wouldn't make a Jupiter Stone." The tone in her voice became one of desperation. "You promised me, you promised Radulf and Livia. You promised everyone!"

"I've got to break that promise." I touched her arm, only to feel her pull away from me. "I have to bring in the lightning. Please just trust me."

"How can I, when you speak like that? If you bring lightning into this room, what do you think will happen?"

"I know what will happen, and I don't want you here to see it! Honestly, for once can you just do as I ask? I'm trying to save your life!"

It should've been enough reason for Aurelia to listen to me, but instead, she waved that away, as if being bound and in Brutus's control was only a slight inconvenience. "Are you saving my life? Or sacrificing yours?"

"I'll have a shield up. I'll be fine. But I can't manage the storm and a shield, and also protect you."

She shook her head. "Something is going to go wrong with your plan. I don't know what it is, but I can feel it. You ask me to trust you, but I need your trust too. I've always been right on these feelings before, haven't I? If you create the Jupiter Stone, something will go wrong."

I put my arms around her and pulled her into a tight embrace. Into her ear, I whispered, "I will not create the Jupiter Stone, but I must bring in the storm. If the dragon is hit with lightning, it will break the curse. It's simple, really."

She pressed against my chest, and when she leaned away, tears were in her eyes. "Nothing is ever as simple as you make it sound. Don't do this."

"There's no other way."

She put a hand on my cheek, the most familiar her touch had ever been with me, except when I had kissed her.

"How can I stop you?" she asked. "Tell me what to say or do, and I will."

"There's only one thing I want from you," I whispered. "Marry me."

Her eyes widened. I knew how long she had waited for me to ask, but now that I had, her reaction was hardly one of enthusiasm.

"If my answer is yes, will you leave with me now?"

"Tell me yes, and when I'm finished here, I will find you again."

She shook her head again, harder this time. "You said you wouldn't offer when your future was uncertain. It's never been more uncertain, and if it is known, then that's only because of how it will end."

I smiled. "Marry me, Aurelia."

"Why are you asking now?"

"Because I want a reason to kiss you one more time. Give me that reason."

The first tear fell onto her cheek. "I'll make you this bargain. Come back from this, and then you can offer marriage in a proper way. Please come back to me, Nic, and hear my answer."

That wasn't exactly a yes, but I leaned in to her anyway, determined to get one last kiss. Before I could, something heavy crashed onto the roof above us. With Aurelia's hand in mine, we looked up to catch a glimpse of a large eagle's wing, and a lion's tail dipped inside the oculus opening.

Caela.

My distraction.

Her arrival sent the Mistress flying in circles beneath the oculus again, ready for a fight if Caela chose to enter the Pantheon.

"Did you call her here?" Aurelia asked.

Before I could answer, I covered my ears when a series of piercing squawks echoed inside the room. I looked over at Aurelia to say something, but she was covering her ears too. The Mistress hissed and spat out rings of smoke, warning Caela to stop.

If I was lucky, then I had just enough magic left in me to temporarily slow the Mistress in time for Caela to get Aurelia and escape. I'd already told Caela what I wanted. Once Aurelia got onto Caela's back, she would protest or threaten or even kick at Caela to make her return to the Pantheon, but Caela was not to let her go until they had arrived in Britannia. Aurelia would forever be furious with me for this, but at least she would be alive.

"Get ready to jump on her back," I said to Aurelia. "When Caela gets down here, you won't have much time."

"I won't leave you," she said.

I only smiled back at her. "Then Caela will snatch you in her claw. Trust me, it's far more comfortable riding on her back." Aurelia continued protesting, but I'd already left the alcove.

By now, the Mistress had landed on a different coffer, lower on the roof where the concrete was thicker. When her claws dug into it, two bronze sheets fell to the ground, followed by chunks of concrete thick enough to crack the tile floor. I wondered how many chunks of concrete could be pieced away from the roof before the entire dome collapsed. As bad as that would be, I also wondered how much more damage would be done in this elegant room before the night was over.

I no longer had enough magic to do any harm to the Mistress, and that wasn't really the point anyway. All I had to do was get her out of the way for a few seconds. It would empty my magic completely, but once I got the amulets back, it would quickly return. No matter how angry he'd be after Aurelia escaped, Brutus would still allow the vestalis to return the amulets to me. What other choice did he have?

I climbed onto the altar in the center of the room and checked again that the Mistress's claws were dug into the bronze sheets. I wasn't sure that anyone even noticed me; they were still distracted by Caela's awful cawing.

I aimed my hands toward the Mistress, or rather, to the bronze sheets, and used magic to tear them from the concrete roof. The Mistress fell with them, struggling to regain her balance in the air. She might've been more successful, except that I was rotating in a circle, pulling down several other bronze sheets still in the dome. Some landed on her head or wings, their heavy weight throwing her off balance again. Those that missed her still kept her from flying properly since she was trying to avoid them.

There were only a few places in the Pantheon that were safe right now. Directly beneath the oculus, I was safe. The alcoves were safe — Aurelia was still in Saturn's alcove and, unfortunately, Brutus was hiding in another of them too. I didn't know where the vestalis had gone, but Callistus would keep her safe.

Caela flew into the Pantheon, trailing behind the Mistress where the bronze sheets had already fallen. After making a half circle around the dome, she landed on the floor and cawed out for Aurelia to run toward her.

Aurelia didn't come out at first, and I wondered if above the sound of bronze sheets clanking onto the marble, she even heard Caela. But this was her only chance. She had to go.

I was out of magic. Whatever was done was the most I could do. And I was also out of strength, though I refused to fall. If I did, Aurelia would try to help me and I couldn't allow that. So I forced myself to remain standing, just until I could gain enough energy to get down from the altar.

Finally, Aurelia ran forward, but it was a moment too late. For by then, the Mistress had regained her balance and crashed directly into Caela. They rolled together on the floor, wings tangling with claws, while one screeched and the other growled.

Caela had lionhearted courage, and talons far sharper than the Mistress's claws, but puffs of flame kept erupting from the Mistress, which forced Caela back. Once they untangled, the Mistress took to the air first, though Caela shot up immediately after her. From below, Brutus cried out his support for the Mistress. I found just enough magic within me to send him into a coughing fit. I'd have caused him to choke on his heart instead, except that I wasn't sure he had one.

Overhead, Caela was screeching again, and the Mistress had smoke billowing from her nostrils. From what I could see, Caela had more than her share of wounds. She was losing.

I needed to do something to help the griffin, though I knew I wasn't up to it. I tried sending up bursts of magic, but they came from me with little more force than whispers and feathers.

"Stop this!" Aurelia yelled it loud enough to get everyone's attention in the room. Even Caela fluttered to the ground and the Mistress returned to the coffers, her claws digging into the bare concrete.

I turned to her and raised my hands, but not to fight. It was in surrender.

Amidst the confusion, Aurelia must've found Callistus and gotten her bow and arrow from his saddle. An arrow was nocked and aimed directly at me.

THIRTY-FIVE

Aurelia pulled the arrow back even further, and the tone of her voice made it clear she would not hesitate to release it. "I warned you, Nic, that I would not allow you to make a Jupiter Stone. Even if it requires me to become your enemy, for your own good, I will stop you."

I didn't particularly want to be shot with an arrow tonight, but if that happened, I knew I'd come back from it. Despite the heavy tone of Aurelia's voice and her threatening posture, this was not the act of an enemy. Aurelia would shoot me, bringing me down, and then once I was given up for dead, she would help me heal. If I could figure out the plan this easily, then so could the Mistress. This trick would never work.

"Shoot him if you wish," the Mistress said with honest indifference. "We have the amulets. It won't be hard to find someone else with magic who will be more cooperative."

That wasn't entirely true. If finding someone else were as easy as she made it sound, they'd already have killed me.

The Mistress continued, "The same is true for my Praetor.

Stop him tonight, and another Praetor will rise in his place, and another, and another. Diana's war will continue on."

I looked up at her. "None of this is necessary, Mistress. I've said I will bring in the storm. Let Aurelia leave with the griffin, and I'll do as you ask."

"I have a different plan," Brutus said. "Tell the griffin to leave, and I won't kill the girl."

I turned and saw he must've snuck up behind Aurelia and had a knife at her throat. Aurelia's face was set in a tight grimace, and the knuckles of her hand holding the bow were white. She was clearly angry with herself for failing to hear his approach, and I worried that anger would overshadow her wisdom. "Drop the weapon," he said.

Aurelia shook her head, her stare fixed on me. She wanted me to use some magic to stop him, but I had nothing to offer her.

"Do as he says," I said. Unlike her gesture just now, Brutus was not playing any tricks. She closed her eyes, lowered the bow, and let it clatter to the floor.

With the knife still against Aurelia's neck, Brutus addressed me. "Order your griffin to leave."

Caela was watching me, waiting for my instructions. "Go now," I said. It was all I could do.

Caela gave a soft caw, one of sadness, I thought. But I nodded at her as well. With a long final look at me, she spread out her wings and lifted into the air on a steep climb out of the Pantheon. She kicked at the concrete with one talon before leaving the oculus, and a chunk fell down, almost hitting the

Mistress, who left her perch in the dome to avoid being hit. I thought Caela would be equally upset she had missed that opportunity.

Once Caela was gone, I said, "Now let Aurelia go."

"I think not." The Mistress swooped down and grabbed Aurelia within her claw. Aurelia flailed and tried to loosen the grip, but there was nothing she could do. The Mistress carried her high into the dome.

I raised a hand. Some magic had returned from the Divine Star, but not enough to force the Mistress to release Aurelia. All I could hope for was to protect her fall, if necessary.

The vestalis had entered the room again, though this time Callistus only walked along behind her. She gave Aurelia and the Mistress little more than a passing glance before walking over to me, still on the altar.

"You know how to save her, Nicolas." The vestalis placed the amulets at my feet. "You can save everyone here."

Aurelia cried out. It looked as if the Mistress was squeezing her.

So I pulled the white rock out of my pocket and held it up. "This is what you want, Mistress." That got her attention as her black eyes focused on the rock, hungry for its powers. I took a step forward. "If you harm Aurelia in any way, I will destroy this rock. Let her go, or it will become dust in my hands."

"You've had the rock all along?" The Mistress snorted, smoke rising from both nostrils amidst her disgust and anger. "You tried to trick me?"

Technically, Aurelia tried to trick her. I had outright lied. But whatever she called it, I wasn't bluffing with my threat, and she knew it.

I picked up the bulla and put it around my neck first, then put the Malice on my wrist, loosely lacing it up, which was all I had time for. The flow of magic into me was swift and strong.

I sent a ball of magic up to the Mistress, aiming at the wing. It hit in the softer flesh between the bones and sent her sideways.

"Release her!" I shouted. "I can do worse to you, and you know it!"

"What if you could stop the Mistress, do you think it would matter?" Brutus laughed at the thought of it. "Just as I will be replaced if something happens to me, the Mistress will be replaced if something happens to her. Diana can always find someone new to curse. The only way to end this war is to allow Diana to win. Stop fighting us, Nicolas. Pledge your magic and the amulets in service of Diana. Then all our troubles will be over."

My eyes narrowed. "If I make the Jupiter Stone, will Aurelia be safe?"

Aurelia shook her head. "Don't listen to them!" She started to say something else, but the Mistress squeezed her again.

"He must listen," the Mistress said as she flew in circles overhead. "He will serve me or face the consequences!"

"If I still had my bow, I would stop you!" Aurelia cried.

The Mistress laughed. "You have the heart of a hunter, girl. You wield the bow and arrow as fiercely as a goddess. The blood of a dragon can flow through your veins as well. If you bring any harm to me, Diana knows exactly how to use this girl."

Even from where I stood, I saw Aurelia's eyes widen as she understood what the Mistress was saying. That's why Diana had been watching Aurelia all this time. If I killed the Mistress, Aurelia would become her replacement. If I ended one curse, another would begin.

"Make the storm, Nicolas," Brutus said. "Do it, or the Mistress will drop the girl back to the floor."

"Do it the way you described to me." Tears streamed down Aurelia's face. "Only that way."

"Break the curse," Atroxia said into my head. "I beg you to end my suffering."

And in doing so, I would likely cause Aurelia's suffering. She loved me, more than I had ever deserved, and in a way I had never been loved before.

"Of course he will do it," Brutus said, then looked directly at me. Satisfaction gleamed in his eyes in a way that infuriated me. "You are the sacrifice to the gods, are you not?"

I had not thought of it that way, and yet that was exactly correct. Why had Caesar's ghost marked me in the caves, and allowed me to steal that bulla? The magic I held wasn't a curse or a punishment. It was given to me so that I might carry out a purpose Caesar wanted. It was the same reason the Malice of

Mars had come to me, even though there had been other Romans with magic, including Radulf, who had wanted a Jupiter Stone for years. Mars intended the Malice to fall into my hands. Why? Would he care that I had greater powers or the ability to defeat any attacker? No, the only purpose for the Malice was that it gave me the strength to challenge the lightning for a storm.

This must also be the reason why every attempt to escape my fate had failed. Because as far as I might ever run from the empire or from magic or even from the gods themselves, I could never run from my own destiny.

When I came here, my plan had been to make a storm, and only that. To bring in lightning targeting the Mistress while I stood protected within a shield.

But that was not my fate. It was always intended that I make this Jupiter Stone.

An amulet that carried the power of Jupiter himself. One that could only be created to benefit someone else. Never for the person who created it.

When my father had attempted it, it was to save my family and our ragged town from the Roman invaders. He had the right motives, but lacked enough magic.

Through me, Radulf had enough magic, yet he had always wanted the Jupiter Stone for himself. If he had attempted to create the stone, he would have failed too.

Above me, the Mistress had deposited Aurelia on a narrow cornice high above one of the alcoves. There was nowhere for her to go from there, and it was too high for her to jump down. But if she kept her balance, she would be safe.

What if I were only making the stone to save Aurelia's life? Would that allow me to survive it?

"You will not survive it," Atroxia said into my head. "But you must create the storm."

I looked up at the Mistress, who had landed on a cornice at the opposite side of the dome. For all her greatness and grandeur, the dragon looked remarkably lonely. Alone. Empty. Somewhere behind the Mistress's fiery eyes, Atroxia was also awaiting my decision.

I directed my attention to Brutus. "Whatever happens at the end of this, I want your solemn vow to release Aurelia."

"When I am holding the Jupiter Stone, she will go free," he said.

"Please don't do this," Aurelia said. "Nic, you know what will happen."

"You will go free; that's what I know."

Before she could answer, I looked away. I had to while I still had enough courage to move. I stared up through the oculus, noticing for the first time that the moon had shifted its position in the skies just enough to bathe the altar in its silvery light. Diana was at work in here tonight.

Caela was no longer visible, but I knew she wasn't far away. I whispered a call to her. "Find Aurelia," I said. "When this is over, find Aurelia."

Finally, it was time to begin. I looked down, gathering magic into my hands and arms, letting it fill my chest and the hollows of my legs. The storm I wanted was no ordinary rainstorm. I wanted dark clouds to obscure even the brightest star, winds that would uproot the strongest trees, and sharp sparks in the air, tangible enough that any Roman with the sense of a clay pot would race to be indoors.

For all its showmanship and grandeur, Rome had never seen anything like what I was about to bring.

Above me, the heavens began rumbling. My show had begun.

THIRTY-SIX

I knew when enough clouds had gathered above us because darkness filled the Pantheon. Torchlights still glowed where they had been placed on the walls, but they flickered in the wind that filtered down from the oculus, giving the room an even more ominous feel.

Ahead of me, Brutus had backed into the alcove directly beneath Aurelia. With the bow near his feet, it wouldn't be hard for him to upset Aurelia's delicate balance if he thought I was tricking him in any way, but that was not my intention. I simply needed to ensure I didn't lose control of anything I brought into this room. I hoped Aurelia was balanced enough on that cornice to withstand what was coming.

Outside, we heard the scratches of tree branches against the sides of the building, and the tumbling of loose objects as they blew down the roads. I hoped everyone outside had cleared from the area because it was only about to get worse.

When I looked up, my arms raised with me, high as I could reach. Then I pulled them low, and with that, I pulled rain down to the earth. It came in fat, flooding drops of water, so heavy that they fell like tiny silver balls upon my head and my shoulders. Within only seconds, water began building on the Pantheon floor.

Knowing what would likely come next, Brutus climbed onto the statue, getting his feet out of the water. That disappointed me. I wouldn't have minded if he were in the water when the lightning came down.

The Mistress also launched herself into the air, though she was becoming agitated and finally touched down on the head of the statue of Jupiter. Something about that seemed appropriate.

Most of the time when I used my magic, I felt it draining me, slowly weakening me. Even with the Malice, that happened. But not tonight. Something in this storm was building the powers already within my chest and shoulder. I was stronger than I had been when the storm began.

For whatever it was worth, I'd have to trust my own instincts, and hope the magic was powerful enough to sustain me until it was over.

Until all of it was over.

Through nearly every hour of my turbulent life, I'd gotten by on the insistence that I had no intention of dying that day.

Tonight was different. Tonight I would die. I knew that now.

I removed the bulla from around my neck and wrapped the cords around the Malice, holding the amulet itself in my hand. Beneath the bulla, safe in my palm, was the stone. It was only a rock now, but before I was finished, it would be different. Everything would be different.

I lifted the rock over my head and shouted up through the oculus, "I am marked by Julius Caesar, bearer of his bulla containing the magic of Diana, and wearing the Malice of Mars! They give me great powers, but tonight I seek the greatest power!"

"Diana will receive that greatest power," the Mistress said. "For she is the greatest of all the gods."

I didn't accept that. "Is that why her temple is a full day's ride from Rome? Why her twin brother, Apollo, sent me the griffin, and why Mars sent me an amulet that makes hers seem like a toy? Is that why the other gods have always favored Venus over her?"

"She has been wronged!" the Mistress scowled. "Who is Venus? A goddess of love? What is that compared to Diana, who blesses the hunt?"

I lowered my arm, even as hard rain continued falling, and I had to shout above the noise. "It's everything. The hunt is death, the end of a life. But life exists because of love, something Diana knows nothing about. It saved my life when Gaul was invaded, and helped me survive the mines. Love kept me going when the world literally crashed down upon me. That's why Venus is the favored god. She builds and sustains and gives. Diana only takes."

"Diana should be the ruler of all gods!" the Mistress said. "And with the Jupiter Stone, she will prove it!"

"Diana has betrayed the gods!" The vestalis had seemed content to be forgotten in this room, but now her voice boomed louder than mine had ever been and her finger pointed accusingly at the dragon. "Diana deserves no honors!"

"You only want Atroxia!" the Mistress said, and even in the rain, smoke blew from her mouth. "You want me gone!"

"You are a curse that never should have existed!" the vestalis said. "You are a symbol of the crimes you have committed, but Diana will haunt you no more. I have come for Atroxia. The vestals will reclaim her tonight."

More smoke puffed from the dragon's nose. I couldn't risk her attacking the vestalis, although I had greater faith in the old woman's abilities to take on this dragon than my own.

Yet I shouted, "Turn to me, Mistress! I am the one who angers you! I freed you from the temple only to trick you with the Malice."

Fire burst from her mouth. It was immediately doused by the rain, but her growing anger was evident. That was good. I wanted her angry.

So I yelled even louder this time. "I fought you again and locked you inside the cave, not for Atroxia's sake, but to punish *you*! You were the one I entombed there!"

The Mistress began flying around me, her circle coming ever closer. "I defeated you in the cave and brought you here."

I shook my head, holding up the Malice again, with the bulla and rock still in my hand. "With this Malice, I cannot lose. So if you think you defeated me —"

"Another trick?" the Mistress screeched with anger. "Why?"

"Because I intend to break the curse tonight. I intend to destroy you."

"No!" the Mistress shouted, and somewhere farther away, Brutus shouted it too, though his shouts were for different reasons. Brutus had seen through my plans. In her anger, the Mistress did not.

She charged directly at me, fire blazing from her mouth, and eyes nearly as hot with rage. As soon as she was within the moonlight, I brought my arms downward again, but not to bring in the rain.

I brought lightning.

It didn't touch me, for I had ducked low on the altar, and the Mistress had flown directly over me. She was between me and the lightning when it struck her back. With lightning searing her from wing tip to claw, she continued forward under her momentum and crashed into the far wall of the Pantheon. At least two statues toppled over, and most of the paintings on the walls fell. Every remaining bronze sheet that had been in the dome crashed with her, all of them falling to the ground.

And suddenly everything went quiet.

Because what landed on the floor of the Pantheon was not a dragon, cursed and terrible in its greatness.

What landed there was a young vestalis who had been imprisoned in a tomb since the death of Julius Caesar. And a prisoner of the dragon every day after that.

The curse was broken.

And impossibly, I was still alive.

The Jupiter Stone had not been made. More important, it did not need to be made.

I was still alive.

The rain continued to fall, though the drops were lighter now than before. Brutus jumped back onto the floor to survey what had become of the Mistress.

He stopped when he saw Atroxia lying there, on her side facing away from us, and moving, though only a little.

The vestalis rushed over to Atroxia, helping her slowly get to a seated position. As she did, she said to me, "She is forgiven, Nicolas. She will rejoin the vestals and spend the remainder of her days helping to build the best of what it is to be Roman."

Now Atroxia met my eyes. The only time I had seen her before was in the catacombs of the temple on Valerius's land. It had been dark in there, and her grip on my wrist had been so painful, I'd barely noticed her appearance then. But I didn't see how I could've missed it.

Atroxia's hair was as red as the scales of the dragon had been. Her lips were equally red, though the rest of her skin was pale, perhaps the consequence of centuries without seeing the sun. But her beauty could not be denied. She might've even been lovelier than Livia, something I'd never thought possible for anyone.

"You saved me," Atroxia said, almost in disbelief. "After all I've done wrong, you *saved* me."

"No!" Brutus shouted, not to the vestalis but to me. "You've ruined everything!"

I used enough magic to punch him back to the wall, then said to the old vestalis, "You both must leave! This isn't over."

The vestalis immediately got Atroxia to her feet and then helped her onto Callistus's back. He would get them safely away from here. If only I could get Aurelia out of here too.

"I told you what would happen if the Mistress were destroyed," Brutus snarled. "Didn't you believe me?" He cried out to the heavens. "There must be a new Mistress." His gaze lifted to Aurelia.

I wasn't sure how to get her safely down from where she stood, nor if that was enough. She needed to get out of the Pantheon, as far from Brutus as possible.

Suddenly, the cornice beneath Aurelia crumbled and she screamed. Her arms flailed until she found a chunk of rock protruding from the wall. It was holding her for now, but it wouldn't for long.

Diana must've done that, upon Brutus's request. Nothing else should've caused that piece of wall to collapse on its own.

"The moment she loses her grip, Diana will curse her," Brutus said. "It will be the only way she survives that fall. She will become the new Mistress."

"I won't let that happen!" I shouted.

Brutus ignored me. "And when she becomes the Mistress, will you destroy her with a bolt of lightning too? No, of course not. For you will obey this Mistress just as I was sworn to obey the last one. Once the curse is in place, she will demand the amulets from you, and you will give them to her!"

"You promised to let her go!" I said.

"And I will, if you save her from the curse!" Brutus said. "Pledge your loyalty to Diana, swear to use the amulets to serve her, and there will be no need for a Mistress. I will take the Jupiter Stone in her place."

I stood tall on the altar again and raised my hand. "Hold on, Aurelia, please."

She kicked against the wall, still trying to save herself. "Don't make that stone, Nic!"

All I said to her was a mumbled "I'm sorry." Upon my silent command, the rain fell heavier than before, and thunder rolled overhead. Then I looked over at Brutus. "And when the stone is made, I will use it to end this war. If there are no amulets, there can be no rebellion in the heavens. No curses. No Praetor War. Everything ends tonight." I raised my arms and saw sparks of light dance in the dark clouds above me. I felt their tingle in my fingertips.

"You will not destroy those amulets," Brutus said, moving forward. "I can still get the Stone. I can still give it to Diana and earn my rewards!"

My attention returned to Aurelia. "Whatever happens after this is no longer my story to tell. But I hope you will."

"No!" Brutus lunged for me, intending to grab my legs and pull me down from the altar. But just as had happened with the

Mistress, the moment he touched me, I called in the next bolt of lightning. My final bolt.

This one did hit me.

It entered my hand, starting with the bulla and running down my arm through the Malice. It raced through my shoulder and exploded inside my chest, then spread from there into every limb, and into my head, where I felt as if my brain had ignited with a power such as I never had understood before.

Brutus had vanished. He'd gotten one hand on me, which normally would've taken every bit of magic I had to continue with this storm. But the lightning took him first. Jupiter himself carried the Praetor back to the heavens. Brutus was gone.

Yet the lightning had not finished with me yet. Perhaps in the skies, a bolt lasted for only part of a second, yet it lingered in my body, weaving itself between every fiber of my existence. Raw, perfect energy poured into the rock held in my palm, filling it with a light that could only compare with the brightness and heat of the sun.

This was a Jupiter Stone, the power of the gods. Jupiter's powers, superior to all other gods. For that moment, standing within the bolt of lightning, I had that same power too. I felt everything, knew everything, and finally understood everything. I saw in my mind the past and future interwoven as one long thread, and myself in the center of time, holding both halves together.

Rome would fall, eventually, and much of civilization

would collapse with it. But not yet, and, more important, not because of me. Other civilizations would gradually rise in its place all over the globe, achieving glories I never could have imagined on my own.

In my hand, the Jupiter Stone had drawn from the sheets that had fallen around me to become a sphere of bronze. Angular cracks split through the bronze like the antlers of a stag, while beams as bright as lightning shone through. It looked as if the lightning wanted to escape, but I knew what this really was. Jupiter, the ruler of the skies, was showing his power as greater than Diana's. It was the greatest magic both in the heavens and on the earth, the magic of the gods. At least for this small moment, I was one of them.

And all I asked of the stone was one command: Destroy the amulets.

The bulla responded first. It widened from the center, the gold stretching ever thinner and distorting the carved image of the griffin until it was unrecognizable. Finally, the seams burst, and when they did, the entire bulla exploded with it. The leather cord that had kept it around my neck fell harmlessly to the floor, the only proof that would ever remain of the bulla's existence.

The Malice went next. The silver melted down my arm in a long line that dripped in heavy beads onto the altar. Every falling drop landed like the clang of a hammer and then melted into the stone.

Finally, the Jupiter Stone enlarged until the room was bathed in its light. The beam it sent up through the oculus would be visible throughout all of Rome, perhaps throughout the empire. Perhaps as far away as wherever my family was now.

The Jupiter Stone had become bright enough to blind me, but nowhere I turned could shield me from its light.

Where was Aurelia? Was she still here? Was she safe?

"Destroy yourself," I whispered to the stone, fully aware of the consequences of my order.

Somewhere in the room, I thought I heard Aurelia crying out my name. She seemed so far away.

Lightning came down again, a bolt that filled the room. I took hold of it, drawing all of its powers into myself. When the stone exploded, the lightning entered my heart. I felt its final beat. I felt the moment it stopped.

And before I had fallen onto the altar below, my world had ended.

THIRTY-SEVEN

AURELIA

If you hold a wolf by the ears, eventually you'll get bit.

Isn't that what I tried to tell Nic, over and over? Why hadn't he listened?

My name is Aurelia. I suppose this is my story . . . now. It's one I never wanted to tell, but I will.

If I had to describe what I saw, I would first speak of the noise, echoing throughout the Pantheon with such violence that it should have shattered the walls. But for me, it all happened in silence.

The lightning disappeared as suddenly as it had arrived. And for a spare moment, I thought Nic would survive it. He looked at me, though I wasn't sure he saw me. Then there was a great flash of light, brighter than the lightning itself.

When the light vanished, he fell.

I screamed when it happened and lost my own grip on the wall. But before I landed, Caela appeared from out of nowhere to catch me. When we were a little lower to the ground, I jumped off her back, splashed into a full inch of water on the floor, and ran to where I could better see Nic.

His collapse onto the altar broke it into three pieces. The three pieces of his heart, I imagined. One for his family, who meant so much to him that he had repeatedly sacrificed his freedom for their protection. One for Atroxia, a young vestalis who was connected to him in ways I still didn't understand. But I did think she reminded him of himself, of his hope for forgiveness and mercy. The third piece was for me. He loved me. He had told me so, and I had felt it in his kiss.

Long before that, I had known how he felt. Even when he denied them, his feelings were never much of a mystery. Nic probably didn't even realize how often he stared at me when his mind was drifting off into other places. He stared, as if my face was the way he could rest from his troubles. I didn't mind that. I liked the expression in his eyes when he watched me. Besides, he always needed more rest.

He was resting now, just in a very different way. I hated this. His heart was torn apart on that altar. My heart felt torn apart too.

I screamed out again, my cries echoing throughout the Pantheon as a reflection of my pain. Smoke rose in quiet tendrils from Nic's body, and although some light rain had fallen for the first few seconds after he fell, it had stopped now. Everything had stopped now.

At first, I didn't dare go any closer to him and looked at him only from a distance. Not because of any danger to my life, but because of the danger to my emotions. I couldn't bear to see him this way.

Yet he had asked me to tell his story, and so I knew I had to go to him. He lay on his back between the three shattered pieces of the altar, with two arms and a leg over each of the three shards and the other leg lying on the floor.

The lightning had completely destroyed the sandal on his right leg, which was bare now, but the left sandal was still there. I noticed and thought this was important because it was how I'd known Nic ever since our first meeting: With one foot in the life of a free man and the other still in bondage. I wished I had another pair of sandals for him. Wasn't he free now, finally? Maybe not the way he wanted, but he was free.

With that thought, I collapsed beside him, nearly blinded by hot tears that stung my eyes and ripped at my heart. I had never known pain like this, never known it was possible to feel this way and still survive it.

It took a bolt of lightning to end Nic's life. I felt as if I had been struck with the same force of destruction, except I would have to go on.

But not yet.

I took Nic's hand in mine. The tips of his fingers were still smoking and felt warm to the touch, but only for the intense heat that had just traveled through him. Nothing more.

As the dark clouds overhead finally parted, the moonlight shone again through the oculus. I couldn't look at his face, couldn't make myself do it. If I did, I'd see it empty of the passion and humor and energy that had drawn me to him so strongly.

I really had loved him. At least he had finally understood that, just as he had wanted me to understand his feelings.

That brought on more tears. I was grateful to be alone. Anyone who thought of me as strong and warrior-like would never have believed it to see me this way now. I didn't care. The sorrow I felt was as much a part of me as my bow and arrows. But I still preferred to be alone. Nobody else would ever mourn for Nic the way I did, so nobody else should be here.

I brushed my hand upon Nic's arm, and as I moved it into the moonlight, I saw something new. A dark red scar covered his arm, like the stems of a fern, or tiny branches of a stag's antlers. Through the pattern, it was obvious at every point where the lightning had moved through him.

I checked his other arm and saw the same thing, as well as on his legs, though the patterns were lighter there. They would be on his back and chest too; I was sure of that. But I would not check. It didn't feel right to roll his body away from where he fell. Even if moving him didn't matter anymore, I wasn't capable of doing it. I could barely make myself move.

So I knelt again beside him, this time maneuvering my body so that I was close enough to lay my head against his shoulder. The heat from the lightning was fading, and I didn't want that. I didn't want to feel him go cold. That was worse.

A squawk sounded behind me, sad and quiet. I had forgotten Caela was here. When I turned, she was looking at me as if confused, curious about why Nic didn't rise up to greet her.

Then she must've realized the reason for his silence. She bowed her head, sat near the altar, and looked at me.

"What do you want me to say?" My tone was unkind, which wasn't fair to Caela, but I'd forgotten how to speak any other way. "I couldn't save him, and you didn't. Why did you leave when the storm began? Why didn't you fly in and take him away from here? You could've saved him!"

I grabbed a chunk of rock from the altar and threw it toward Caela, who only ducked and then glanced behind her where it landed with a small splash. The rainwater was already draining from the room. By morning, it would be gone.

Caela probably hadn't even understood me. She belonged to the gods, so she must be more intelligent than other animals, but she gave no sign of understanding. She only tilted her eagle head, brushed her lion tail across the floor once or twice, and then lay down near the altar.

I put my head back down on Nic's shoulder and let the tears continue to fall, each one disappearing into his wet tunic. A hole had been burned through the fabric near his chest. He'd destroyed these clothes too, as he had every other tunic Crispus had given him.

I wouldn't marry Crispus. Livia loved him, and when they both were ready, it was right that they should marry. As for me, I doubted I would ever love again, but I could accept that. Once I made it to Britannia, I would improve my skills with the bow and learn other weapons too. Defend Nic's family if it ever became necessary. He would want that.

I better understood now the guilt Nic had felt for not being able to save my father, or Valerius either. None of that was his fault. Nor was it my fault that I couldn't save Nic. But still the guilt pricked at me. How I wished I were stronger.

Nic had probably understood for some time he would have to break the curse on the Mistress and that he would have to destroy the amulets. Despite his protests and his promises, he must've known he would end up making the Jupiter Stone. Nothing I would've done could have changed that.

Hours seemed to pass before my tears finally dried. I was still as sad as before, but my tears had run out. I wondered how long it would be until morning came, and what would happen once it did.

Temple worshippers would come. Or worse, people who had seen the storm and the light beaming up through the oculus. They would come out of curiosity and a desire for gossip. They would disturb Nic's body, carry him before the emperor as proof of his crimes against Rome.

I would have to find a way to stop them, somehow. That seemed like a very big job, so for now I decided to sleep. Suddenly, nothing in me cared about what might happen tomorrow. I wasn't even entirely sure tomorrow would still come. Why should it?

My swollen, tired eyes could not be held open a minute longer. I closed them and finally let myself sleep.

THIRTY-EIGHT

AURELIA

Sunlight entered the Pantheon slowly, as if the new day were ashamed to begin after what night had taken away. But it wasn't anything so poetic, and I knew it. I was no dreamer of such things. The dim morning light was only because of the oculus at the very top of the building, and the torches that had gone out during the storm. Until the sun was high in the sky, this room would sit in shadow. For now, everything was faint and almost blurry, and I preferred that.

It didn't help that my eyes were still swollen. Until I realized that, I had allowed myself to think this was a dream. That last night had not happened, and that Nic and I had only fallen asleep near each other, as we had in Caesar's temple shortly after we first met. In that imagined dream, I would lie here on his shoulder, enjoying the comfort of his arm around me, keeping me safe and warm and —

Nic's arm was around me!

I started to sit up, then kept my place. Perhaps *this* was the dream, and I was a dreamer after all. Perhaps I was only imagining that there had been enough magic within him to give him a faint spark of life.

I raised my free hand to his chest and gently felt for a heartbeat. If it was there, I couldn't feel it, but his chest was rising and falling. Only a little. I wouldn't have even noticed if I had not been so close beside him. But he was alive.

He was alive!

I wanted to sit up and scream out his name and tell him he was alive, just in case he didn't know. But I wondered if suddenly hearing his name screamed out in this echo chamber of a building would actually frighten his heart into stopping again. I couldn't take the risk.

So I kept my hand where it was, counting every rise and fall, and waiting between the long pauses for it to rise and fall again. It was so faint, so shallow, maybe I was imagining it. But there, it rose again, a little better this time! It was real!

The reddish scars were still on his arms, and also on his neck, I noticed. The delicate branches imprinted onto his skin were beautiful in their own way. I wondered if they'd ever fade.

We lay there for some time. He remained asleep, or half-alive, or whatever he was. I was afraid to move in the slightest, lest anything get worse. But something would have to change soon, when the worshippers arrived. What then?

I decided to wait as long as possible, letting him rest and gather strength. If necessary, Caela and I would defend him once people started to come. I had a reason to defend him now.

Where was my bow? I'd dropped it when the Mistress lunged for me, and the rainwater must've washed it into one of the alcoves. I wanted to find it, but I wouldn't leave Nic alone, not even for that long.

How odd it was to realize that the people of Rome might never know what he had done to save the empire, or even the world beyond it. Last night, Nic had halted a rebellion of the gods. He had stopped a war here on earth and in the heavens.

Maybe that was why he had asked me to tell his story. So that people would understand why everything had to happen the way it did.

"Wake up," I whispered into his ear. "Wake up and tell your own story. I'm a terrible storyteller, you know that."

He stirred a bit, though my soft whispers couldn't have been enough to wake him. His arm tightened around my shoulder, and his fingers twitched a little.

"Nic?" I was louder this time.

He didn't move.

"Nic?"

"Shh." His whisper was so quiet, I barely heard it.

Still, I smiled, and sat up on one elbow. "Don't tell me to be quiet."

"Then hush."

I wanted to nudge him, just to tease him back. But I realized perhaps it hadn't been a tease at all. He was nodding, and his lips seemed to be moving slightly. He was listening to someone inside his head.

Was it Atroxia? I knew he had a special connection to her, but he had freed her from the curse. Their connection should have ended. As far as I was concerned, she needed to get out of his head and stay out.

After a moment, his arm moved again. I took his hand in mine and gave it a squeeze.

"Aurelia?" He asked as if he didn't know the answer. Why weren't his eyes opening?

"I'm here. Just rest."

"Did I die?"

"Yes." I scrunched up my face. "Or you mostly died, I'm not sure."

"Did I come back?"

I brushed my hand against his cheek. No scars were on his face, though I wouldn't have minded if there were.

"Look at me, Nic. Open your eyes."

They fluttered a bit, as if he was trying and not quite succeeding. I leaned in to him and gave him a light kiss. He might not have even felt it, but I wanted him to know I was here.

When I sat up again, his eyes were open, just barely, but it was definitely him in there. He was even smiling a little, and that alone made me happier than I ever thought I would feel again.

His smile quickly faded as a hollowness filled his eyes. He said, "My magic is gone. Whatever I had left, it took everything to bring me back."

"I don't care about that," I whispered.

"I think I destroyed the amulets. And the Divine Star is empty, if the scar is even still there."

"You don't need them. The war is over."

"It is?" He raised his head, appearing genuinely surprised. How could he not know?

Explanations could wait until later. For now, I squeezed his hand. "It is."

He laid his head back down on the altar. "That's why everything hurts."

"It also doesn't help that you did battle with a bolt of lightning last night."

"I lost that battle." Another weak grin tugged at the corner of his mouth. "To win, I had to lose."

"You did win, Nic. You're alive. All battles are over."

His eyes closed, and when they opened again, a hint of mischief was in them. "So will you marry me or not? Before you answer, you'd better plan to keep your promise, because I won't let you out of it as easily as Crispus did."

I jabbed my elbow into his side, though not too hard this time. "All of a sudden promises matter to you? Like your promise not to make a Jupiter Stone?"

"Like my promise to come back from it if I did." He drew in a slow, deliberate breath. "Help me up."

He started to rise on his own, but it was clear he had no strength. That didn't matter to me. I would be strong enough for us both until he could keep himself standing.

Caela got to her feet too. I forgot she had stayed near us last night. But Nic turned to her as if he had known all along that she was there.

"I think I called her here, before the . . . well . . . before," he said. "When did she come back?"

"After it was over."

"Of course." He started in her direction, but his legs failed him. I laid one of his arms over my shoulder and then wrapped my arms around his waist to help him climb over the altar rubble. "Caela will take us out of here, before anyone comes."

"Where are we going?"

He looked over at me. "Britannia. We're leaving the empire."

My heart leapt. Before now, every time Nic had spoken about Britannia, there was always doubt in his voice, even when he tried to convince me otherwise. But he seemed firm in his plans now. "How will you know where to go, without magic to guide us?"

"Radulf was in my head. He's the one who woke me up. Caela brought him and Livia to Crispus's home. She will bring us there too."

I did a double take. "Radulf? How could he be in your head?"

"I don't know. Maybe I dreamed that too. But wherever my family is, Caela will get us there."

By then we were on the solid floor of the Pantheon. Caela had to crouch very low so that Nic could roll onto her back. I got on behind him, and this time I would be the one to ensure he did not fall.

Caela normally took off at steep angles, requiring her riders to hold on tight. This time, she rose gently, gliding into the air in wide circles around the Pantheon, with each round taking her higher and higher. By the time we reached the height of the dome, the first patrons of the temple had entered.

"What happened in here?" someone asked.

"Look, a griffin!" someone else said, pointing upward. "Wasn't that the animal the slave boy used to ride?"

They couldn't see Nic or me on it. Caela's wings were spread too wide, and we were both low on her back.

"That slave boy was executed the other day, wasn't he?" a third person asked. "I think he died."

Ahead of me, Nic chuckled softly. "I came back."

I wrapped my arm even tighter around his waist. "Yes, you did."

THIRTY-NINE

AURELIA

Caela didn't fly as quickly as she usually did, but neither of us were in any hurry. The longer we flew, the stronger Nic became. After an hour, he began describing what he remembered from the previous night. It wasn't much, and I found he was asking more questions than he could answer of mine.

"The Mistress — I really broke the curse? Did that happen?"

"It happened. Atroxia thanked you. The vestalis promised to take care of her."

"I don't hear her in my head anymore," he said. "I think when the curse broke, that ended our connection. Or maybe we'd still be connected, if I had any magic."

He seemed sad every time he mentioned his lost magic. But his hand was holding mine and it remained just as firm, so maybe he was beginning to accept what he'd lost.

"You did more than give Atroxia her life back," I said. "The empire forgave her because of you. That's an even greater gift."

He nodded and went silent for a long time. I noticed his knuckles dig into Caela's back, but only in the most loving of ways.

After another hour of flying, he was sitting up without needing my support. Sometime during that hour, his fingers had become intertwined with mine. I liked that.

"I need to find honest work in Britannia," he said. "The only thing I really know about is mining, but I won't do that anymore, even as a free person. I do like the idea of working with my hands."

"Crispus wants to design buildings," I said. "Maybe you can build from his designs."

"That's a good idea." He seemed to mean it, or at least, his voice sounded a little happier. "I've destroyed so many buildings. It might be nice to create them instead."

We talked about that for a long time, and about our hopes and dreams for what Britannia might be like, becoming so involved in our plans that it scarcely occurred to us Caela was flying lower than before. The air around us was clear and the morning sun was bright and crisp.

Crispus had described Hadrian's Wall to me before, as the current boundaries of the empire. I saw it when we passed overhead, a gray brick wall winding up and down through autumn grasses, and with occasional groups of Roman soldiers as sentries. They pointed us out, but Nic didn't notice so I didn't tell him. I only said a few minutes later, "We're out of the empire."

"I thought so," he mumbled. "Despite everything, I'm sad to think I'll never see Rome again."

"At least Rome will still exist, thanks to you. And who knows, perhaps one day we'll go back."

His hand tightened around mine again. "Yes, we'll go together, one day."

One day, and every day from now on, we'd be together.

Gradually, a home rose up in the distance, more square than the villas of Rome, but elegant nonetheless. Smoke rose from a chimney, and farm animals roamed within its fences.

The front door opened upon our approach, and a very pretty girl exited with a basket in her arms, perhaps to gather eggs or to feed the animals. Her curly blond hair was pulled up in a bun, and she was speaking to someone still inside the home. I knew her, and when Nic recognized her too, he tapped my arm, just in case I hadn't yet seen.

Then Livia heard the flap of Caela's wings and looked up to see us. Her cry of joy was so loud we could hear it from as high up as we still were, but every second brought us closer.

By the time Caela had landed, Livia was right beside us. She hugged Nic, even as he was sliding off Caela's back. Then, from almost nowhere, Nic's mother appeared. She wore an apron with flour handprints on it. Did that mean there was fresh baked bread nearby? My stomach ached with hunger, and Nic must be worse. He hadn't eaten much lately.

"I never allowed myself to hope for this moment," Nic's mother said as tears welled in her eyes.

"What are those marks on your arms and legs?" Livia asked.

Nic probably hadn't even noticed them until now. Or at least, he looked at his arms when she mentioned that and seemed genuinely confused.

"They're evidence of his victory," I quickly said.

"It was a victory, then?" Nic's mother whispered. "How did you survive it?"

Nic eyed me sideways, warning me not to answer. Instead, he asked, "Has Crispus arrived yet?"

"We received word from an advance rider," Livia said. "He and his mother will be here soon. Perhaps by the end of the week." And no one looked more excited about that than her.

"Nic?"

He turned. Radulf stood in the doorway of the home, balanced on a cane, but otherwise much healthier and stronger than when I'd last seen him.

When Nic stepped forward, Radulf walked to meet him, and the two stared at each other for a while. Radulf's eyes flitted from Nic's chest to his wrist, checking for both of the amulets.

"You destroyed them?"

Nic's hand brushed up to his chest, where the bulla used to be. Finding nothing there, it only fell to his side again, and even if he didn't say it, I knew it made him sad, like remembering a lost friend. "They're all gone."

"Ah." Radulf walked around Nic, surveying him. "You'll need a new tunic."

"I hope it's the last one I'll need for a while." Nic drew in a sharp breath. "My magic is gone. Not gone, in the way that it's been empty before, but truly gone. I destroyed *everything.*"

"And yet you heard my voice in your head this morning. Interesting." Radulf smiled at that.

I stepped forward. "How? If neither of you has magic anymore —"

A twinkle sparkled in Radulf's eyes. "As I said, that's very interesting. Nothing more." He clapped Nic on the back, just below his right shoulder. When he did, I was sure I saw him flinch, maybe just a little.

Nic smiled back, a real smile, and the most natural smile I'd seen from him since we met. He held out his hand for me, which I gladly took. "Yes," he said. "Whatever comes for us now, it will be . . . interesting."

ACKNOWLEDGMENTS

The close of any series is difficult. By the time I write the final chapter, I've gone on quite a journey with these characters, not only following their ups and downs in the books, but also in events that never make it into the pages. It takes several bumps, bruises, and scars for Nic and his family and friends to reach the ending of this series, but they are all stronger for it. Maybe the same is true for each of us. Life is a series of ups and downs, and if we get a few scars of our own, then it proves we can heal.

There are several people who have walked this journey with me, my family most closely of all. Jeff, I could not do this without you, nor would I want to. Here's to the day you came to me. To my three kids, you bring joy to my life beyond what you can imagine. Each of you amazes me.

I am also infinitely grateful to the Scholastic family for your countless hours of hard work, much of which doesn't get appreciated as it should. I thank you for all you do. To my editor, Lisa Sandell, you are everything a brilliant editor should be and a wonderful friend beyond that. I am so lucky to work with you and look forward to many more exciting years together.

It is also an honor to work with a talented agent such as Ammi-Joan Paquette. Seriously, if I heard a rumor that you could spin gold, I wouldn't even bat an eye.

There are many more writing projects still to come — please watch for upcoming titles! And there are dozens more ideas in my head with characters fighting for my attention. I can't wait to share all of them with you!

ABOUT THE AUTHOR

JENNIFER A. NIELSEN is the acclaimed author of the *New York Times* and *USA Today* bestselling Ascendance Trilogy: *The False Prince, The Runaway King,* and *The Shadow Throne.* She also wrote the Mark of the Thief trilogy: *Mark of the Thief, Rise of the Wolf,* and *Wrath of the Storm;* the historical thriller *A Night Divided;* the fantasy adventure *The Scourge;* and the sixth book of the Infinity Ring series, *Behind Enemy Lines.*

Jennifer collects old books, loves good theater, and thinks that a quiet afternoon in the mountains makes for a nearly perfect moment. She lives in northern Utah with her husband, their three children, and a perpetually muddy dog. You can visit her at www.jennielsen.com.